G000128428

To Ernie

Blind Cupid

As a twisted mind unravels
hope redeems
love kills

Max Brandt

'Safe pair of hands'!
All best Ernst.
Max Brandt

This is a First Edition of the paperback

Blind Cupid:
as a twisted mind unravels, hope redeems, love kills

ISBN: 978-1-910094-18-1

eBook ISBN: 978-1-910094-19-8

Published February 2015

By Magic Oxygen

www.MagicOxygen.co.uk

editor@MagicOxygen.co.uk

Edited by Izzy Robertson

Cover drawing by Shaunagh Radcliffe

A catalogue record for this book is available from

the British Library.

Printed by Lightning Source UK Ltd; committed to improving environmental performance by driving down emissions and reducing, reusing and recycling waste.

View their eco-policy at www.LightningSource.com

Set in 11.5pt Times New Roman

Titles set in Distressed and Secret Service Typewriter

Thank You

('Acknowledgements' is far too grand!)

Everybody who ever told me that I should write 'properly'
(not sure if that was encouragement or a gentle hint to give up
and get a real job!) they know who they are
and if I named everybody, well…long list!

But particularly and especially:

Janie – who puts up with more than a soul should have to bear

My three lovely daughters
but Arwen's the one who pointed me in the right direction

Rissole – don't ask

All my friends in the Inn Theatre Company

Will.

Things base and vile, holding no quantity,
Love can transpose to form and dignity.
Love looks not with the eyes, but with the mind,
And therefore is winged Cupid painted blind.
William Shakespeare
'A Midsummer Night's Dream'

You're neither unnatural, nor abominable, nor mad;
You're as much a part of what people call nature as anyone else;
Only you're unexplained as yet -
you've not got your niche in creation.
Radclyffe Hall
'The Well of Loneliness'

CHAPTER ONE

1960

Lying quietly was best. Or sitting. Or standing. It didn't really matter, as long as it was quietly. He was lying now, straight and rigid, blanket drawn up underneath his chin, hands at his sides. He could feel his nails biting into his palms. It was quiet downstairs as well. No radio, no talking. If there had been shouting, that might have been really bad. But quiet, well… that was bearable.

Perhaps he had dozed off for a while and Daddy had gone out. That might be really bad, if Daddy had gone out and he hadn't heard him go. If Daddy had gone out, he wouldn't have any idea when he might be back and he would have to stay awake just to be sure that everything would be okay.

A door closed below and he heard footsteps across the lino in the kitchen, heavy footsteps; Daddy walking to the back door. Daddy hadn't gone out, Mummy had, and that was really, really BAD.

The back door opened and he heard muffled voices and then the loud, rough Daddy laugh.

He felt his bladder let go and he leapt from bed, feeling the warmth gushing down his leg. His five year old mind was seething and blinded by panic; just get the sheets, get them, hide them, get them. He fumbled frantically, patting at the mattress, hoping that it wasn't wet. He could lose his jammies, that was easy, but, but oh, oh, oh, if the mattress was wet, Daddy would know. Little yellow boys don't wet the bed, whatever happens. That means they're girls. Only girls do that.

He thought it would be all right.

He peeled off his pyjamas and threw them in a ball under the bed. More laughter from downstairs. And a cough. That was special Uncle George. That was bad. Mummy hated special Uncle George. So did he. Special Uncle George smelt strange. Flowery.

His mind veered away from the other bad stuff, clamped down and concentrated on hiding his pyjamas.

He tiptoed to his chest of drawers and opened the middle drawer quietly – quietly, quietly, always quietly - and looked for his other jammies. He sobbed. Mummy hadn't put them back. He could feel his throat going sore with barely restrained tears. His eyes stung and his stomach clenched and unclenched. He needed to go to the toilet, badly. But Daddy and special Uncle George would hear him. They would know he was there.

He hugged himself and danced from foot to foot. He froze. The bottom stair creaked and the third stair popped. They were coming.

He leapt back into bed and pulled the covers up under his chin, lying straight. He closed his eyes and tried really, really hard not shake. He heard his bedroom door open.

'Hello little man,' George said. 'What have you got for your old Uncle tonight then?'

More rough Daddy laughter from the landing.

'Only twenty minutes Georgey boy. You only paid a fiver, remember?' Daddy's footsteps clumped back down the stairs.

He couldn't help it. He started to shake.

CHAPTER TWO

1990

The faint scratching at the lock, as somebody fumbled a key, brought Rob out of his light doze. He had been dreaming of home.

A quick look at the bedside clock told him it was just after three a.m. and he could see the square shadows of the lead lights in the window being cast by the full moon. Somewhere an owl screeched and he heard the hiss of tyres passing on the wet road outside.

Rob tried to disentangle himself from the sheets, knowing what was about to happen, but the door flew open and three shadowy figures tumbled into the room. No light was needed, the intruders knew these rooms by heart.

The prancing phantoms fell on him. The first took hold of Rob's head, tugging his hair viciously and twisting; the second grabbed his ankles, digging nails into the thin flesh at the heel; the third phantom heaved the sheets up and began to roll Rob, squeezing him more firmly into the cocoon in which he had parcelled himself.

And not a word was spoken. The only sounds were the assailants' heavy breathing and Rob's own panting, whistling between his teeth as he fought to be free; a lost cause.

The third shadow, having checked their handiwork, moved away to the washbasin in the corner of the room.

'Hold him.'

Now soft giggles joined the laboured breathing. The wrapper stood over Rob, weighing something in either hand, looking from one to the other, trying to make a decision.

'Your hair needs a wash.'

Rob felt the cold, sticky liquid hit his forehead and begin dribbling down the bridge of his nose. He closed his eyes, but the stinging had already started. The shampoo trailed across his cheeks, over firmly clenched lips and back up into his hair.

'Need to clean your teeth as well, you scuzzy fucker.'

Rob could smell the sharp tang of toothpaste, and then felt the slime as it mixed with the shampoo on his lips, face and eyes. All he could hear was barely suppressed laughter, breathless and a little panicky.

'Massage now, I think.'

Rough hands pounded his face and scalp, rubbing the mess in. Chewed and ragged nails caught his nostrils and ears and scratched his chin, while fingers poked him in the neck.

It stopped, and there was silence. Even the breathing became subdued. The owl screeched again.

'Aah, what a mess.' A different voice said. 'Think we should help him clean up a bit?'

Rob heard zips ripping open and braced himself, fighting to turn his head away from what he knew was coming.

The smell and warmth made him gag and thrash, but he managed to keep his mouth and eyes firmly closed, knowing that it would soon be over.

Zips up. He could hear the choked hilarity as one or other of the attackers jumped up and down, crowing under his breath. He felt warm air against his ear.

'Welcome to Freeways, toss pot. Remember, there's a pecking order here and you just been pecked by the top man, okay?'

A fist crashed into his groin and, trussed as he was, he couldn't even double up in agony. The punch had the desired effect. Rob's mouth opened and he let out a soft cry. The mess trickled over his tongue, hit the back of his throat, and he retched painfully.

'Aah now, Wilkesy, Wilkesy, don't cry. Shall I get Mumsy to come and kiss it all better then? Oh dear! I can't, can I? Never mind.'

Rob heard the door open and he rolled toward the sound.

'Sleep well Robbo, busy day tomorrow.'

The door clicked shut and anger, silence and darkness closed in.

It took him a while to get out of the wrapping and across to the sink, wiping as much of the stinking mess from his face and hair as he could. Rob's eyes stung fit to kill and the smell of mint, piss and mixed fruit kept his stomach busy, trying to hold a lid on supper and stop it making a guest appearance on the bedroom floor.

He turned on the tap and waited for it to run hot. He avoided looking at himself in the mirror and stared at his feet, trying not shiver. And not for the first time, he cursed his father and mother for bringing him into the world and then dumping him at Freeways, and all the other children's homes where he had stayed.

And not for the first time, Rob Wilkes wished them both dead and burning in hell.

CHAPTER THREE

1962

So this was going to be home. He wasn't sure what to make of it. Huge, cavernous, all polished wood and staircases. The garden was nice. He had other children to play with, some of whom were standing with him now, waiting in the office for somebody important.

He held his breath, fighting the tears that had suddenly decided to blur his vision. He knew he was away from Daddy and the special uncles, but he still felt a terror every time the tears stung his eyes. Only yellow boys cry. Girly boys.

He sneaked a look down the line. Three other boys and two girls, all shuffling and looking nervous. They had all arrived together. They had been told by the stern lady with glasses that they were lucky, lucky children, to be chosen to come and live here. He missed his Daddy, despite everything, and his Mummy, but they had gone away. Had the other children's Mummies and Daddies gone away too, he wondered?

There were voices outside, where the stern lady was, that echoed in the oaken hallway and sounded like booming monsters coming to see him. The door opened.

The stern lady was there, followed by two men. They were very old. One had funny, wild white hair and wore a white suit and the other had a black pinstripe suit and his hair was almost gone. What was left was plastered to his head and shone like the sun on water, or so he thought.

The stern lady and shiny-haired man stood by the door as their companion walked down the line of children, looking closely at them, smiling.

He could smell cigarettes and a strange, sweet smell, like Mummy's perfume. The man's shoes squeaked as he walked by them. They were almost as shiny as the other man's hair.

'My name is Mr. Milford,' the man with wild white hair and shiny shoes said. 'This is my business partner, Mr. Dickens and this is Miss Crick, who looks after the running of this house.' He smoothed his hand over the top of his head, pressing his white mane down. As he put both hands in his pockets, the hair rose up of its own accord, as wild as before. The children stared, open mouthed, and tried not to laugh. 'You are new arrivals at The Lawns; our second intake. Behave, work hard, do as you're told and you will find your time with us to be rewarding. And you may even find a new family.'

He paused, watching their reactions closely. Good. A few surprised looks and one or two of them were close to tears, but that was to be expected.

'Pay heed to Miss Crick. Her word is our word and that is the law here at The Lawns. Now, get your bags and Miss Crick's assistant will take you to your rooms.'

They followed the trio out of the office and collected their meagre belongings.

His room smelt funny; a sharp smell that leaked from the drawers and wardrobe. And his bed sheets were all stiff and white and cold. No lights were shining through the windows or stretching fingers beneath the door. It was pitch black.

He lay in bed, covers to his chin, ramrod straight. This was really bad. He had nothing to measure anything by. It was all strange and unfamiliar. He had no routine, nothing to understand and react to. He was adrift and scared.

His eyes widened. There were footsteps in the corridor. He heard the door handle turn. Gritting his teeth, he willed himself not to wet the bed, not so soon. The door opened.

'Come with me.' A voice he didn't recognise.

Outside, light from the downstairs hallway leached its way into the gloom, and he saw it was Mr. Dickens. With him were two of the other new arrivals, a boy and a girl. They all followed Dickens downstairs, but instead of going into the office, they turned left and went into another, dimly lit, room.

At the far end of the room was a large leather wing-backed chair, in which sat Mr. Milford.

'Come here children. Line up in front of me.' Mr. Milford took a sip from a large glass and placed it on a small table at his side. At his feet were three pairs of shiny shoes. He heard the door click, glanced round, and saw that Dickens had gone.

'Look at me boy!' Milford leant forward; his hair seemed to rise up and fall round his face like claws. 'Always at me!'

All three of the children jumped and moved closer together, not daring to see if they all felt the same.

'Now then.' Milford leant back in his chair. 'We're going to play a game, and it will be fun. Take off your night things.'

His pyjama trousers puddled at his feet and somehow, he felt better. Calmer. He was back in a place he understood. He was still scared, but he understood now.

He felt the other children next to him and wondered if Mr. Milford knew special Uncle George. They smelt very similar and that too was comforting.

CHAPTER FOUR

2007

Chief Inspector Montgomery Flute locked his car door, checked his watch and took a deep breath of the spring scented Devon air. It was one of those mornings that, to use the old cliché, made you glad to be alive. He took a moment to just enjoy the soft breeze that curled through the trees in the police station car park and playfully rattled sweet wrappers and the previous night's take-away boxes across the tarmac.

The school run was in full swing and cars were crawling along the main road towards the school that was the station's next door neighbour. Gridlock as per usual, but Flute only had to raise his eyes a fraction and look in pretty much any direction to see trees and fields and wish himself somewhere else. It would be a perfect day for walking on the moors.

Drumming his fingers on the bonnet of the car, he considered the possibility of just climbing back in and making a run for it.

Two constables came from the main building and made their way to a patrol car parked next to Flute's old Saab. They nodded and muttered a greeting, which Flute acknowledged with a terse nod. He sighed. It was Friday, the weekend lay ahead and there would be all the time in the world for stomping across the wide open spaces.

A brief but powerful pang hit him in the gut. Wide open. Empty. He had to grit his teeth to stop himself tumbling into the gaping pit. It had been nearly a year since Tom had died and although the hurt was now a dull, continuous ache, every so often it flared and caught his heart unawares. That was painful.

Raised voices from the street made him look, dragging him back from the brink of an attack of the maudlin monster. Two lads from the local comprehensive were squaring up to each other, fists bunched at their sides, faces red and angry, whilst a gaggle of six or seven other kids circled round them, not quite sure, or so it seemed to Flute, what to do.

The language was pure Anglo Saxon, mixed with a healthy dollop of the current street patois, which sounded faintly ridiculous to Flute's ears. But what would he know? He came from an era when 'man' and the phrase 'rip off' were the sole territory of the hippies. He supposed 'wicked' would eventually find its way into the wider vocabulary of the nation as a whole.

He caught the eye of one of the protagonists and jerked his head, indicating that they should clear off. The two lads looked at him as if he had just dropped from a dog's mouth and sneered. Flute took a step or two towards them and the whole crowd moved away, scooping bags and backpacks from the pavement and rejoining the general flow of adolescent humanity towards that tower of academia that passed for a school.

Flute shook his head, bemused, and made his way to the front door. That dull, lonely ache still hung in the back of his mind, waiting for its moment to resurface, as it undoubtedly would. It was a daily occurrence.

Two more officers were heading towards him as the door banged shut. They were deep in conversation but when they saw him, one of them, an old time bobby with twenty odd years' service, raised his voice slightly and said as they passed,

'… and of course there was a time when 'gay' meant happy and cheerful, not perverted. But that's so-called progress for you…'

The door banged shut again as they exited and Flute stood stock still in the corridor, reminding himself that it wasn't as if it hadn't happened before, it would happen again, inevitably, and that by now he should be used to it. Water, duck's back and so on. But by God, it still grated. He glanced up and saw Sergeant Bill Rockingham standing behind the front desk, studying a piece of paper with deep concentration.

'Morning Bill'

Rockingham looked up, his face a study in feigned surprise. No Oscars for him.

'Oh, hello Sir.'

They stared at each other for a moment. The sergeant sagged and tossed the paper onto the desk.

'I'll have a word with them when they get back. And Alan Turpin should know better, he's been in the force long enough.'

Flute shook his head and puffed a breath out.

'Rocky, I've got better things to worry about and...'

'That's as maybe, but if we can't get it right in these four walls, what the hell hope have we got out there?' He nodded in the general direction of the town. They stared at one another again. 'How's things?' Rockingham cocked his head to one side, waiting, knowing that Flute knew what he was talking about.

Bill Rockingham was another stalwart of the local constabulary, who had been a sergeant when Flute arrived from training school, smart in blue and green with enthusiasm. Rocky, who thought life had thrown him all the curved balls he deserved, until his brother Tom had announced that he was gay; until Tom also announced that his new partner was none other than Monty Flute. And now both he and Flute were desperately trying to come to terms with Tom's pointless death.

'Things will be better when next Wednesday's been and gone, Rocky.'

Rockingham nodded and looked down at the desk, in search of something interesting to study, not wanting to see the expression on Monty's face and not wanting Flute to see the sadness in his own eyes. He cleared his throat, looked up and grinned.

'I know something that'll get your juices pumping, my lad! Came in last night. I've put the full monty on your... sorry, the full report on your desk, but it seems that one of the lads in the Torquay office might have something of interest with regard to your old mate Nick Sloane.'

The corner of Flute's mouth twitched and his eyebrows went up a notch, the closest he ever really came to showing an emotion that resembled surprise or pleasure. Rockingham nodded, pleased with the effect.

'Sloane, eh? That's put a sparkle on the day, Rocky. Thank you.'

Flute almost floated to his office and even managed a halfway civil greeting for the uniformed inspector he passed on the way. His plain clothes sergeant, Derek Cavannaugh, met him as he paused by the coffee machine to get a polystyrene helping of the sludge that passed for tea.

'Morning, Sergeant Cavannaugh, what's the news on Sloane? I'm assuming that you've had your customary rifle through the papers on my desk?'

Cavannaugh opened his mouth to protest, and then thought better of it. Flute could be a pain in the arse at times, but there wasn't a better

Inspector to work with in the whole of the Devon and Cornwall Constabulary.

'They had an unidentified GBH victim wheeled into Torbay Hospital last night. Nasty, painful and messy, but not life threatening. One of the local boys, who was at the scene first, found a screwdriver nearby with blood on it, so he brought it in. It's the one that was used in the assault. Here's the bonus though. They got a positive match from a fingerprint on the handle of the screwdriver; Nick Sloane.'

Flute put his cup on the desk and sat down, beating a triumphant tattoo on the desk diary with his fingertips. He looked at the clock on the wall and gave a satisfied sigh.

'Look at that, just look. Not quite eight o'clock and already the day's becoming one to remember.'

CHAPTER FIVE

2007

It was on mornings like this that Mike Soloman knew why he had retired early. The sun was a hazy disc lying just behind the trees and the air, though chilly, held the promise of another glorious day to be spent wandering by the river or sitting in the garden with a large glass of wine and a good book.

Sheila was away up-country visiting her useless sister, whose even more useless husband had buggered off with some floozy or another, and Mike could live life at the pace he wanted to. Him and Colin.

The black and white mongrel came crashing back through the long grass at the side of the river, as if he had known that Mike was thinking about him. He dropped a stick the size of a small tree at his feet, watching and waiting expectantly as Mike just ambled past him, head up and gazing out at the countryside.

The trees were starting to burst into leaf, the flowers already peppering the meadows and hedgerows with colour, a reminder and promise of longer and warmer days. Along this isolated stretch of the river he rarely saw another living soul. The peace was complete. Mike Soloman wasn't given to deep thought, not in the intellectual sense of the phrase, but he liked to be able to get lost inside his own head, just swimming around in the warm and friendly waters, relaxing. If anyone had asked him what he had been thinking about on his long treks through the pastures and fields that made up the estate of Domington House, he would look at them askance and tell them it was none of their beeswax. The fact was he couldn't really recall thinking about anything in particular.

Colin made another concerted effort to attract Mike's attention by pushing his way between the man's legs and trying to drag his tree with him.

Mike laughed. 'Get off y'daft bugger! I can't throw that!' He bent and snapped off a decent sized stick and hurled it into the grass, aiming for the river. Colin bounded away in a high state of ecstasy, barking loudly.

Somewhere above Mike heard the echoing tap of a woodpecker working on the bark of a tree, hunting for its breakfast. People would say that a walk along this part of the river was quiet but if you actually stopped and listened, really listened, it was anything but. The whole place was alive whatever time of the year you chose to stroll by.

Mike tried to locate the woodpecker up in the branches of the horse chestnut, but the weave and clutter of the tree defeated his best efforts. He meandered for a while, wondering what was missing. Colin.

He whistled and called but there was no familiar answering bark or crashing of the undergrowth, just a couple of blackbirds chittering out a warning. Even to Mike's ears it seemed unnaturally quiet.

'Bloody dog! I'll give you twenty to one he's found a pile of fox shit to roll in, dirty little bugger.'

Soloman retraced his footsteps and found the tree that Colin had dragged to him. He whistled again and listened. He thought he could hear a faint growling.

'Colin! Here boy, c'm here!' There was a short, sharp bark in response, but no sign of the dog doing as he was told. Unusual for Colin. 'Where are you fella? Colin!'

Mike pushed his way through the long grass, heading towards a huge willow that leaned out over the water. The grass round it seemed to be moving. A large patch of nettles and thorns blocked his path, so he veered off to the right and came to the river bank. It dropped about three feet to a small strip of sandy gravel and, off to his left, he could see Colin's tail wagging in the undergrowth as his rear end hung out over the strip. He'd put a rat or some such into a hole, daft idiot.

Mike jumped down onto the sandy strip and scrunched his way along to the brave hunter.

'Come on you soft sod, leave him alone.'

He pushed aside the grass and froze. He could see Colin's back and ears, but the dog seemed to be lying between someone's legs. He could see the legs - and the soles of a pair of shoes.

'Hello?'

He patted the dog's rump and tugged gently at the pelt.

'Move it Colin… shift y'arse!' He gave the dog a mild slap on the behind. Colin came out backwards, twisting nimbly and landing on all fours on the beach. Mike shook the grass. 'Hello! Who's there? You all right?'

Colin barked and made to jump back up onto the bank. Mike pushed him away and started to move the grass aside, calling all the while.

Shoes. Black Oxford brogues. Shiny and brand new from the look of them. White socks and bare calves; the hair looked matted and wet, the flesh white and cold. Mike shivered and took a deep breath; then he pushed the grass fully aside.

And wished he hadn't.

CHAPTER SIX

2007

Nick Sloane dropped the car into third gear and accelerated away up the hill. Although it was dark, he could see the waning moon spread light from a cloudless sky across the softly undulating vastness and smell the sea through the open window.

It was a long detour he had decided to take to get home, but the road that ran along the shore above the sea from Dartmouth to Kingsbridge was spectacular at any time of the day or night. And he needed the solitude.

His grip on the steering wheel was relaxed, unlike his state of mind. It boiled and seethed where it normally simmered. Ferdy Epstein had managed to turn the heat up and because of him it was more than probable that Sloane would face a lot of questions from the police.

Epstein was a first-class wanker and it never ceased to amaze Nick that the man had managed to hang on to his 'business interests' as long as he had. The fact he had hung on to them was due in the main to Nick's hard work and loyalty.

He watched Epstein's back and just recently that had taken a deal more time than Nick thought useful - or wise.

There was an interesting conundrum that had come to occupy Nick's thoughts a great deal of late: if he, Nick Sloane, was considered by the authorities - and the majority of people in Epstein's employ - to be a psychopath, then what were the two new 'bodyguards' that Epstein had recently put on the pay role? Über-psychos?

Sloane considered himself to be pretty well balanced. He did the job he did because he was able to.

The only pleasure he got from it was that of seeing someone who deserved justice get it meted out to him - and it paid a damn sight better than stacking shelves in Asda or sweeping the streets. Others would see his whole life as a conundrum, a complete mystery, but Sloane was relatively comfortable with the way things were.

Well, almost.

One of the new boys had been sent out with Nick that evening to, in Ferdy parlance, have a quiet word with somebody. There were four things that Ferdy usually asked Nick to do: have a chat, have a quiet word, give somebody a ticking off or kill the fucker. Last night should have been a quiet word, but Mr. Over-enthusiastic-new-boy-arsehole had turned it into a ticking off scenario.

Nick was having a quiet word with the recipient's kidneys when… what was the idiot's name... Calum?... when Calum had disappeared. Nick made the assumption that Calum had lost his bottle. Never make assumptions.

No, the stupid twat had gone to Nick's car, grabbed a screwdriver from the toolbox, come back and, without a by your leave, proceeded to try and unscrew the client's kneecaps. Jesus, the noise had been enough to wake the dead. And Calum had laughed. That was the thing that had really pushed Sloane's boat out. Then, to crown it all, he had chucked the screwdriver out into the darkness of the alleyway and walked back to the car.

Sloane had followed, slipped into the driver's seat and calmly driven away, although he felt anything but calm.

They had made their way out of Torquay, along the front, heading for the ferry at Kingswear. Sloane said nothing, but sat, biding his time, listening to Calum giving detailed descriptions of previous acts of derring-do.

They had turned off the main road, heading out to the Ferry, when Sloane suddenly swung the car off the road and onto a farm track. Which was where, he presumed, Calum still was, nursing a severely bruised ego and upper body. Nick had caught the last ferry across to Dartmouth by the skin of his teeth and also managed to catch last orders in The Windjammer.

The landlord had obligingly filled his hip flask and Nick had spent a quiet hour or two at the castle, watching the sea crash into Castle Cove by moonlight.

Sloane changed down into second and negotiated the hairpin bends down to Slapton Ley, opening her up as he came out of the last and shooting off down the arrow-straight road, listening to the engine roar and feeling the wind whipping round his head. It felt much, much better now.

The problem of the screwdriver had been quietly turning over in the back of his mind as he had been watching the waves and driving. The solution was hard. Nick loved his car, but if it meant that he would stay out of the clutches of the old bill, so be it. Epstein could bear the financial cost of getting his wheels fixed.

He revved down and swung into the car park on the sea shore, by the war memorial. Killing the lights, he sat for a minute, checking the surroundings.

It was close to three in the morning now and very few people would be about, but there might be a late night tryst happening in the car park. Some folk were such romantics.

Nobody around. He opened the boot, climbed out and found the tyre lever. Shutting the boot, he jammed the lever under the lock and wrenched it open. One by one the tools ended up far out in the sea, along with the box itself.

He had retained another screwdriver and proceeded to loosen the screws that held the CD multi-changer in place. Once they were loose enough, he ripped it out. That too went for a swim. By God, Epstein would pay for this.

With his trusty tool, he sat back in the car to prise the radio from its resting place and pull the SatNav from its holder on the dashboard. Nick walked a little way up the car park and watched the splash as the two top-of-the-range pieces of kit hit the ocean.

He locked the doors and ducked from sight as he saw the approaching headlights. Nothing to worry about, just a late finisher or early starter.

He rammed the tyre lever between the door and frame and wrenched it open. It still shut, but it was a mess. The tyre lever went swimming too. Nick left a message on Epstein's private office line to the effect that, if the law contacted him tomorrow, then he, Nick, had finished work at, he checked the time, 12.55am.

If Epstein was worried, good job. It might teach him to be a tad more selective when hiring his hoodlums.

Sloane made one more phone call, to Torquay nick, and reported the break-in and theft, telling the duty officer that he was heading home and if they wanted to speak to him and see the damage, he'd be at home in the morning.

He pulled a small, silver, Edwardian hip-flask from his jacket pocket and took a sip. The Hallsands Lighthouse sent its lonely warning across the sea and Nick wondered, not for the first time, what the future held. If anything.

CHAPTER SEVEN

2007

Simon Nicholson could hear the noise bellowing from the open window of the children's home. That was Jasmine. It sounded as if she had started whatever was happening, he could tell from the strident, shrill tone of her voice, and, following close behind was Jasmine's little shadow, Krissy, her deeper pitched, adenoidal chatter echoing everything Jasmine was screaming. He could hear several different voices laughing - that would be the lads - and occasionally, he could make out Hamish Smith's dark, border burr telling them to calm down.

Nicholson sighed in resignation. It seemed it was going to be one of those days. But they had, as a staff team, already discussed the likelihood of disruption today. They had just managed to get Freeways back onto some sort of even keel when David Trelawney's care manager had dropped the nugget that she had found David a foster placement.

Trying to get kids who were accustomed to chaos settled was hard enough. They seemed to have been getting on top of it, but the thought that their carefully balanced little world was about to be upended yet again was bound to send the kids off on one.

Chaos was where these youngsters came from and it was, in pretty much every case, where they felt most comfortable. Causing chaos, planning upheaval, was the only form of control these kids had over their lives.

David was leaving, which meant another new figure was about to be thrown into the equation. It was so hard for them.

Simon had seen it happen many, many times since he had been at the home; close on twenty years, almost as long as the place had been open. He was one of only two of the original staff team. Not bad, considering the burn out rate for R.S.W.s was reckoned to be about five or six years.

He hefted his over-night bag and walked across the car park and up the path to the front door. Glancing into the garden at the back of the house he saw David sitting under the tree, a huge old fir that had been there longer than any of them. He remembered how many kids had sat in just that same place, thinking, crying, kicking the trunk in frustration, climbing into its lower branches. It was a great tool to have, that old tree.

The front door flew open and Jasmine, closely followed by Krissy, flounced past him, shouting back over her shoulder.

'Yeah? Well you can fucking stick your fucking fine, you manky old fucker!'

'Yeah, fucking stick it!' Echoed Krissy, trying hard to copy Jasmine's head flick and swinging hips.

'I didn't take your fucking keys. And if you don't believe me, ask that little tosser Kevin, yeah?!'

'Yeah, he's a tosser!' Krissy scuttled past Simon, giving him a sly smile.

Hamish strode out, red in the face and huffing.

'Afternoon Si. Happy days. Jasmine! You leave the grounds, young lady, and you know what's going to happen don't you?'

Simon could predict exactly what was going to happen. He silently cursed the TV.

Jasmine stopped in her tracks, turned on her heel and pointed at her face.

'Look at this face, Scotty. Is it bovvered, eh? Do I look bovvered? I ain't bovvered!' The last word was screamed at the top of her voice.

'Yeah, we ain't bovvered,' said Krissy. She looked worried.

Hamish turned his head slightly and stared into the middle distance, deciding what would be the best course to take. 'I could cheerfully throttle Catherine Tate,' he muttered. 'And the stupid thing is, these kids don't even understand that she's taking the piss! Ah sod it.' He looked to Jasmine. 'Suit yourself Jas, suit yourself. We'll see you later.'

Simon nodded and followed Hamish back into the house. That had been the best course to follow, he reckoned. Although they needed the attention, these kids, it had to stop somewhere, otherwise you'd spend your entire day following them around asking what was troubling them.

'Kevin!' Hamish roared, patting his trousers for his keys. 'Get yourself down here young fella m'lad, we need to talk.'

Simon opened the office door. He dropped his bag on the floor and flopped into a chair, nodding a greeting to the other two staff members who were already there, waiting to enter the fray on the next shift.

'Kettle's just boiled if you want a brew,' said Hamish as he came into the office. He sat and opened the day-to-day log book. 'One of the little buggers had Mo's keys off his belt I'm afraid, so youse guys are going to have to keep a very weathered eye on the lot of them...unless I can get Kevin to give them up.'

Simon stood up and stretched.

'Shall I go and have a word?'

'Aye, okay. Give it a whirl after we've had handover. You're all here and Deidre and I will be around for a while anyway.'

Simon nodded and made everyone a coffee as they settled in to hear of the previous shift's events.

Hamish cleared his throat. As assistant manager at Freeways, he was the most senior RSW on duty. Most A.M.s made themselves office bound, but not Hamish. He was definitely hands-on, taking his fair share of the sleep-ins and covering shift illness, something that was happening more and more frequently these days. Hamish scrubbed his face with both hands and leant forward, consulting the log book. It was where everything got written down. Telephone calls, minor messages, incidents, everything. It was the most effective back-up system they had. They all wrote reports, in triplicate, but this old A4 diary was their lifeline to what was going on in the house. The first thing they all did on arriving was consult it.

'Right, here we go then. I've been here with Mo and Eileen, Mo and I slept in last night. As we know, young David leaves us this afternoon, so Ray's laid on a special tea and made a cake. That'll be nice.' He gave the other three a wry look and they smiled. 'Lee's due in court tomorrow, so we need to try make sure that he doesn't flit off tonight. Pauline and Tamsin will be back from school later and I think it might be an idea to get them all out this evening. Ice skating might do the trick.' The others nodded.

There were more mundane things that were discussed, but the handover went quickly. Simon decided to go and have a chat with David in the back garden and as he left the office, saw Kevin heading towards the kitchen.

'Kevin!' he called.

The boy turned and looked. Simon held out his hand and moved his fingers; come on, give me the keys, the action said. They stared at each other for a second or two, then Kevin shrugged, dug into his pocket and threw Simon the bunch.

'Thank you,' he said. 'You've just ensured your place on the ice skating trip this evening.'

Kevin smiled and went into the kitchen to pester Ray for some toast.

Deidre Cochrane came out of the manager's office and walked towards him. She had been in charge at Freeways for nearly two years, and it showed. Only today, it seemed to be weighing on her with even more destructive pressure than usual. She gave Simon a distracted smile.

'Can you step into the office for a second please Si? I need to talk to all the on-duty team before you head off.'

Hamish and the others glanced up from what they were doing, but only Hamish recognised the look on Deidre's face.

'Guys, I need to talk to you. Hamish, can you hang on for a while? You might be needed.' She dry-washed her hands and perched herself on the edge of one of the desks.

'Do you remember Terry Faulds?'

Everyone nodded or muttered yes. Terry had left the home for supported lodgings almost a year ago. He had a history, but then all of the kids who ended up at Freeways had a history. Terry's had been a deal more terrible than most.

Both parents killed in a road accident when he was six, he had come to Freeways. His folks had been only children and his grandparents were dead too.

Si remembered the frail little fella, all knees and eyes and red hair. They had found him a good foster home, with every chance that he would be adopted in the long run. He had been sent off and marked down as one of their successes.

Two years later, he was back. And his foster parents were doing a very long stretch for abuse. The photographs still occasionally surfaced on the Net when the police broke up a ring.

He had stayed for three more years and, at twelve, had headed off to another foster placement. He was happy, he was hopeful. He had a future.

He had returned, briefly, when he was sixteen, having been found in

Plymouth, selling blow jobs for three quid a time. The money went to his carer. That one was still waiting to go to court. There had been a lot of evidence to correlate.

He flatly refused any more placements - who could blame him – and with Simon's help had managed to start a college course and get supported lodgings in Torquay.

In their various ways, everyone in the room knew that the news was going to be bad, although they all hoped for something positive, some small spark in the expected gloom.

'What's happened Deidre?'

'They found his body down by the river this morning. I'm going over to see the Inspector now. This is NOT to go any further, is that understood? We stand to have enough problems tonight with David going and we don't need this added to the mix.'

They all nodded. Simon cleared his throat.

'How did… what..?'

'He was murdered. God help the poor little sod. His throat had been cut.'

CHAPTER EIGHT

1990

Rob Wilkes sat with his back against the old fir tree, knees drawn up, with his arms folded across them. The sun was warm on the back of his neck and he let himself drift a little, feeling the book between his fingers and the bark of the tree rubbing against his back. He was trying hard not to concentrate on either of these sensations, yet remain aware of them. There was the low drone of a bumble bee somewhere above his head and, in the distance, were the summer-muffled voices of kids in the fields.

When the house was empty, as it was now, it felt almost perfect. He could sit and dream or read, or he could get the attention of one of the staff members, like that new bloke, Simon.

He'd tried to fit in, become one of the mob, especially after his 'initiation' ceremony, but it just wasn't right. He wasn't like them... well, he was like them, if being in care boiled down to that, but they weren't the sort of kids he would readily mix with if he had the choice. They didn't read, unless it happened to be a porno mag that one of the other lads had found, and the music they listened to, well, it wasn't music as far as he was concerned.

But that didn't mean they could push him around; Scooter Lennox had found that to his cost after they'd raided Rob's room. He didn't like having to do things like that, but they forced him. Nobody pushed him around, nobody. That was about the only thing he had learned at his father's knee. No, wrong; he'd learnt plenty at his father's knee but had decided to ignore most of it.

And now he was leaving. He wasn't sure if he was happy or not. It would be good to have more independence, but he'd miss these moments of solitude and he'd certainly miss being able to chat with

Simon when the chance arose.

He opened his eyes and leant his head back. 'Lord of the Flies'. His favourite book of the six that he owned; all bought with his meagre pocket money allowance; all hard back and all in pristine condition. He'd had seven, but Scooter had got to them on one of the other occasions that he and his crew had managed to get a set of staff keys.

Rob had just got back from the cinema with a couple of other kids, as Scooter and Justin were going in and out of their rooms, helping themselves to anything they fancied. Harriet, the member of staff on duty, had been chasing them around. Useless she was, useless. Scooter had already started tearing pages out of 'Moby Dick' and scattering them along the top floor landing. Rob had known the moment they got up there what the pieces of paper were.

He saw Scooter throw the book to Justin as they came up the stairs and heard him say,

'Stop it Jus, he'll kill you if he sees you doing that.'

Simon had put a restraining hand on Rob's shoulder. He shrugged it off and collected all the torn pages, staring at Scooter all the time.

'Don't try and stare me out, y'wanker. Weren't anything to do with me. It's him.' He jerked his head at Justin.

Rob had thrown the book away and waited. Several weeks later, Scooter's prized possession, a skate board, had been found in the garden with words 'Call me Wanker' carved into the footplate; and later that evening Scooter had to be taken to the local hospital with a severe case of diarrhoea and sickness. Something he'd eaten.

Rob smiled without humour at the memory. Simon had chatted with him about the incident - Rob knew that Simon would probably be the only one to pick up on the 'Moby Dick' paraphrase - but he had just sat, pretty much as he sat now, smiling and shaking his head, denying all knowledge.

'Call me satisfied,' was what Rob had said to Simon, who had had trouble suppressing a laugh.

Now Rob was leaving. He heard footsteps on the path at the side of the house and Simon's familiar tuneless whistle.

'Must be time to be packing up the old black plastic bin bag and heading off into the sunset,' Rob thought.

It summed up his whole experience of being in care; he arrived with nothing and was leaving with a few clothes and some books, all chucked into a waste sack; a metaphor for his entire life to date.

'Hey Robbo.' Simon plonked himself down at the boy's side. 'Shufty over, let me have a bit of the backrest action then. Ta. So, how's it going?'

Rob grimaced and spun the book in his fingers. 'Okay I s'pose. When we leaving?'

Simon rubbed his chin. 'Whenever you're ready mate. All packed?'

'What? My designer council sack? Did it last night.'

'Sack? I asked Mo to get you a case of some sort when he was in Paignton last week.'

Rob laughed. 'Mo? He's got a memory like an amoeba, non-existent. Tosser.'

Simon sat quietly and fumed for a minute. Mo Palfrey had started at Freeways about the same time as him and had managed to make an enemy of pretty much all the kids at the home... and not a few of the staff team too. The man was thoughtless and he and Simon were going to end up having words.

'Sorry about that old son. Not much I can do now, unfortunately. What you reading?'

Rob tossed him the book and leant forward between his legs, plucking idly at the grass.

'Whoa! 'Lord of the Flies'; I'm impressed. It's...'

'What? That some kid in care can actually read something that hasn't got pictures? Or's got something to do with something other than tits and cars or makeup and Vanilla Ice and George fucking Michael?!'

'Steady on mate! Blimey. I was going to say, I'm impressed, it's a difficult book to get into, for anyone, let alone...'

'A twat like me?' But this was said with an audible smile. Simon gave him a gentle push.

'Yeah, a twat like you.' He pulled his tobacco tin out of his shirt pocket and began to roll a cigarette. 'You seen the film?'

Rob shook his head. 'Not yet. I was going to see it back along but the girls decided on 'Ghost'. Out voted.'

Simon took a quick look over his shoulder and handed Rob his tin.

'Thanks. You'll get yourself a bollocking from old wotsit if you're not careful.' Rob rolled an ultra-thin ciggy and lit it. 'Yeah, maybe I'll treat myself to the film when I get a bit of money. Is it good?'

'Dunno, I haven't seen the new one.'

'New one?'

'Oh yeah. The original was made back in... what, 1963? '64? Early sixties anyway. Black and white and scary as hell. At least that's how I remember it being when I first saw it, and that must've been in the early seventies.'

'Wow. Really? Best book ever, I reckon.'

Simon stopped himself from asking how many other books Rob had read and stuck to just nodding and smoking.

'And, as far as I recall, William Golding had a hand in the script, although I could be wrong about that. Did you know Golding was born in Cornwall?'

'No, no I didn't.' Rob inhaled thoughtfully on his cigarette. 'D'you s'pose there's a video of that one around?'

'No reason why there shouldn't be. I'll have a look in the rental place at the top of town. If anyone will have it, they'll be the ones.'

Rob flicked his miniscule butt-end away and stood up. The set of his shoulders told Simon he was angry. Rob took the book from Simon, slapped it against his palm and began to walk back to the house.

'Ready then?' He called, without looking round. Simon sat where he was, waiting. The boy got on the path and turned. 'What?'

Simon tucked his chin in and looked at Rob from under raised eyebrows. Wait, he told himself. This may be a seventeen year old lad, just, but he's got the emotional maturity of a twelve year old. Just wait. He stood up.

'Never mind the film, I'm not going to be here, am I? And you got better things to do, looking after these morons. And once I'm gone, well...' He stared out over Simon's head, watching a seagull wheeling overhead. 'Out of sight, out of mind, that's right isn't it?'

Simon could see the tears threatening to spill down Rob's face. He didn't go to him, but finished his cigarette and ground it out on the grass.

'I thought you'd know me better than that, old son. I'll see if I can find the film, then, if you fancy, you can come round mine and watch it. Okay?'

He knew he was breaking the rules and could end up in all sorts of shit, but he'd made an instant decision and knew that he would stand by it if Rob decided to take him up on the offer. Besides, there was something about this lad. He thought he could trust him.

Rob watched the gull disappear over the roof of the house.

They stood, Simon watching Rob and Rob trying to avoid his gaze, for a minute or two. Then Rob said,

'So, what's this woman like where I'm going?'

Simon took his cue and walked across the lawn.

'Mrs. Slattersdyke. Marie Slattersdyke. She's very nice. Stickler for the rules…' He saw Rob raise his eyes and start to sneer at the mention of rules. '… but… but, she's fair. You'll have an outreach worker, she's due to come and see you tomorrow and help you start looking for work…'

'Work?! What about my college?'

'That too, if it's what you want.'

'And what about Tim? Can I get to see him when I want?'

This was the bit that Simon had not been looking forward to. Tim, Rob's younger brother, was being fostered by a family in the town who were none too keen on having Rob turning up on their doorstep. It would take some careful negotiating, despite the fact that there was an agreement to let Tim see family once a week.

Rob and Tim's parents never bothered and the foster carers assumed, wrongly as it happened, that the agreement did not include Rob. They lived by the adage that the fruit never falls far from the tree. And maybe they were right, in some respects.

Although Rob appeared to be a nice enough youngster, there was definitely something there that reminded Simon of Wilkes Senior. He couldn't put his finger on it, but he only had to think about Scooter, and…

'That, old son, will be something that we can discuss with your social worker. I know, I know!' He held up a hand to stop the outburst he could see rising to Rob's lips. 'But I'll work on it, all right? It's the best I can do at the moment. And you've got a part to play in this too, you know. Show the powers that be that you can do this independence thing and…'

'Yeah right! Independence, hah! Same old rules, do as you're told and we'll see. Behave yourself and we'll see. Just hang on while we discuss it and we'll fucking see! Change the fucking record Si! You know it'll never happen while Tim's where he is. But hey, what the fuck, right? C'mon, let's get my bin-bag and go.'

He walked away into the house, hands clenched in his pockets, pushing past Mo Palfrey.

‘Hey, what’s your hurry? Never heard of excuse me?’

Simon heard a muffled ‘Bollocks!’ waft out of the door and thought how fortunate it was for Rob that he’d be away from Palfrey’s pettiness. Mo caught sight of Simon and pushed his round, thick lensed glasses back up his nose, blinking like a malevolent owl.

‘You taking the little reprobate then?’ Simon nodded, not sure he really wanted to speak to Mo at all. He made him want to shout, and tell him what an idiot he was. ‘Good riddance; won’t be sorry to see the back of him. He’s a nasty one, that kid. See it in his eyes.’

‘Very professional assessment, Mo. I must remember that.’

He walked out to the car and waited for Rob to reappear. As he sat, he thought about what Palfrey had said. And he was right. It was Rob’s eyes. They were dead. And if the eyes were the window to the soul, it didn’t bear thinking about.

CHAPTER NINE

2007

Simon looked in the mirror over the sink as the toilet flushed and thought about getting the grey hair seen to. After all, they were in the 21st century, the age of reason and enlightenment, and if females could get their hair coloured because they were worth it, then why not him?

The hammering on the toilet door made him jump.

'Come on Si! What you done, fallen down the hole in the middle or you having a wank in there?!' There were loud guffaws at the remarkable wit of Lee Hensley, followed by group chanting. 'Wan-ker, wan-ker, wan-ker!'

Simon sighed, but before he could open the door to respond, he heard the office door crash back on its hinges and the dulcet tones of Mo Palfrey screeching down the corridor. Remarkable, he thought, that so much had changed in the last seventeen or so years, but Mo was still here, causing the same old grief. The first manager they had worked with, David Sloane, had not managed to get rid of him, and neither had successive managers, right up to the lovely Deidre Cochrane. And she had enough to worry about at the moment.

He stared at himself again, thinking about Terry Faulds. And too much thinking along those lines would only lead to one place - not a place he really needed to be at the moment. Plenty of time for that.

Mo ranted at the group in the corridor and then Deidre came out of her office and grabbed one of the girls to take her into town; divide and conquer.

Simon took one last look at himself and left the security of the cloakroom, wondering at the mysterious ways in which Social Services worked. Not only was he about to take David to his new foster home, but, in the middle of the kerfuffle surrounding Terry, he had taken a phone call to tell them that Lee had been found a place in supported lodgings; Marie Slattersdyke had come up trumps yet again. The woman was amazing.

So now the house was two down and, in the coming weeks, could expect more than a few sleepless nights and disrupted days as the new pecking order was established.

Simon ignored the remainder of the group and went to the lounge to collect David, who sat flicking through the TV channels with a black plastic sack between his feet. He looked up.

'Ready then?' He asked, flicking off the TV and flinging the hand-set onto the settee.

Simon raised his hand in a wait-a-minute gesture and went back to the office. The more things change, the more they stay the same. David had arrived at Freeways with his meagre possessions in a cardboard box and now he was leaving with a luggage upgrade. Simon had lost count, over the years, of the number of kids he had moved on with the ubiquitous black plastic sack. It made him seethe; and, once again, it was good old Mo who had stuffed up.

He opened the office door and stuck his head in.

'Congratulations Mo! You've managed to save us £5.99 on a bag for David. Carry on like this and we can get a new set of pans for the kitchen.' He slammed the door on Palfrey's reply, but smiled in satisfaction at the watery look of surprise on his face, amplified by those coke-bottle bottomed glasses. Now Simon felt stupid and petty himself, and cursed Palfrey for bringing him down to that level and making him feel even sillier.

He banged on the lounge door.

'Come on then Tiger, let's hit the road!'

As they made their way to the car, they passed Lee Hensley's care manager. Simon slowed.

'Hi Keith. What..?'

'Come to collect Lee.'

Simon turned on his heel and held Keith's elbow.

'Whoa, whoa, whoa! Lee? We haven't even broached the move with him yet. It's far too soon to be…'

'Strike while the iron's hot, mate. Places at Marie's are like rocking horse shit, you know that.' He pulled away from Simon's grip and shrugged. 'See you.'

Simon stared at the social worker's back, stunned.

'You catching flies Simon, or are his looks too much to cope with, eh?' David Trelawney laughed.

After they were on the road, heading out to the small village of Stockington, Simon turned on the radio quietly and waited. They had made attempts at small talk; football, downloads, girls, or women as David insisted on calling the children he knocked about with, but now the lull had set in. Not exactly the quiet before the storm, but it was a silence that Simon recognised.

Kids in care, the ones he worked with anyway, didn't talk about themselves a great deal, unless it was to boast about some small triumph or to exaggerate and expand upon a deed of heroic bullying. They might confide in each other, tell snippets of their personal stories to the other residents, because they were kindred. Unlike so many other aspects of their lives, in this they didn't try to out-do one another. History for these kids was painful; not something to wear like a badge. Every so often, when the burden of their past got too much, or they felt safe, they would grab a worker and then more of their story would come tumbling out like a poisonous waterfall, a torrent of muck that had been backing up inside them for who knew how long. Disclosure.

Eye contact was hard for most of them. Sitting in a car, on a one to one basis, provided the perfect opportunity to talk. Not always to disclose, but to try things out; test the water. This was one of those silences.

Simon tapped the steering wheel, rehearsing what he might say to David, because he had a pretty good idea where the conversation might go, if David started talking.

'They don't get it, do they?'

Simon let out a long breath and started to concentrate. Here we go, he thought. Get your listening ears on. That was what a lot of this job was about, listening. Hearing what was going on underneath it all; like trying to pick up a song on a badly tuned radio.

'What's that old son?'

'Blokes like him.' David jerked his head back in the direction they had come. 'Just pitches up, grabs Lee and…what's he think he's playing at, eh? Pick him up and dump him somewhere else. Has he asked Lee? Does he know what Lee wants? Does he care what Lee wants? Course he don't. Just shift 'em round. It's cheaper to keep one of us at somewhere like a B and B than in a place like Freeways, isn't it? Get more people like him and Piggy and you could save the social a fucking fortune.'

He slumped down in the seat, an angry, resigned expression creasing his face into a dark thunder cloud.

Simon let the speech hang in the air for a while and gathered his own thoughts. Mo Palfrey's nickname still hung round like a bad smell. Who had given him that one? One of the other kids… years ago now. What had his name been..? Richard, Roger..? But the lad had been a reader, that much he could remember. 'Lord of the Flies.' That was it… 'Call me Wanker.' Simon smiled; he'd been a sharp lad, like this one.

And that was it, wasn't it? You could listen all you like, make the right noises, but the problem was, and he was probably as guilty as the next person of this, you still treated them like kids. Right and proper, in many respects, but these kids had been through more in their short lives than many of the adults around them were likely to go through in the entirety of theirs. But the kids, they knew. They were savvy and they listened and watched and sensed and knew things, almost intuitively, about what was going on around them. Yet for the most part, they were pretty much invisible to all the adults in their lives.

'And what about this lot?' David pushed himself upright. 'What are they getting paid for having this lout in their home then, eh?' He thumped his chest. 'Cos they're sure as fuck not doing it for love, are they?'

There was the crux: fear. New people, new surroundings, new rules, just…new. And this move had been handled as properly as Simon knew how.

'Of course they're getting paid.' Simon shrugged. 'No kid's cheap to run, Dave, you know that, you said it yourself. But the Shadracks are a great family. You met them. And Warren's about your age, isn't he? Not everybody's about the money, mate, believe it or not.'

'Maybe not. Am I going to be able to get over to town and meet my mates?'

'No reason why not. Warren and his brother play footie a couple of times a week and you'll see the guys at school too. I think this is a great place for you to be, mate. Really.'

'Yeah, right. Don't really have a choice, do I?'

'Hey, come on Dave, we've been through this. We discussed it with

Kathy…'

'That bitch.'

'Put a sock in it fella. She asked if you wanted to go to a foster placement, you said you'd be happy to get out of…'

'The shit pit. Yeah, yeah. I know. It's all down to me.'

'It was a joint decision Dave. You had your say. And, as I recall, Kathy gave you any number of chances to back out. Am I right?'

He waited. This needed to be resolved, as far as possible, before they got to the Shadracks.

'Am I right?'

David huffed and puffed and folded his arms and drew his knees up to his chest.

'Can we change the radio station?'

'Am I right?' Simon needed an agreement.

'Yeah… I s'pose. I'm just… just… just a bit nervous, y'know?'

Simon kept his expression neutral but punched the air in the privacy of his own head. For nervous, read scared shitless. And who could blame the kid? He'd never met his mother - although Social Services knew who she was - didn't know who his father might have been, and his mother wasn't saying, and had spent his entire sixteen odd years getting shunted from pillar to post. He had been adopted at about eight months, then dumped back with Social Services when he was three because his 'dad' had decided that he would be happier living in Saudi with a different partner. His 'mum' decided she couldn't cope and disappeared off the face of the earth. Two foster homes and various residential units later, Freeways had inherited a very angry young man. But things moved on and now David was, it seemed to Simon, much, much better and ready for the change. A change he desperately needed.

'Nervous? Mate, if I was in your shoes, I'd be more than a little nervous. Bloody hell, I remember when I first started at Freeways, I was…'

'You can remember that far back then, can you?'

'Nice. Thanks for that. Dave, seriously, it doesn't matter where you're coming from, any sort of change is stressful, scary. Meeting new people is a big thing for anybody, obviously more so for someone in your position, and anybody who tells you any different, well, sorry, but they're lying.'

'You reckon?' Simon could hear the hopeful cadence in David's voice; wanting to believe what he was being told, but still listening to that small voice that he had come to rely on over the years; the one that said 'They're all full of crap', the one that said 'Keep your head down', the one that said 'Nobody cares for you but you, so get on with it.'

'Without a doubt. Ooops, nearly missed. Here we are.'

Stockington was your archetypal Devon village. Old buildings marching up a winding main street, a mix of thatch and Victorian; a few shops; a pub or two, but in this case, three; a war memorial and a tin hut that passed for a village hall. There was a new build estate on the outskirts and a few grander houses on the edge of the village as the road climbed steeply away towards Dartmoor.

The Shadracks lived in one of the more modest houses that climbed with the road; a lovely old, rambling place that looked lived in, but cared for. They pulled into the drive and, as Simon switched off the engine, the front door opened and Brian and Aileen Shadrack stepped out. They had two children of their own and ran a successful stables a few miles from Stockington. Brent and Warren were at school, so David had the chance to find his sea-legs before having to get to know them properly.

They got out of the car and Simon retrieved David's 'luggage' from the back seat. Aileen Shadrack, veteran of many foster placements, didn't bat an eyelid, but came over, took the bag and extended a hand to David.

'Hello David. Good trip?' She paused momentarily as David touched her hand quickly and dropped it back to his side, staring down at his shuffling feet. 'Come and have a look round, see what you think, cos it's been a while since you were here last, hasn't it?' Without touching him, she put an arm round his shoulder and guided him towards the house, chatting all the while, but pausing occasionally to let David speak if he wanted. He stayed silent, but Simon could see him looking around surreptitiously.

'Hi David,' Brian Shadrack said, careful to use the boy's full name until they found out what he preferred to be called. He and Simon shook hands. 'Good to see you again Si. How's our lad then?'

'Nice to see you too, Brian. Dave? He's scared, but that's stating the obvious, otherwise, I think he'll do okay. You might even have a bit of a honeymoon period, which is never bad.'

'Tea? Coffee?' Brian glanced over his shoulder and saw that Aileen and David had disappeared into the house. 'Or shall we stroll in the garden to discuss the new addition and sample a glass of the homemade that's secreted in the shed?'

'It's a lovely day and you have such a beautiful garden, I think it would be a crime not to take advantage, don't you?'

CHAPTER TEN

1990

Rob Wilkes stood at the gate and looked at the house. There was nothing remarkable about it; a perfectly ordinary, mid-terrace Victorian pile with white painted window frames, red window sills and a matching front door. Paved front garden with tubs, stuffed to overflowing with begonias, pansies and other mysterious blossoms.

White net curtains in all the windows, with odd knick-knacks peeping through, and a gold knocker and letter box. It was the epitome of ordinary, suburban normality. And Rob was quietly shaking as he looked; it scared the living daylights out of him.

The front door was open, revealing a porch with some coats hung there and a closed, glass-fronted door beyond. Hung between the glass and the inevitable nets was a sign that read 'No Vacancies.' Rob hefted his sack like a small Santa and looked over his shoulder at Simon.

'Must be a mistake, Si. Look, they're full.'

The porch door opened as if on cue and a woman, wiping her hands on an apron, stepped out, smiling. Simon gave Rob a gentle push.

'There you go mate; that's Marie. But you will call her Mrs. Slattersdyke until she tells you otherwise. Clear?'

Rob nodded and pushed open the gate, trying a smile on for size. It felt uncomfortable and tight, like a shoe that was too small, pinching, but Marie Slattersdyke seemed not to notice. She walked right up to Rob, took his baggage and said,

'You must be Rob… hello Simon… come on in and have a look around. It's not fancy, but it's comfortable…' She ushered him through the door, still chatting, but glanced back at Simon and indicated that he should follow.

Simon, even in the relatively short time he had been at Freeways, had been out to Marie's any number of times. Bringing new residents or coming to see newly ensconced ones, he always felt at home in Marie's kitchen.

It was, to him, a conglomeration of everything that a homely kitchen should be; warm, welcoming, smelling of baking and with all sorts of arcane paraphernalia hanging on hooks and sitting on shelves throughout the small space. The rest of the house had a similar feel.

As he sat at the kitchen table, he heard Marie's voice and footsteps coming down the stairs.

'… to settle in. Just pop your things in the wardrobe and lay your books out, then come and have a cup of something. I've just taken a fruit cake out the oven.' She breezed into the room on a waft of warm, cake-scented air, and sat opposite Simon. 'Now then, young Simon,' she said, and leant across to pat the back of his hand. 'How are you?'

'Young Simon'! It always made him smile; she was probably no more than two or three years older than he was, yet she had the demeanour of a woman at least a decade older.

'Good as ever, thanks Marie. So, what do you think?'

'Scared little chicken, but he'll be fine, I think. Don't you worry, young Simon, we'll look after him. What's the story?'

'I thought that David had…' She held up her hand and gave him a sad little look that said 'Just tell me, please.' He saw a world of experience in those eyes and knew why the kids that came to her trusted her. 'You know I like to hear it fresh and you seem to have a lot more common sense than most of the oiks they send along with these kiddies. So…'

He gave her a potted history and she listened intently, shaking her head and uttering small noises of shock, even though she had probably heard tales much worse than this. But she didn't just give the impression of caring and being genuinely saddened; something in the way she looked and sat told you that, despite everything, she actually did care. No lip service here.

'What are your first impressions?'

Marie sighed and sat back in her chair, staring at the kitchen wall. When you had been doing something like this for as long as Marie Slattersdyke, you could usually get a pretty accurate idea of how the young person in question would fare.

'Might be bumpy, young Simon, but I think we can cope with anything our Rob can chuck at us. He needs some feeling in his eyes.'

She sighed again. 'Why do people like his parents ever bother to have kids, eh?' And that was the end of the conversation. Marie always ended this part of the new intake chat with a comment about the youngster's past.

They heard an upstairs door close and Rob coming down to join them. Marie stood and went to put the kettle on the gas ring.

'Come on, young man,' she called. 'Kettle's on.'

Rob tried not to shuffle into the room, but walk in confidently and appear to be at ease. The two adults smiled at him and at each other; it had almost worked.

'Now then,' she continued, pulling plates from a cupboard, 'We'll have a brew and a piece of cake, then young Simon can get on his way and we can settle down and have a chat about what we're going to be doing. Okay?'

Rob nodded and looked at Simon, who smiled and gestured, carry on.

'Thanks, yes, cake would be nice, thank you, Mrs. Slattersdyke.' She turned quickly from the cake cutting and looked at him sternly.

'Not telling you again, young Rob. What did I say upstairs?' She cocked her head to one side, waiting.

'Sorry… Marie. Thanks Marie.'

'That's more like it.' She smiled and made the tea, heaping three spoons of sugar into the mug for Rob, somehow divining that this was what he would want. As ever, she was right.

The conversation stuttered along and Rob began to look more and more uncomfortable, until Marie told him to disappear back upstairs and finish what he had been doing. He needed no second invitation, even though they all knew he had no more to unpack. He retreated, looking embarrassed and angry.

Marie nodded, more to herself than anybody else, and tapped the table top, standing as she did so.

'Off you go then, young Simon… no, no, don't fret, we'll be fine. Just keep on going, regardless, and we'll see you in the week, okay?' She peered into his face and waited for a reply. 'Okay?' He nodded. 'Good. Now, away, go on, scat.' She looked thoughtful, reminding Simon of someone who had forgotten something, not important, but was vexed at having forgotten whatever it was. 'Shame about those parents.' she mused, patting Simon on the arm. 'See you soon, my love.'

He found himself on the front path, feeling uncomfortable about leaving Rob, and wondering, if he was uncomfortable, how Rob was feeling. He heard a loud crash from within the house, as if in answer to his question. He turned on his heel and was met by Marie, closing the front door firmly and saying,

'Go on, get lost! I can manage. Done this more times than you've had a wee.' And she was gone.

Simon sat in the car and rolled himself a cigarette, craning his neck to look through the passenger side window at the upstairs of the house. He couldn't hear anything, but knew in his gut that he should go, although his heart told him to hang around just in case. Half an hour and two cigarettes later, he started the engine and headed back to Freeways.

~~~

Marie made a subtle amount of noise as she climbed the stairs, simultaneously knocking and calling out 'You all right Rob, my love?' as she quickly opened the bedroom door.

Rob had all his clothes piled in the middle of the floor and, scattered around and on top of them were his books. He stood staring stupidly at the flame that danced at the tip of his fingers. A Zippo. His farewell present from the kids at Freeways. He looked up.

'What's the point, eh? What's the fucking point? New start? Okay, all right, if it's a new start, let's do it proper. What do you say, Marie? Fancy a fire?'

She didn't show a flicker of emotion, just stepped forward, snapped the top of the lighter shut, scooped all his belongings up in her arms and turned to leave.

'Oi! What you doing? Where you going with my things then?' He was too surprised even to move. Marie turned back to look at him. She tilted her head to one side, seeming puzzled.

'If you want a fire, that's fine. But we do things properly at mine. I've got an incinerator in the back garden and we can go there and do the business… if that's what you want. But you are not losing me my no-claims bonus on the house insurance, clear?' She waited a second and made to go. 'Coming?'

A small sob made her turn around. She breathed a sigh of relief; that had been a gamble and, normally, she was not a betting woman. Walking back to him, she threw the clothes and books onto the bed and put her arms around his shoulders, keeping her own shoulder pressed gently to his chest. Even giving these poor little buggers a cuddle had to
~~~

be done to the rules these days.

She just stood and held him, feeling him quake in her arms. But apart from that initial sob, he uttered not another sound.

'I'm sorry Marie, but… but…'

'Ssh, ssh, ssh.' She patted the back of his head. 'We've got plenty of time. Just you calm down and get tidied up. No harm done now, young Robbie, not a bit of it.' He seemed to collapse into her at the mention of his name.

'My Mum used to call me that.'

'Sorry my love, I didn't want to…'

'No, no, no, it's all right. Honest. It's… it's sort of nice, really.' He shivered a bit as he took a deep breath. 'What am I going to do, Marie? Everything's so big and… they just kicked me out and… I had to say it was all right, didn't I? They say… they say…' He took a step back, wiping his eyes with the heels of his hands, keeping his gaze fixed to the floor.

'They say to you… yeah..? They say 'Tell us what you want. Is this Okay? You must tell us.' So you do, yeah? You tell 'em. You tell 'em what you want. You tell them how you feel about being dumped out cos it's cheaper. You say what you feel. Think. Yeah? Then they look at each other and tell you why what you want isn't possible. Realistic, that's one of their favourite words.' He flopped back onto the bed and fiddled with his books. He held up his copy of 'Lord of the Flies'. 'Tell you what; this fucking book's got more idea about what's real to me than they have.' He looked up at Marie. 'I'll behave while I'm here, Marie, and try to get along. But looking at this lot just now…' He flicked some clothes into the air.

'… well, I decided. If they can say something and just go ahead and do it regardless, then I've learnt a good lesson, eh? I wanted to get rid of it all, you know? Everything about me, even my books. Clean sheet. And that's what I think I'm going to do.'

Marie was watching his eyes as he spoke and silently agreeing with most of what the lad said. As he spoke of clean sheets and new beginnings, she saw that final, tiny spark flick out. And Marie knew, almost certainly, that it was probably going to be too late to save little Robbie Wilkes. Even from himself.

CHAPTER ELEVEN

2007

For a day that had started out with so much promise, it was staggering how fast it had turned into a pile of crap, thought Flute, banging his feet up on his desk and twirling a biro between his fingers. He looked at the wall clock - nearly eight. He'd been at it for close on twelve hours; it felt like twenty and would probably end up being so.

He threw the pen down in disgust. They'd had him! Bloody had him, right there in the palm of their hand, and somehow the smooth little bastard had crawled back under his stone and got away.

He supposed he only had himself to blame, in some respects. He'd been so caught up in the report about the screwdriver that he'd ignored all the other bits of paper. And it was that little scrap that had lain in his tray, that he'd ignored, that had been his undoing. Nick Sloane was a crafty bugger.

And then something even more unpleasant had slithered into his town. A murderer, and what was more, a child murderer. No, that was wrong. The poor sod had been eighteen, but in Flute's book that was still a child.

In the years that Flute had been stationed at the nick, he'd had many dealings with the kids at Freeways; petty stuff on the whole, a lot of it aggravating and time consuming beyond belief, but never anything like this. Ever.

Bill Rockingham had seen the SOCO's pictures right at the start and had called Flute straight away.

'The lad's name is Terry Faulds, Monty. He was living at Freeways up until seven or eight months ago. I'll get hold of Deidre Cochrane, she'll have all the relevant information.'

Flute sat up and reached for a sheaf of papers on his desk.

Preliminaries. Speculation. Possibilities, he supposed. But it didn't look helpful.

The lad had been dead for about six hours when he'd been found and from what they could gather, he had been in the river; yet the clothes he had been wearing, whilst undoubtedly his own, were dry. Well, dry on the outside. It seemed that whoever had killed him, had... what? Dumped him in the river post mortem, then re-dressed him? As strange as it was, that appeared to be the case. But the biggest puzzle, well, one of the bigger puzzles, were the shoes. What the hell was a lad like Terry Faulds doing wearing a pair of brand-new Oxford brogues? Derek Cavannaugh was in another office chasing that one down, or trying to.

Puzzle number two was how did he get there? No car tracks lead to the scene, so he had either been dragged or carried there, which given the location seemed highly unlikely, or else he had been dumped from the river. Yet the man who had found the body - Flute rifled through the papers - Michael Soloman, couldn't remember seeing a soul.

Flute picked up the pen and circled Soloman's name on the sheet. Thus far, he was their only suspect and a pretty damn flimsy one at that. No. Flute knew, in his heart of hearts, that Soloman wasn't anything to do with it. He scrabbled under the pile and pulled out the pathologist's prelim. It made uncomfortable reading and started Flute down a path that he really didn't want to be travelling right now.

How alone was this young lad? How scared? And having started thinking like this, it was inevitable that he thought of Tom and how he was at the end. Flute would never have the answers to those questions, for Terry Faulds or Tom, but he had his imagination, and that was more than enough.

The infernal mobile in his jacket pocket warbled at him. He hated the tone but had yet to find out how to change the damn thing - and a certain stubborn pride precluded him asking Cavannaugh or Bill Rockingham to change it for him.

'Flute.'

'Monty; Rocky. Still at it then?'

'Absolutely. Treading treacle at the moment.'

'That's sounds about par for the course. You leaving soon?'

'I should think so. I can't do much else but sit and stare at the paperwork really. All the people I need to talk to have gone home.'

'Then follow their example and meet me at The Goat for a jar.'

'It is tempting, I admit…yeah, go on then, I'll see you in about half an hour, okay?'

'Anon. Bye.'

'Yeah, bye.' He flipped the cover back and slid the phone across his desk, already half wishing he had declined the offer. He wasn't really in the mood for socialising, yet maybe he needed to get lost a little in cheery mundanity rather than the morbid variety.

Cavannaugh tapped at the door and came in, wearing the harried expression of one who had spent a fruitless few hours on the telephone. Flute gestured to the chair in the corner.

'And?'

Cavannaugh threw up his hands and slapped them back down on his thighs.

'I suppose that means you were frustrated?'

'Very. That's the problem with the internet, isn't it?'

'Sergeant, I have yet to unravel the mysteries of mobile phone technology, so don't ask me to comment on the efficiency of something about which I have not got the first notion.'

'Ah. Too much information is the basic problem. There must be thousands of manufacturers, makers, distributors, sellers and painters of the Oxford brogue. Black. Size nine.'

'Painters?'

'Precisely. Anyway, I managed to narrow it down to the manufacturer, but they supply so many different people, they could have been bought anywhere. There are over seventy outlets in Devon alone for this particular brand.'

'Well, we have to start somewhere. What about young Terry's background, anything to pull us in the right direction there?'

'Now that's a deal more helpful. Deidre Cochrane gave us copies of the file from Freeways, with her bosses' permission, and I've had a couple of P.C.s wearing their fingers to the bone. But the offices are closed now, so we'll start again in the morning.'

'What's his story?'

Cavannaugh gave Flute a brief picture of the life that had been Terry Faulds' and watched as his boss's face crumpled into an expression that he could only describe as weary sadness.

'Dear God, poor little… what about the carers who are waiting to go to court? Anything there? Could they have done this to keep him from testifying?'

'Not likely. The bloke's inside for a different offence and his wife's now in a hospice with bowel cancer. She's out of it regardless.'

'Maybe there is a crude sort of justice then. Have you read the pathologist's initial thoughts on what happened to him?'

'No. But I get the impression, by the look on your face, it wasn't nice.'

Flute pushed the paperwork across his desk and tapped with his forefinger.

'Not required reading, but I think you should know. He was tortured before he had his throat cut, basically. Mr. Kent will be carrying out a full examination tomorrow.'

'Why? Why... what's the point, Sir? I just can't fathom what sort of motivation lies behind somebody doing something like this.'

'I doubt even the killer really understands what's going on. The human psyche is much like the mobile phone as far as I'm concerned.' He stood and put his jacket on, dropped his mobile into the pocket with a grimace and looked at the clock. 'I'm off for a beer and if you've got any sense, you'll do the same. Good night Sergeant.'

'Night Sir.'

Flute's footsteps echoed down the corridor of the nearly deserted police station. They had a civilian night clerk on the desk, but these days, any calls were all routed through the Exeter switching centre. During the night, the mobile patrols could use the station if they needed, but the public couldn't gain access. All they had was a telephone outside that connected to Exeter as well. He had a thorough dislike of this place at this time of night; it seemed even more institutional than it did during the day, a typical example of late fifties building. Square, by all accounts functional and very much soulless.

He nodded to the clerk at the desk and let himself out into the cool night air. It was a clear, breathless evening, with the westering sun throwing a soft, gold light across everything.

The Goat seemed an even less attractive proposition, now that he was outside, but he'd promised to meet Bill.

The roads were quiet and he arrived at the pub in good time. It seemed fairly busy. The picnic tables in the garden had huddles of people enjoying the last of the sunshine and the whole place felt relaxed and welcoming.

He took the first parking place he came to and, as he was locking the Saab, a black Porsche that looked as if somebody had set about it with a sledge hammer pulled into the car park.

The driver slid out from behind the wheel and stood, pushing his sunglasses up onto his head, looking at the garden and the people.

Flute felt his stomach clench and gripped his keys until they bit into the palm of his hand. He could get back in the car and drive away; he'd come for a quiet drink. But he decided to hang around.

It might be interesting to have a chat with Nick Sloane.

CHAPTER TWELVE

2007

So good to live by the river. Calming. So good to live near the countryside yet be close enough to a town so as to not lose touch with the pulse, the life, the vibrancy.

So good to have the river running through the town, cutting it in two, effectively separating the good from the bad and ugly. So peaceful was the garden as It stared at the lights in Eastown, imagining all that was happening over there.

It chuckled, relishing the sound it made and how it felt in It's mouth. Everything had a flavour, a unique taste…everything. Soon, It would prowl and hunt again. There had been too much time wasted, and the struggle for their souls and salvation had lost its momentum. It felt the tears well and the emptiness bloom as It thought of all the children that needed to feel It's love and benediction; so many that could have been shown, were it not for the interfering, meddlesome…It clenched It's fists, willing the fury back behind the bars, bidding it wait.

It laced It's fingers, feeling the delicate bones and soft sinews, marvelling at their intricacy and wondering how things that felt so fragile could wield so much power. It could feel them stretching, reaching; they were remembering their work, being awoken; as It's heart was being awoken, stirring, beating in time with the desire to be known, to be alive once again. It needed to pass It's love on to those that were deserving. And there were so many. So very many.

It felt the rage battering at the bars, howling to be free. Sometimes It felt that It should allow It's wrath free-rein, just let it go and watch it run amok in the ranks of the Others; those who refused to try and understand the purity of It's crusade. They who would try and stop that very crusade and place It behind the same bars where It caged It's power.

For the Others, the acts alone were not enough. They were dull of mind and spirit; unenlightened. It would have to spell things out for them.

It shivered in anticipation, relishing the thought of their confusion; how they would try and quantify and qualify and explain, when all they had to do was look at what would be in front of them to understand the purity and humanity of the mission.

They would have proof of It's divinity before very much longer, as It gathered the poor lost souls to Itself and gave them the freedom they so deserved. It stared up at the stars for a moment, shivered and made It's way down the steps to the river.

It sucked the air into It's lungs, smelling the mud and green decay; the faint, coppery residue of love spent and love reborn. It was the scent of prophecy, the bouquet of divination and its taste was spectacular.

The boathouse was a clever construction, hidden by reeds at low tide, but rising with the water as it came in. The structure rested on purpose built blocks when the tide was out, giving It the privacy It required. This was It's way-station, It's halfway-house, the place where they all came to realise It's magnificence and generosity, the place where they came to know that their journey to a loving, carefree future was nearly over.

It sat in a straight-backed chair in the corner of the boat-house, watching the oily rise and fall of the water and hearing it suck at the pilings with a lasciviousness that made It smile in fond remembrance. The atmosphere was restful, gave It space to think and ponder upon aspects of the mission that had been troubling It. The problem was, in the greater scheme of things, a minor one, but it was a puzzle, one that was both pleasing and annoying. How could It define Itself? Annoying as it was, It had to have a way to describe Itself for the Others, to better lead them to understanding; things had to be classified, delineated, labelled for the uninitiated.

The smile faded from It's lips and It's mouth tightened. It knew what It was, but It would need a name; things had to be signposted for the fools.

It laughed. The notion was exquisite and, like all good ideas, all great ideas, so very simple and obvious; they might even be granted a glimmer of understanding. It would be Cupid.

~~~

Success allowed many things, indulgence being one of them,
~~~

anonymity and power being just some of the others. He was unsure which of these he enjoyed most but thought that all three were perhaps dependent, one upon the other. He certainly wouldn't be able to indulge his...proclivities, without his power and wealth, and these perfectly natural tendencies had afforded him even more wealth and power. All rather neat and comfortable; almost like being paid for doing something you loved.

He reached across his desk and opened the lid of his hand-crafted Chavin humidor. The aroma rising from such a thing of beauty made him smile broadly. Things of quality and class, things that reminded him of his less-than-humble beginnings, were things to be cherished and prized. Possessions were trappings and, generally speaking, that didn't impress him, but possessions that screamed expense and excellence were to be prized. The rarer and more beautiful they were, the better he loved them. Beauty was his creed; beauty in all things, and if he could own it, so much the better.

He let the aromatic smoke slide into his lungs, relishing its mildness and perfume. He watched the blue billowing haze roll lazily from his mouth as he exhaled, floating with the fumes across the tastefully decorated study.

Checking his watch, a Rolex naturally, he stood up and stretched, deciding that he would have a massage before he went to the warehouse. He needed to be relaxed and prepared before he slid into his other skin and presented himself to the world of lesser mortals.

He flicked a switch on the intercom and a solicitous voice answered at once.

'How may I help you, Sir?'

'I'm showering. Bring Melissa and Briony to the blue room for my massage. Ten minutes. And Frank?'

'Sir?'

'Make sure they wear their leather collars, the Moroccan ones, and the wrist and ankle straps.'

He cut the connection, knowing that all would be ready and waiting for him when he emerged from the shower. Another advantage of success: no one questioned him. It was power in one of its many guises.

A gentle, four-note warble disturbed his reverie, warning him of a call on his very private line. Either a customer or supplier needed soothing or encouraging. He felt a tinge of annoyance that his anticipation had been interrupted by the mundane necessities of something as coarse as business; he wasn't properly prepared. In his mind's eye he needed to put the correct picture in the frame, his notion of how others saw him, before he could deal with things in that world. He was wearing the wrong skin, which always put him in a less receptive mood.

He grabbed the handset, taking a deep breath as he did so.

'Yes.'

'Is that you, Tantalus?'

Very few things made his skin crawl, but the sound of that voice, soft and wheedling, leaking sincerity he knew to be as false as his own façade, made his gorge rise. He disliked anger intensely and became, paradoxically, furious when someone made him feel that way. Someone would pay for spoiling what he had hoped would be a relaxing hour or so before he ventured out. He waited, bringing his thoughts under control; nothing must betray his repulsion. No quiver in the voice, nothing. They had a mutually beneficial arrangement, each making the other a great deal of money. Strange that he, of all people, should have qualms in dealing with this… person.

'Tantalus? It's me. Are you there?'

'Who else would it be? What do you want?'

'I will have… merchandise for you very soon.'

'The market is contracting. I'm not sure if I can…'

'Now, now, Tantalus…' The voice paused, allowing the inflection used on his name to burrow home to where, the caller knew, it would sit and fester. Where it would ripen and swell until it split and spilled its poison over whoever happened to be on hand. 'Let's not be hasty or uncooperative; besides, Daddy would want you to help me, now wouldn't he? Mmm?'

Tantalus closed his eyes and tried to concentrate, repel the thoughts and emotions that were rising in him, threatening to drown him in a river of stagnant, malignant memories. He clamped his teeth together, trying not to grind them in impotent rage.

'Not grinding our teeth, are we?' Asked the voice in an artless fashion. Tantalus could almost hear the smile that was sneered across the speaker's face.

'Don't try and invoke that particular ghost to get your own way! He was your 'daddy', not mine. You and your like were the special ones. This is the last time, alright? Call me again and I promise you I'll make sure…'

'Promise me what?' Hissed the voice. 'I have people too, you snake. There are ways…'

'Ways! Ways?! You really have no idea, do you? You think your sick little world will always turn, don't you? One day, and the way you're going that day is not very far off, one day you'll discover just what the nature is of the bear you poked with your sharpened stick. Do you honestly think I've become who I am and remained where I am, without having friends? I could…'

'Oooh, now I'm really scared! The things you've done have been the terrors of the earth. Daddy would be proud.'

'That man had nothing to do with anything here, anything I've achieved…' Tantalus could feel the sweat on his brow and the utter, all-encompassing fury boiling in his gut. How dare this creature impugn him in this way, hold him accountable for what created them all? This bastard was due a lesson. He took a long, deep breath, pulling himself back under control.

The voice at the other end of the line laughed softly.

'I'm still good, aren't I? Still able to find your soft spot and squeeze until you squeal.'

'When?'

'It's already begun. I'll be in touch… and remember: I've got you by the balls as much as you have me. Be nice.'

The gentle burring of the disconnected line drove Tantalus over the edge. He threw the telephone across the room and screamed. The tormented noise echoed round the house and in their rooms, the children cowered, knowing that He was upset. And that they would suffer for it.

Tantalus sat down slowly and removed his shoes, holding both of them to his chest and crooning to himself. He would polish them now. It always calmed him a little.

As he polished the black Oxford brogues, he sang himself a little song, letting his mind drift and explore new ways that he might vent himself on his most precious possessions.

CHAPTER THIRTEEN

2007

Ed Peterson did what he did best; creep. Not deliberately, but he did. It was the way he went unnoticed. He crept everywhere. He was stealth personified, which was how he had come by his name at Freeways. Of course, he was long gone from there now, glad to be out. But he still kept in touch with a couple of the kids; saw them in the field, behind the cricket pavilion or down the old branch line station every so often, when they congregated to have a drink or had got enough dosh together to buy some weed. It was they who had given him his nickname, 'Creep'.

He liked it; because, even at twenty one and living on the streets, it gave him a feeling of belonging to someone or somewhere.

Which was why, he supposed, he'd never left the town when he was moved into independence lodgings. He managed a couple of months away at Old Mother Slutty Bikes, but missed the old place. He couldn't understand why the kids who went there liked her so much. He scratched his arse through his grubby great coat and patted his pockets for his tobacco; no accounting for taste, he reckoned.

Creep walked in the shadows, kept to the back streets whenever he could, always kept his eyes on the pavement. Rarely spoke, even when spoken to, which was a problem when he went to collect his dole, but the people whose gardens he tended on an irregular basis had no cause to complain. He worked hard, did as he was told and went away - for minimum money.

Nobody knew where he lived, which suited Creep just fine. Having hopped over the wall from the small industrial estate, he headed along the riverbank towards the back of the local supermarket. It wouldn't be long before the night stackers rolled up the doors and trundled out all the throwaway goods that they couldn't sell. It was cheap and he didn't have to speak to anyone. In actual fact, apart from the few kids he met up with, the only person he ever said more than a couple of words to was Andy Hopkirk, the local off-licence manager. Creep was a good customer.

He liked it along the river at dusk, especially at this time of year. All the trees had leaves and cast shadows. He should have moved to his summer place back along, but the weather had been lousy up until a few days ago, so he'd stayed under his pallets for longer than usual.

He disappeared into the bushes as he heard some people approaching on push bikes. He'd grab some food, go to the offy and then head back to the yard. Few ciders, then kip. He had to get an early start, Mr Pruitt was expecting him at the top of town to do his vegetable garden.

And that was what he did. It was what he did most days and nights.

Early the following morning, he was up and over the wall and heading down the path, actually quite enjoying the early morning quietness. He stopped and listened, head to one side. Odd.

He peered between some overhanging branches, down to the river that drifted serenely by, heading under the town's two bridges and on, to the sea. Blimey, he thought, he's enthusiastic. Creep looked down river, under the first, modern bridge, to the second, 19th century version. The tide was going out fast, and the bloke he'd just seen in the rowing boat was going to have to be pretty careful going under Eastown Bridge, because you could already see the rocks hidden below the surface when the river was full.

Creep thought about calling a warning and decided better of it; he just watched the man pulling hard and heading, ever more swiftly, towards the second bridge.

He heard somebody whistle a dog and call. That was Mr Soloman and Colin. Creep sometimes did a bit of hedge trimming for him. He'd have a word and see if there was anything in the offing.

Always good to have more than one string to your bow.

CHAPTER FOURTEEN

1990

Rob had held on to the idea that things could, and would, get better. It seemed to be working. Marie Slattersdyke was a difficult person to live with, but, as time had gone by, Rob had come to understand the expression 'hard but fair'. Simon Nicholson had kept his word, despite Rob's niggling doubts, and had been in contact often. They had, eventually, managed to sit down together and watch both versions of 'Lord of the Flies'. Simon had been right, much as it annoyed Rob to admit it, that the original version was by far the better; less glossy and more immediate. More real.

And in the real world (although sometimes Rob wondered), what he couldn't get his head around was how slow everything was. Anything and everything that he wanted or needed had to be cleared by, it seemed, half a dozen people and there was always some precondition with regards to his behaviour or what they expected him to do in return. There never seemed to be a straight 'yes' to anything.

Marie worked hard to try and compensate a little for that and, every so often, would leave a gift for Rob on his bed. Usually a book. He had a good collection now, but his favourite was still 'Lord of the Flies'.

The slowest, most frustrating aspect, was getting to see his brother. Tim was fostered by a local family, not half a mile from Freeways, while Rob was in Torquay, at least fifteen miles away. Rob's social worker, it seemed to him, was dragging his heels about contact. Everybody involved had to give consent, and that included Rob and Tim's parents. And Tim's foster carers. And his social worker. And the link worker. The list was apparently endless. Every fucking social worker and their bosses and their boss' bosses and their cousins seemed to have a say in what was and wasn't right and proper for Rob to do - or not do. Or see.

Rob was slowly coming to grips with the speed of things generally, but this was ridiculous. He had been with Marie for nearly three months and nothing had happened. Despite the promises he had made to innumerable people, this morning, he had decided that all the to-ing and fro-ing was coming to an end.

He had a feeling that it was his parents, mainly his father, who were blocking the visits. Ian Wilkes had a hatred for all things official that out-weighed everything else. If he could do anything to thwart the social, the police, the government, anyone in authority, then you could bet your life he would.

Rob had been rehearsing this for days now; running through the order in which he would approach people, always remembering to keep his temper and manners, try to be reasonable with, and respectful of, others, but just get to spend some time with his brother.

His first stop was his Mum and Dad's place. He hadn't called it home for as long he could remember. He didn't think it had ever been home, not in the way he had come to understand the true sense of the word.

He stepped off the bus in the centre of town, aware that he had already broken his word to Marie. She thought he was at the library in Torquay. There was no way he would have been able to explain to her what he intended to do and have her understand, even though she said she did.

He headed across the old bridge, turning right opposite the 'Bull and Horse', his old man's favourite pub - probably because it was closest to home - and found himself in old Eastown, a random mishmash of old farm-workers cottages, rambling Victorian piles and Thirties middle-class homes, all crowding haphazardly around St Boniface's church. Eastown as it had been, before the Sixties had come cavorting into town and demanded new housing. There had been plenty of landowners who had seen a way to a quick profit and the unloading of land that was not much use, other than to graze a few sheep on. There were always fields elsewhere to do that, and the views from the hillside were lovely. Or had been until the planners and builders got to work.

Rob crossed the road and headed up the hill into the heart of the estate. It spread for what seemed like miles; long twisting roads, lined with houses that had an air of defeat hanging from them, like the washing that hung limply in the yards. Cul-de-sacs branched off in various directions, dead ends, even though some of them had crescents leading off them.

Occasionally, there would be a ray of hope in the line of despair; someone who had taken a little time over their small plot of land, arranging strips of flowers or placing hanging baskets on the walls. They were few and far between.

Rob crammed his hands into his pockets, pulled his head down into his shoulders and stared at the pavement as he walked. Uniformly drab and dirty houses filed past him on either side, with little to distinguish one from the other apart from the different coloured front doors.

He felt the angry, leaden lump in his gut grow as he approached number 19. The loud and violent memories clamoured in his head; the smells, the noise, the pain. He stood for a moment, waiting at the gap where a garden gate had once been, looking miserably down the path to the dusty red front door.

The windows stared back. A local radio station sticker, peeling off at one corner, sat in the centre of one of them, giving it the appearance of a malevolent, one-eyed beggar, hoping for a hand-out but knowing that none would be forthcoming.

He took a deep breath, gritted his teeth and walked to the door. He pushed the button and heard the distorted sound of 'Lara's Theme', painfully out of tune because the batteries were almost flat. It was his Mum's favourite film. The door stayed shut. He heard no footfalls coming to answer the summons.

Rob felt like just turning round and walking away. Perhaps if he had, his life might have taken a different path, but he pushed at the door with his forefinger, knowing, or vaguely recalling, that it was often left on the latch for his Dad, who forgot his key more often than taking it with him to the pub.

The door creaked open.

With his head still down, the first thing he saw was the coconut mat, worn bald in places, with the legend 'Welcome to our Happy Home' still legible. There was the telephone table, just inside the door and, hanging from the wall, an assortment of coats, with an army of old boots and shoes piled haphazardly beneath. He looked slowly up the stairs and down the hall towards the kitchen. The daylight that spilled in through the front door did nothing to brighten the interior, it merely emphasised the drabness of the surroundings.

White painted banisters and woodwork, faded and yellowed, chipped and tired; wallpaper, torn in places, also faded, that had hung there for as long as he could remember; carpet, once green and patterned with yellows and browns, that tried to hold you to the spot, almost begging you not to go inside; all these clawed at his senses, making him feel small and helpless again. And the smell, insidious and vaguely threatening, of old biscuits and long dead dog, wrapped itself around his head, smothering him with memories. He could almost hear himself screaming at his father to leave mummy alone, whilst in the background, little Timmy, in his nappy that hadn't been changed for days, screamed almost as loudly.

Piles of old newspapers and unopened mail marched up the stairs and in the hallway four or five black plastic rubbish bags huddled in the shadows, like frightened dogs waiting for a beating.

Rob closed his eyes and took a deep breath through his mouth, trying not to gag, then stepped across the threshold, wiping his feet like a good boy, and trod on the carpet that tried to hold him back.

A layer of dust coated everything, from the gaps in the banisters to the telephone table, whilst great nets of old cobwebs hung from the corners of the ceiling.

'Hello?'

His voice fell flat, yet seemed to echo through the ghost-laden house. The air was thick with sadness and stale hatred. Nothing could survive in this, nothing could thrive and grow, least of all two little boys whose parents' lives revolved around alcohol and hating each other.

He decided to look upstairs, knowing that if anyone was in, it was likely to be his mother, probably still in bed, sleeping off another night of vodka. Her way of 'relaxing'.

The landing was littered with cardboard boxes, half-full of old clothes and board games that had never been played. This was from the era of the car-boot business, something else that had never actually got beyond the big idea stage. Ian Wilkes had been, and still was, as far as Rob knew, a great one for hitching himself to a money-making bandwagon and falling off before the wagon had ever reached full speed. His father's creed was: if at first you don't succeed, give up straight away.

Rob tapped gently at his parents' bedroom door and waited. Nothing. Clenching his fists and trying to stop himself shaking, he pushed it open. The uniform mess had found its way here too and the smell was foul. Even the sunshine through the grimy windows seemed dirty as it fell to the floor, across piles of clothes and old magazines, like a tired old yellow cat that couldn't be bothered to curl up to sleep.

His mother, wearing a bra and panties, with her jeans half-way down her legs where they had been when she had passed out, lay spread-eagled across the bed. Rob looked at her, wanting to feel something, anything. Even hatred would have meant that there was a little left inside him, but he couldn't even feel pity.

A nearly-empty half bottle of vodka sat on the bedside table; this was the love in which Helen Wilkes got lost these days, only now it was more than mere infatuation. Her harshly blonde hair lay in matted tails across her face. Her blue eye-shadow, also harsh, was smeared and mixed with black eye-liner, giving her the appearance of wearing a mask. No superhero this, no wonder woman. She was thirty five, this much Rob knew, but lying there oblivious to everything, she would have passed for a ravaged fifty.

Rob picked an old dressing gown off the floor and threw it over her, knowing that to try and wake her, let alone speak to her about Tim, would be an impossibility. He didn't feel disappointed, just resigned.

As he reached the bottom of the stairs, he heard a noise from the living room. He stopped, listening. Television? It sounded too real, too un-amplified. He suddenly felt cold, distant. Everything zoomed into sharp, monochromatic focus. He knew Father Fear when it hit him, and this was it. He could feel the sweat chilling on his forehead, and his thigh muscles starting to twitch almost uncontrollably. A groan and cough. Another drunken sleeper, he hoped.

His head shrieked at him to get out the house but Rob needed to see. Needed to conquer his fear. If he wanted to achieve anything today, then this would be a thing to do. This was no pig's head on a stick, no dead airman, this was real. It was his Lord.

He turned the handle and eased the door open just wide enough for him to get his head and shoulders through the gap.

He was so hot now, he thought the plastic would melt between his fingers; he could feel the rough pattern of the flock wallpaper in the lounge scratching at his back as he pushed through the opening; his breathing sounded harshly in his ears.

Ian Wilkes lay face down on the sofa, wearing only dirty boxers. His jeans and an Iron Maiden tee-shirt were on the floor, hanging like a limp flag from the neck of an empty Jacky D. bottle.

Rob felt sick.

Lying beneath his father was a girl, naked but for a bra. As the door opened and his face peered round, her eyes shot open and she pulled one arm from beneath the sleeping man.

Rob froze. His father muttered and stirred and rolled slightly to one side, easing a hand across the girl's stomach and resting it on her crotch.

'Still lively, eh my little Rosie?' He belched and opened bloodshot eyes to peer down at her. 'Nothing like a bit of morning nooky, and I'm your man for that.'

The girl struggled briefly, pushing her free hand against Wilkes' shoulder; she looked at Rob in the doorway, great dark eyes pleading with him to help her. Wilkes half turned his head. Rob expected him to explode from the sofa, in a whirl of fury and stale whiskey.

He just gave a cigarette choked chuckle and winked at him.

'Fancy a threesome then? Let your old man teach you a thing or two.' He looked back down at the girl. 'That's right, innit Rosie my Rose? Still a few tricks in the old dog yet then.'

Rob flew out the house with his father's laughter slapping him about the head and the only words he ever heard the girl speak ringing in his ears.

'Help me, pleeeeeease!'

~~~

How Rob managed to keep his voice on an even keel, he never knew, but he succeeded. He had permission from Marie to go into town and meet a couple of old friends. Back by eleven was the only proviso. He was only grateful that she couldn't see his face. Marie had an instinct for lies, on a face to face basis. Thank God for telephone boxes.

After he'd run from his parents' house, he had no clear notion of what he intended to do. The rage and horror and utter emptiness was all consuming.

On the town side of the bridge, down some steps next to the river, was a small spit of land. It stretched, like a triangle, for a few hundred yards, with the river on the left and a channel on the right, where a host of small boats were moored. LeCroix Island, named for the town with which the area was twinned, was a pleasant place for people to eat their lunches and stroll in the sunshine. And in the evening, it had enough bushes and trees to hide some of the local ne'er-do-wells from prying eyes. It was known by the kids as Cider City and was also many people's permanent address.
~~~

He sat on a bench at the far end of the island, staring across the water, down towards Quay Marsh and the rolling hills beyond.

Blank; totally and completely blank. He could have been a cardboard cut-out, placed on the seat by some joker. He barely moved the entire time he sat there and how long that was, he had no idea; only that when, in time, he became aware of his surroundings, the sun had moved across the sky and his stomach was telling him it was way past the time to eat.

Sitting in isolation had accomplished one thing; he was calmer, he felt less empty and his head was clearer. He decided to stroll into town, grab a sausage roll or a pasty, then go up to where Tim was living and see if he could persuade them to let him and Tim spend a bit of time together. He was not going to let this day become a complete waste.

He allowed himself to day-dream as he walked up the hill through town, heading toward the edge of the Domington Estate, where Tim was living with a family whose jobs were all on the land attached to the Estate.

He let himself imagine that he and Tim had a place of their own. A flat somewhere, away from town but not in the countryside, so they could lead their own lives. Sure, he knew they'd need help and money, he wasn't naïve enough to think it could happen without other people being involved, but it would be just them; him 'n' Tim was what his head told him they would be. Him'n'Tim. The other kids at Freeways would sometimes sit in each other's rooms, late at night, and talk quietly about what the future held. Most of them wanted a family, simple as that. The majority of the girls had already decided that their route to happiness was having a baby. A little one who would love them unconditionally.

If there was one thing Rob agreed with workers at Freeways about, it was that the girls were daft - his words, not theirs. It was kids having kids and not a thing Rob relished. They all reckoned that they could do so much better than the sad excuses they had been saddled with. But Rob knew they were doomed to failure.

They'd end up in a hostel for young mothers, watched over by well-meaning women, and they would have no real idea what being a parent was all about. Disaster. It was not something that Rob ever wanted to experience.

His dreams of Him 'n' Tim began to waver as he approached the house where Tim lived with the Crooks, Don and Melanie. He knew this was the closest Tim had ever come to a real family, with or without Rob. His daydream flashed up in his face and wind blew the ashes away.

He rang the doorbell, waiting for any number of responses to his arrival, and as ready as he could be with an equal number of carefully thought-out and rehearsed replies. He was relieved to hear Don Crooks call that he would get it. Good. Don was fair, like Marie, and a bluff, friendly Geordie.

Don Crooks opened the door, newspaper in hand, calling back over his shoulder.

'Aye, I've got it.' He turned to see who was there, and Rob saw his smile falter.

'Well, well, Robbie. Why man, there's a surprise.' He folded the paper under his arm and stepped outside to stand in front of Rob. He looked him up and down and his smile surfaced again. 'Well yer grown and no mistake man. Was it Tim y'wanted?'

Rob just nodded; he couldn't think of anything sensible to say.

'I'd best check wi'the boss first.' He winked, turned to go, then turned back again. He sighed. Rob didn't like the sound of that. He heard sighs like that from too many people to think that it boded any good. 'Nay, Robbie man, I canna pretend that. Look son, have youse checked wi' anyone that it's okay t'be here like?' Rob stared at him, caught in the headlights of Don Crooks' concerned face. 'Truth is son, y'old man was here a couple a weeks ago, with his and Tim's workers like, 'n' they said... well, it was y'old man actually... said that you'd told 'em that y'dinna want t'see Timmy again like. That it was unfair on him. Timmy was devastated, man. That's why I was a bit surprised like, when I opened the door.'

Rob felt his throat closing over and the tears stinging his eyes. Why had they done that? What gave them the right? He swallowed hard, choking back his anger and frustration.

'I never said that.' He kept his voice quiet. He was afraid that if he raised it, he'd lose his temper. 'It's my Dad. It's him. Why didn't my social worker tell me? I've... I've been waiting for them to arrange a visit. They told me not to just turn up on your doorstep. So I waited.'

Don Crooks laid a hand on Rob's shoulder, feeling the barely suppressed emotion quivering below the surface.

'More power to y'lad, for waitin'... but I dinna think your Tim's going to want to see youse... not right away like. Are y'still at Marie's?'

Rob nodded, ducking his head as he lost the battle with his tears. He buried his face in the crook of his arm, mashing them away.

'They can't stop me, can they? I mean…'

The front door flew open and Tim hopped out, grabbing Don round the waist and peering under his arm.

'Who is it Dad? Is it…' His face froze when he saw his brother standing there, red eyed and wet faced. Tim's own face crumpled and his chin trembled, his breath coming in short, angry gasps. 'What do you want?' he screamed. 'What do you want, you shit bag, eh?! Get away from me.' He took a step round Don, lashing out with one clawed hand. 'You… you…' A feral, uncontrolled screech flew from between his gritted teeth.

Don scooped him up round the waist and pushed the door open with his free hand.

'Away now son,' he called over his shoulder. 'Away 'n' I'll call y'at Marie's, soon as I might.'

Rob stared at the closed door, unable to take in what had just happened. He walked away, but, as he walked back to the bridge, he knew that he had an appointment with his father. And the sooner the better.

~~~

The sun was a grey and orange memory in the western sky, closing everything in stealthy shadows and warmth, as Rob sat on the bridge parapet diagonally opposite the 'Bull and Horse', listening to the noise filtering out from the public bar. And above the general hubbub, he heard Ian Wilkes' drunken laughter.

He stared down at the piece of wood from which he was picking the bark. He could wait. He had all the time in the world.

Rob had spent the rest of the day and most of the evening sitting on the bench at the end of Cider City, drinking, pacing himself, not wanting to get so pissed that he was useless. But he needed the courage. Time and thinking were a rage's bitter enemies. The fury was still there, but muted. Four cans of cider and a small bottle of vodka (the Wilkes' poison of choice, so it seemed) later, he was here, peeling a stick and waiting.

The public bar door opened and the noise spilled out onto the street, closely followed by a reeling Ian Wilkes. He stood, hands on knees, staring back at the bar. Raising his middle finger to whoever it was that
~~~

stood in there, he shouted,

'And fuck you too!' He straightened up and waved. It seemed that this was his friendly way of saying goodnight. 'See ya!'

He staggered round in a small circle, relying on his homing instincts to set him on the right course, fumbling in his pocket for his cigarettes as he did so. He eventually found his mouth and shielded the flame of his lighter with a flourish. The flame cast an eerie blue and orange glow across the thin, stubbled face. He saw somebody watching him, sitting on the wall next to the bridge. Stuffing the lighter back into his pocket and removing the cigarette from his mouth, Wilkes swept it extravagantly away to one side and let the smoke leak out over his face.

Rob watched quietly, feeling the hatred bubbling to the surface as this arrogant, ignorant man stood, hip shot and cocky, watching him.

'Got a problem m'buck?' He called, taking what was meant to be a threatening step forward which instead turned into a messy stumble. Wilkes' Devon accent always came to the fore when he was drunk.

Rob slid off the wall, tossing the stick over his shoulder into the river, gave his father a slow up and down look, spat, and walked away towards the riverside steps. What happened next depended upon how punchy Wilkes was feeling. Rob reckoned that what he had just done would be enough provocation.

He was right.

'Oi! You! What be your problem then, eh?'

Rob could hear the footsteps picking up speed. He got to the top of the steps and looked back. Wilkes was halfway across the bridge, flicking his half smoked cigarette into the river. 'Problem, you old fuck? Problem?' He gauged the distance between himself and his father and decided it was worth one final shove. 'The only problem I got is you, you old cunt.'

He didn't wait to see what effect his words had, taking the steps down to the river two and three at a time, and turning quickly back into the shadows cast by the brickwork. Crouching down, Rob felt round for the lump of wood he'd salvaged earlier from the industrial estate, hefted it, and waited.

His father reached the top of the steps and stood there, swaying, looking down the footpath. He took a couple of steps down and stopped, waving a dismissive hand.

'You'm not worth it, y'useless piece a...' His voice trailed off, head incapable of coping with staying upright and talking at the same time.

Rob leant the wood against the steps and walked out into the dim light cast by the street lamps over the bridge. He looked up as the figure he had held in so much dread over the years, turned back to the road.

'You're not fit to eat what drops out of a dogs arse. Piss head.'

Wilkes wheeled round and squinted down at Rob, who picked up a handful of gravel from the path and hurled it at him.

The stones peppered his face and Rob nearly laughed out loud as Wilkes' arm wobbled to protect himself after the stones had all dropped to the ground.

'What's the matter, old man? Lost your bollocks?'

Rob's fury and frustration at the years of humiliation and pain took him back up the steps. The drink he had consumed, whilst stoking his fires, had made him foolhardy. The thought filtered through too late, because his father recognised who it was on the steps. Rob saw his eyes clear and his mouth become the thin slash that he knew so well when Ian Wilkes really lost it big time.

'You little arse-bandit. You'm say your prayers, cunt, cos you'm not getting away from me this time.' He hawked and spat at Rob. 'Even your own mother won't recognise you when I'm done, you dick.'

'She wouldn't recognise me anyway. She's too busy getting hammered and fucking anything that moves.'

There was no warning. And it was the last thing that Rob was expecting. Wilkes threw himself down the stairs; seven steps, straight down. Their heads clashed as they cannoned into the railings at the turn in the stairs. The weight of his father and the momentum almost took them both over the top and into the river below.

Rob nearly puked as his back screamed and stars whistled in and out of his vision. His father never spoke; all Rob could hear was the old man's laboured breathing and the only smell was his beer-soaked breath.

Wilkes was stunned too and lay atop Rob for as long as he could, getting his bearings and trying to clear his head. As he pushed himself away from his son, he lashed out with a half clenched fist, catching the boy a shuddering blow on the side of the head. It was what saved Rob. He groaned and slid down the handrail, feeling the nausea and faintness growing like a mad disease in his head.

He tumbled off the end of the railings, landing on his hands and knees. Staggering to his feet, Rob saw Wilkes stumbling down the steps, hands outstretched, clawing at his shirt front, grabbing him and pulling him close.

'Goodbye son,' he whispered.

Malefic yellow light slid poisonously along the blade of the baiting knife Wilkes pulled from his inside pocket. Rob saw it, even felt a moment's fear, but his body's needs outweighed the danger, and he threw up. The sudden outpouring, all over his shoulder and cheek, made Wilkes yelp and take a step back. He slashed out, catching Rob just below his left ear and missing the carotid by scant centimetres. The blood tipped out, soaking Rob's shoulder in seconds.

Rob felt a sharp, momentary pain, but the almost dissipated anger drew down to a pin-point, pulsed and erupted; it saved him. He ducked under his father's next strike and swept up the length of wood, whirling round to face him. They crouched, circling slowly. Wilkes dived forward, thrusting and slashing up. He missed, but Rob swung hard, connecting with the small of his back.

Wilkes went down on all fours, panting and whimpering. Rob stared down at the back of that hated head, twisted the lump of wood round so that the three packing case nails were to the fore, and brought it down on the back of Ian Wilkes' head three times: once for Tim, once for him, once for Him'n'Tim.

They found Wilkes the following morning, the lump of wood still embedded at the base of his skull.

In the privacy of their own homes, most who had known Ian Wilkes sent up a silent prayer of thanks to whoever had done for him. Very few people went to the funeral, including Rob. In fact, very few people in town ever saw Rob Wilkes again.

CHAPTER FIFTEEN

2007

Monday morning found Flute at his desk by seven o'clock, sleeves rolled up, coffee in place and staring at a pile of paper, wondering if this was the way to go about finding a killer.

He had spent the weekend wandering on Dartmoor, visiting favourite places, steeling himself for Wednesday and the coming anniversary. But even this was overshadowed by his encounter with Sloane at The Goat on Friday night. Bill Rockingham had tried to divert his attention but even Bill's level-headedness had been to no avail when Sloane had caught sight of Flute and raised his glass in salute. Bill had grabbed Flute's arm, holding tight.

'Leave it Monty, let it go. You know what his game is. Don't play.' Flute had pulled free and stalked across the bar to stand in front of Sloane.

'Hello Inspector. Lovely evening.'

Flute gritted his teeth and drew a deep breath.

'What do you want, Sloane? What are you doing here? Gloating?' Sloane pulled his head back, trying to get out of range of Flute's anger, looking genuinely puzzled.

'Having a beer…' he raised the glass as evidence, '… and relaxing. Same as you, I should think.'

'Let me tell you something, Sloane. What we do isn't a game. We're not two professionals who go at each other in office hours and then have a healthy respect for each other's positions when the hooter goes. There isn't a word in the English language that adequately describes what I think of you and your boss and what you do. Don't let me see you in here again. Got it?' Flute held Sloane's gaze, willing him to have a go. Sloane merely shrugged.

'I think you'll find that I'm entitled to drink wherever I feel like it. Don't threaten me unless you can follow through.' He too held eye contact and took a sip from his glass.

Rockingham laid a hand on Flute's shoulder and whispered in his ear.

'Leave it, Monty. You've said your piece. Harry wants a word about next week's quiz. You up for it?' He tugged gently at the back of Flute's jacket. Reluctantly, Flute broke away from Sloane's icy grey stare and followed Rockingham back to the other side of the pub. When he looked back to the bar, Sloane was chatting to one of the regulars as if he was a normal, everyday member of society. Flute felt his gorge rising.

'Monty! Have a drink and leave. It. Alone!'

It had been, at best, an unpleasant confrontation and Flute felt even more annoyed that Sloane had managed to get him down to his level. He took a sip of coffee and raked the top of his head with his fingertips, trying to comb the frustration out of himself. He had to focus now; Sloane would be a problem for another day. As of now, he had a killer to catch.

He tapped a button on his computer and the screen threw up a notepad list of how far they had come. If it had been a journey round the world, he'd still be in the town market place.

The shoes had drawn a blank and there were no suspects of which to speak. Cavannaugh was in another office running the usual checks on people who had a link to the victim, but they mainly consisted of social workers and kids that had known Terry Faulds during or after his time in care. They were even looking into the histories of local foster carers, given the experience that Terry had had with his foster family.

All he could do was wait for the other offices to open and hope that the Path. report arrived this morning and that forensics might have found something helpful. He began to wish he had stayed in bed.

He typed himself a reminder to get in touch with central records to see if the database might come up with something; a similar M.O., other kids in care who had been murdered, dates, times - anything that might give him something to hold on to and drag him out of the mire.

~~~

Nick Sloane rotated his head and felt the muscles and cartilage in his neck snackle and grind. He shrugged and moved his shoulders in opposite directions at the same time, watching himself in the shop
~~~

window. He nodded, deciding he looked formidably dapper enough to go into the club. It was just past lunch time, and Ferdy Epstein would be feeling in a relaxed state; he usually did around this time, just after his massage, a light bite and glass of chilled white wine. Nick planned to see him as he started to enjoy his first cigar of the day.

He pushed through the door of what had once been a regal art-deco cinema; Epstein had picked it up for a song just before the Council had stepped in to demolish it. The area that had been the stalls was now Grable's (Ferdy had a thing about forties film stars, particularly the females of the species), and the walls in the foyer of the club were lined with black and white photos of the good, the bad and the unknown.

Ferdy had tried for plush chic; retro was the word he used ad nauseum, but somehow, he had missed the mark. It was tacky, like the carpets, and sleazy. The entrance funnelled the punters up a small flight of stairs and through two sets of double doors into the auditorium.

At this time of day, it was brightly lit, allowing the cleaners and sundry labourers to go about their business. The artificial neon glare was harsh and unforgiving and the scars on the walls and floor gave witness to many of the less salubrious encounters the club had seen.

All the seats had been ripped out and different levels installed around a central dance floor. The only feature that gave Grable's an edge, compared to all the other clubs in the Bay, was the wall where the screen had once been. It was a labyrinth of metal walkways and platforms, peppered with large screens that showed continuously changing shots of the stars that Ferdy loved, where dancers and the general public could display their limited talents to drunkenly adoring aficionados in the bear pit below.

There were two bars, one to the left at the far end, near the walkways, and one that ran either side of the doors through which Nick had entered. It was black and white and chrome, neon stars and palm trees - an interior designer's manifestation of Epstein's own personal fantasy. It was a nightmare. But the punters kept coming and Ferdy kept taking their money.

Grable's was one of three clubs that Ferdy owned in the Bay area; the others were Caruso's in Paignton and Junk, on the road between Paignton and Brixham. It didn't take much imagination to guess what the sideline at the third of the clubs might be. 'Hide in plain sight' was Ferdy's motto. And it had stood him in good stead over the years.

Nick soft-shoed down the steps and across the dance floor to the bar on the far side of the room. There was a small cloud of smoke hanging at one end of the bar, which concealed the head and shoulders, but not the paunch, of the man he had come to see.

'Nick, Nick, Nick! How are you my friend? Good to see you.' A hand, its little finger adorned with a massive gold ring topped with a large ruby, emerged from the fug and flapped it away.

Ferdy Epstein perched on the edge of a bar stool, resting nonchalantly against the faux gold-plated and padded monstrosity. He looked to Nick like a chubby, less inviting version of a cross between Al Pacino and Richard Gere. Even the expensive suit, which he always wore, and the gold jewellery, could not smooth out the rough edges that managed to poke through. He looked exactly what he was; a thug with aspirations. And, it had to be said, most of those aspirations had been achieved.

Epstein snapped his fingers, to the accompaniment of rattling identity bracelets, and shouted at the man behind the bar to get him a brandy.

'What you having Nick?' He tucked a stray lock of hair behind one ear. The action had a faintly effeminate air to it. Sloane shook his head.

'Too early for me Ferdy, thanks all the same.'

'What can I do for you then?'

'Do you want the list in order of importance or just as they occur to me?' Sloane perched himself on the edge of another stool, planted his feet and rested his forearms on his thighs, hooking his fingertips together. Epstein sipped his brandy and placed the balloon gently on the bar.

'Oh dear. Problems?' Nick nodded.

'Calum, car, coppers. Precise enough for you?'

'Aaah.' Epstein put his cigar in his mouth and puffed and chewed thoughtfully for a moment. 'Calum.' He removed the cigar with his forefingers and waved it around to emphasise what he was saying. 'I have personally had a quiet word with young Calum about his over-enthusiastic shenanigans; trust me, he won't make the same mistake again. And…' He held up his free hand to stall Nick's response. 'And neither will his colleague get the chance to do the same. He is no longer with us. The car? It was good thinking on your part and if you take it to the Shed, Mikey will take care of it for you.'

'Mikey might be very good at what he does, Ferdy, but it'll take more than a lick of paint and a sledgehammer to sort out the damage.'

'Mmmm. Then we'll dispose of the object and get you a new one. Now, the police?'

'Flute's back on my case.'

Epstein's shoulders slumped at the mention of Flute's name. He pulled furiously on his cigar and swilled the remainder of his brandy, rattling the empty glass on the bar to get it refilled.

'If I could do that bloke, I'd do him myself, I swear to God.' He sighed philosophically. 'But I suppose he and his colleagues will always be an obstacle to our endeavours, an obstacle that we will, we hope and pray, always find new and more interesting ways to overcome. It's what you're good at. Nick. And here's the good news!' He rubbed his pudgy hands, sounding as if he was rattling dice as the rings clicked together. 'I think we are in for a small respite from the long noses of the law. They are otherwise occupied with the death of a lad.'

'One of ours?'

Epstein snorted derisively.

'Please! The last time that happened was when Sticks got careless…wasn't it, Nick my friend?' He gave Sloane an arch, conspiratorial look. 'Mmmm?'

'Who was it then?'

Epstein spread his hands and shrugged.

'I should care? It helps us out, that's all I need to know.' He watched Sloane through half closed eyes. He recognised that look. 'My friend at the station tells me it was a lad from the kid's home…well, ex lad from the kid's home. I seem to remember the name vaguely. Did some business with one of our people. Small stuff. But every cloud has a silver lining, eh Nick? Talking of business…' He reached into his jacket pocket and threw a small plastic envelope across the bar to Nick. 'It seems we have some competition.'

Sloane picked up the baggie. Half a dozen pills and a small block of resin. He pushed it back to Epstein and waited.

'It's good quality. Two things, then. One: why am I not getting this quality from my people? Have a quiet word please Nick. Two: find our competition and give him a ticking off if you would. He needs to know that he's treading on toes, and I do not need my corns getting stamped on. Okay?'

Nick nodded. The supplier would be easy enough, but finding the competition would take a little longer.

‘Okay. Anything else?’

Epstein pulled thoughtfully on his cigar, weighing up the pros and cons of saying anything. He’d known Nick for a long time and knew a little of the way he ticked, knew something of the odd moral code within whose boundaries he worked. It was a quirk that sometimes worried Epstein, but it was a small thing in comparison to the good work that Nick did for him. He was prepared to let it slide, but it bore watching. He exhaled a cloud of fumes.

‘Stay away from it Nick, yes? I know how you feel but I need you concentrating on the business at hand. You know what I’m saying?’

Sloane stood up and brushed at his lapels. He stared at Ferdy for moment, then gave him a small smile that touched nowhere but his mouth.

‘Do I tell you how to spend your leisure time, Ferdy?’ He let the sentence hang for a second. ‘But I see what you’re saying.’

Epstein watched him walk back across the dance floor and head out to do his bidding. And not for the first time in recent weeks, he wondered if Nick Sloane was going the same way as young Calum. He hoped not, for all their sakes. Sloane was dangerous at the best of times, God alone knew what he was capable of if the mood took him in the wrong direction.

Epstein decided he would have to give some serious thought to retiring Mr. Sloane.

CHAPTER SIXTEEN

2007

Time had dragged like a boring song when Lee Hensley had been at Freeways, but since he had arrived at this place, well… he didn't seem to have time to do anything for himself. Bloody Slattersdyke had him up in the mornings, eating breakfast and going off to his Connexions worker before he had time to think about it or even protest.

He'd been at Marie's nearly a week and his feet had barely touched the ground. Still, it hadn't taken him long to get the idea of the game and start managing the rules to his advantage, if only a little bit. He'd managed to get a few shots in and the silver sugar bowl had got him a few quid at the pawnbrokers; enough to get some cider for when he met up with Krissy and Jasmine.

Lee slid down in the seat at the back of the bus, in case the old woman was out in the town and saw him hopping a ride back to Freeways. He had yet to figure out how he was going to get back at the end of the evening. It didn't really worry him too much; if one of his mates was about they could 'borrow' a car. Yeah, that had a ring.

He tapped a rhythm out on his legs and hit empty pockets. That might be a problem. His foot tapped the backpack at his feet. He'd bought the booze but it left him with nothing to buy fags. Well, they could help him there. Jas usually had a spare one or two and if any of the others wanted to share the cider, they'd have to pay the price.

Fuck it! He needed a job, but that dick at the Connexions place would only get him training placements or stupid fucking labouring jobs that paid fuck all! He knew what he was worth, and it was sure as fuck a lot more than sixty quid a week. No, he'd have to have a word with Dylan. He was your man and always on the lookout for someone to push a few bits and pieces.

When he'd been at Freeways, Lee had been too scared to get involved. Dylan could be a mean and miserable fucker when the mood took him. But now Lee needed the cash, and if they weren't going to help then he'd help himself.

He raised his leg and kicked the back of the seat as he thought of his useless fucking care manager. Help? The bloke didn't know the meaning of the word. How was it supposed to help him, dumping him in a house with an old twat that baked cakes and got him out of bed in the mornings? It wasn't like he'd had any choice in the matter!

He snorted and spat on the floor. He'd never had any choice. Do this, do that, do the fucking other. Well, fuck the lot of them!

He slid his hand into the top of the rucksack and pulled out a tin of cider. Cheers! He pulled the ring and chugged half of it, watching the distorted image of the top of the driver's head in the security mirror at the front of the upstairs deck.

Still, with a bit of luck, he might get something out of Dylan and, if his luck really held, he might get Jasmine to suck him off. That'd be a result; he probably had enough tins to get that. Besides, the little slut loved it. She'd probably do it for one tin, if she was in the mood. He rubbed his crotch and smiled dreamily. It was going to be a good… no! It was going to be a great fucking evening.

~~~

David Trelawney sat at the kitchen table and toyed with his dinner. He'd been at the Shadracks for almost a week now and it seemed to be going nowhere. His care manager had taken him into town and bought him a leaving care present, which was a joke in itself; he was still in care. Same thing, different label. Still, the jacket was way cool; suede and leather with the Hard Rock Café logo on the back. The catch was that he'd had to sign up at the Jobseekers place and all the jobs there were crap! Apprentice metal worker or something with the local parks department, pulling weeds and chopping back bushes. Hot and sweaty or cold and wet. Some fucking choice!

And now, it was football practice again this evening. He hated bloody football. But Brent and Warren went with their Dad twice a week and they dragged him along. He felt like a spare prick at a wedding. He was tolerated. Not by the adults, but the kids were fucking snotty. Treated him like a dim-witted charity case.

He let the cutlery clatter onto the plate and stood up. Aileen poked
~~~

her head round the kitchen door and asked him if he was ready to go. She eyed the food still on his plate, but said nothing. Dave wished she had mentioned it; he felt like having a right go at somebody, and she was as good as anyone.

The boys, as Aileen liked to call them, climbed into the car, but not before Warren had managed to assert his position by pushing past David and getting into the front seat. Which meant David had to endure the rattling, high pitched chatter of Brent as they headed for the sports field at the back of the school.

'All right Dave?' Asked Brian in that fucking stupid voice he used whenever he talked to him. David grunted and stared out the window. It was torture, this bloody sport thing. Watching the other three running up and down, Brian trying to get him involved, Warren deliberately ignoring him, even when he could have passed the ball to him, and bloody Brent hanging around him like a bad smell, trying to make friends. He was like a fucking puppy. What a pain in the arse the whole thing was.

As they pulled into the car park at the school, Dave saw a group of familiar kids heading across the field to the sports pavilion. It was Jas and Krissy with a couple of the local kids he vaguely recognised and... bloody hell! Lee was with them.

Even after all the trouble Lee had caused him, Dave would have rather spent an evening in their company than running around a plastic football pitch.

Brian pulled a kitbag out of the boot and hoisted it on to his shoulder. Dave tapped him on the arm.

'Brian... look, I'm not feeling a hundred percent tonight. Would you mind if I just sat and watched? I might feel a bit better later. Is that okay?'

Brian put the bag down and put his hands on David's shoulders, holding him at arm's length and looking at his face.

'You all right mate? You do look a little pale. Do you want me to run you home? These two'll be okay for a while. Rest of the lads'll be here in a minute.'

David took a step back, wriggling his shoulders.

'No, no. S'okay. I'll just sit and watch. It's not a problem.'

'Fine. There's a can of Coke in the bag, if you fancy. Don't catch cold sitting around though. See you in a bit.'

Well that had been easier than he'd hoped. Give them another ten minutes and they'd be so caught up in their bloody silly game, they'd never miss him if he just sloped off to meet the others.

He opened the kitbag and helped himself to the coke. It might turn out to be a fun evening after all.

~~~

It strolled through the streets, smiling at people who thought they knew. But It's voice sounded hollow and echoing with lies, even to It's own ears.

How easily they fooled themselves, these sheep; these self-deluding idiots, so proud of themselves; so knowing, so right.

It allowed Itself a small smile, actually quite enjoying the feeling of it curling around It's lips. It was a hunter, seeking out the one who needed It's adoration. For the chosen, there would soon be no more loneliness, no more disrespect at the hands of these monsters. No more tears.

Cupid strolled the streets, poison wrapped, Godhood hidden. Cupid knew just where to find the chosen acolyte.

~~~

Creep sat in the shadows and watched the group lounging around on the grass. He knew them all; some better than others and it was only the fact that Lee Hensley had resurfaced and was there with them that kept him from joining them.

He could smell the joint they were passing round, and laced with the pungent odour was the crisper smell of cider. Krissy was chatting with the local kids and Lee and Jasmine lay slightly away from the group, hands thrust between each other's legs, whispering fiercely. Jasmine was trying her best to keep the conversation between themselves whilst Lee tried hard to give her the same impression. In reality, he wanted the others, particularly the lads, to hear their negotiations.

'You get a hand job for four minging bloody cans, Lee Hensley. I ain't putting that thing anywhere near my mouth for four fucking tinnies.'

'Aw, come on babe. You loved it before. It's good, innit? You know that.' He heard himself being persuasive and caring, but was coming over to all and sundry as whining and desperate.

'Loved it? Fucking loved it?! I've had stiffer things in me spaghetti bolognaise.' She gave him a squeeze that made his eyes water. 'You get what you're given for four fucking cans of gnat's piss, you tight shit.

Yes or no?'

He returned the squeeze and tried to stick his tongue in her ear. Breathing heavily, he gasped,

'I heard our Kev say you blew him for three fags and a promise. What's he got? C'mon Jas, you know you want to.'

'I'll deal with Poundsberry when we get back. Now, yes or no? Hurry up, I'm getting a cold arse sat here.' Lee pushed her further back and tried to kiss her. 'I'll take that as a yes then.'

The rest of the group looked away and carried on their conversation, bored now that the belittling bartering had come to an end. Actually, they were pretty bored generally, hoping something more interesting might turn up.

One of the local lads heard a noise and swung round to look across the field. He saw a shadow walking towards them but couldn't make out who it was because of the street lighting.

'Who's that then?' He called.

'Hello Beano. How's it hanging?'

The group laughed and clapped. They knew that voice.

'Bloody hell, it's Trelawney! What you doing here? Thought you'd given up slumming it with the commoners now you've got a home. Ooh, look at you...natty jacket. Very cool.'

David dropped to the ground and smiled at the group. This was better. He glanced over at the writhing figure of Lee Hensley and shook his head.

'Had a free evening and thought I'd zip over and see what's what, y'know? The jacket's a freebie, care of the social. Nice, yeah? So, what is what?'

There was a moan from one of the participants of the grass wrestling match.

'Is that it then?' Jas coughed. 'You gotta learn to hang on, Lee. Can I go and get a drink now?'

She came over to the others and sat next to David, giving him a small peck on the cheek.

'Nice to see you Dave. How's things?'

They fell to idle chatter about things that only kids of their age can find enthralling. They hardly noticed Lee sit back down amongst them, taking a can from one of the others and eyeing David suspiciously.

Creep sat and listened, drinking his own beer, and enjoying the feeling of belonging. He saw the other figure approaching the group from the river before they did, and shrunk further back in to the shadows. He knew that walk and its owner was not good news.

'Hello kiddies.' The group jumped in unison as Dylan the Dealer, as he had become known, loomed over them. 'Can I help you?' He sat down and lit a joint.

Lee was the first to recover from the surprise.

'Dylan mate, how are you? I've been looking for you.'

'So I hear. What's it about?'

Lee sat up straighter and assumed a sneer as he looked round the group.

'Business. Can we go somewhere?'

Dylan took his time, pulling on his joint. He spoke round the smoke.

'We'll go to my office, away from ears, 'cos ears obviously ain't got any money for me.'

The pair stood up and walked away from the group, heading towards Eastown and the boatyard where Dylan tended to conduct his deals.

The others watched them go, making sure they were out of earshot before speaking.

'He's a twat,' Jasmine said, changing position so that Dave could look up her skirt if he fancied.

'I thought you liked Lee,' Krissy said, trying to emulate her heroine's position for the benefit of one of the other boys.

'No. Well, yeah, but I meant that Dylan character.'

'He's bad news, man,' Beano said, shaking his head wisely. 'Lee'd better watch himself.'

Creep listened for a moment, but the talk veered away from Lee and the dealer. He thought momentarily, then slipped away out of the bushes and back to the riverside path. He had decided it might be more interesting to follow the other two. He might hear something that he could use.

CHAPTER SEVENTEEN

2007

It had been annoying rather than difficult, but Nick Sloane was nothing if not determined. That was the problem with little men; they always got ideas above their limited capabilities and that, inevitably, was their downfall.

He knew who he was looking for now and pretty much where he could find him. He might have to wait, but this Dylan character would eventually show up. It was amazing what a twenty pound note could achieve where threats of pain failed. That's what made Nick good at his chosen profession; violence was always the last resort… but sometimes people insisted on making a reservation.

Nick cupped the lighted cigarette in his hand and sat in the shadows on a pile of mooring rope, watching the approaches and waiting.

Ferdy's supplier had been very cooperative, in the end, but insisted that he merely handed out the goodies to client A. What he did with them after that was not his business.

Nick had not only gained an assurance that the merchandise quality to Ferdy would improve but had also acquired the whereabouts of client A. Dylan the Dealer needed to make sure his supply couldn't be compromised; not that that would be high on his list of things to do, once Nick had given him the proverbial ticking off.

Waiting never bothered Nick, there was always something to think about, something to occupy his mind. Tonight, it was Terry Faulds. Epstein had been right to talk to him about not getting involved. He knew Nick better than most. But Nick was his own boss and conscience when it came to certain things - and kids was one of them.

There was absolutely no word on the street about the murder. Nothing. Which annoyed and puzzled Nick in equal measure. He had many contacts that inhabited the underbelly of life in the Bay and there was always somebody, somewhere, willing to earn a bob or two selling a fellow low-life down the river. Yet Nick's cash had stayed firmly in his wallet.

He hated, deeply and ferociously, anything to do with kids, any form of exploitation. He had ceased to try and talk to anybody about this thing that had become almost an obsession; they couldn't see his view point. They had absolutely no idea or understanding of how his thinking worked. He wasn't even sure that he fully understood it himself... not that he had tried too hard. Understanding came from knowledge and his knowledge was hard-won, too hard-won to analyse. It was and that was more than enough for Nick

He would do all manner of what others would call despicable things. But he would never go near anything to do with kids. He knew Ferdy supplied the stuff, but he was at the other end of the market. An importer, if you like, several times removed from the scum who handed out tricks to entice the unaware. Adults? Well, they were too far gone, in Nick's humble opinion, but he'd rip the spine out of anyone he came across pushing stuff to kids or harming them.

He knew who they all were, pretty much, but had to watch his back. They were paying his wages, indirectly. But, occasionally, one of them might turn up severely traumatised and thoroughly repentant of their wicked ways.

Nick couldn't rationalise it any meaningful way, but there it was. Ferdy recognised that and, he supposed, let Nick get away with the odd infraction - but without ever really understanding why. He supposed that made them equal, on some obscure level.

He heard the voices echoing down the long stretch of tarmac that was the riverside yard before he saw the figures approaching. Their shadows chased after them or ran ahead as they walked between the dull orange pools cast by the security lights.

Nick, watching the swagger of the taller figure, could almost feel the arrogance of a man grown too big for his own good.

As they drew closer, he could see that the shorter of the two was hardly old enough to drive a car, let alone be involved with this piece of shit. The pair stopped no more than ten feet from where Nick was sitting. How thoughtful.

He let them continue with their conversation, nodding to himself occasionally as he heard Mr. Big spouting all the usual garbage about how much the kid could earn and how he, Dylan the Dealer (Nick could almost see the arsehole's chest swell at that point), would make sure that Lee would always be first in line for 'the shweet gear'; that was how he said it, 'the shweet gear'. Dickhead.

Nick could almost hear the words before they were spoken; he knew exactly what was coming next.

'Now then,' said Dylan, expansively, doing a little two step on his toes and moving his shoulders as if he was trying to keep his coat on, 'Here's how we make a deal.' He pulled a small, plastic bag from his pocket and held it up to the light. 'This is to show you I got faith in you, buddy boy. A primo free sample - it's a one off, so don't waste it! - to get rid of however you fancy. Sell it, use it to show the quality of your gear or have a chill on your own account. Get me the business and we will make a fortune.' His hand shot out and grabbed Lee by the hair at the back of his head. He pulled him close until their noses were almost touching. 'On the other hand,' he hissed through gritted teeth, 'Fuck me about and I'll make sure you know all about it.' He held Lee for another moment and gave his head a shake. 'Do we have an understanding?'

That'll do pig, thought Nick, and flicked his cigarette end in a hard straight line, watching it bounce off Dylan's shoulder. He stood up and stepped out of the shadows, clapping his hands slowly and sarcastically.

Both Dylan and Lee jumped and took a step away from Nick. Dylan's hand was still curled into Lee's hair.

'Who the fuck are you?' Snarled the dealer.

'Well, well, nice motivational speech. Impressive.' Sloane pulled a pair of gloves from his pocket and made a great show of flexing them onto his hands.

'I said…' Dylan unwrapped his fingers from Lee's hair and turned to face the newcomer. 'Who. The Fuck. Are you!?' He took another step forward, not feeling as confident as he hoped he looked.

Nick didn't raise his head, but looked at Dylan from beneath puzzled eyebrows, lacing his fingers and pushing the gloves tightly onto his hands as he did so.

'Who am I? Hmm. Well, I am the man that, I think, you hoped you'd never meet. '

Lee took a couple of small, tentative steps away from both of them, glancing over his shoulder at the long stretch of tarmac between him and the bright lights of town. He hoped these two would be too busy to take any notice of him.

'Stand still, Lee.' The stranger raised his head, but still kept his gaze fixed on Dylan. 'I'll need to talk to you in a minute or two, once Mr. Big and I have concluded our little chat. Come here Dylan. Please, don't make me walk over there.'

Dylan, despite all his front, was not afraid of a fight, but, in the greater scheme of things, adhered to the old saying 'He who fights and runs away, lives to fight another day.' So he intended to get a couple of good kicks in and then hoof it. Then he'd find out exactly who this arrogant fucker was and take him out.

He stepped forward, swaggering slightly, pulling his gut in and spreading his shoulders. His fists were bunched at his sides, ready to fly.

Nick watched him coming, the corner of his mouth hooked up into a wry smile. So many of them thought to get a good punch in first, then hightail it. Did they really think that he'd not done this before?

Dylan was fast, he'd give him that. He was strolling one moment and the next, he was charging, head slightly down, fists raised to face level and snarling. Nick side stepped, brought his knee up and his left fist crashing down on the back of Dylan's head. The man's nose sprayed blood. Nick stood, leg raised, supporting Dylan. Grabbing the scruff of his neck, Nick pulled his leg away, pushed the man to the ground. Dylan groaned and tried to get up on to all fours. Sloane slowly and deliberately stood on Dylan's right hand and twisted.

'Stay on the floor, there's a good fella.' He pushed him gently with his other foot.

'Lee. I said wait. Stay there and learn a lesson.'

Lee froze. This was beyond his experience and it terrified him. He'd had fights before, but they'd been kid's scraps by comparison, usually ending up with him and whoever rolling around on the ground, arms wrapped round each other, trying to stop punches landing. This was so casual and so deliberate. He crossed his arms and hugged himself, staring at the floor.

Sloane heaved Dylan to his feet, blocking a feeble punch and grabbing the offending fist. He laced fingers, quickly and efficiently, and slowly bent Dylan's hand back towards his elbow. He gave a sharp jerk and Dylan screamed. Sloane let go and watched dispassionately as the man crumpled to the floor, clutching the damaged wrist to his chest.

Low moans bubbled in his throat.

Nick hunkered down next to him, rubbing his hands together, balancing lightly on the balls of his feet.

'Now then, Mr. Dylan the Dealer, let me tell you what's going to happen. You don't have to speak, just nod or whine. You brought this on yourself because you are a silly boy who thinks the world owes him a living. You earn your living son, no problem. But do not ever, ever earn it at the expense of my employer.' He sniffed and touched the back of Dylan's head. The man bunched up into the foetal position. 'You can whine now.' He did so.

'Good. Stay away from that supplier, you know who I mean. That sensible man knows which side his bread is buttered, and if you go anywhere near him, I'll be coming to have another chat. Right?' Nod.

'And finally…' Sloane pulled him to his feet once again. 'If I ever, ever, hear that you've been anywhere near the kids at Freeways, or any of them that have left, believe you me, you'll wish I'd killed you tonight.'

He turned his back and walked into the shadows where he had been sitting. Lee waited, sensing that something was about to happen.

'Lee.' The voice startled him. He couldn't see the stranger but felt his eyes upon him.

'Turn around, start walking back. Don't run. I'll join you in a moment. Okay?'

The boy nodded and shuffled off in the direction of the town. He heard a scrape of metal. If he had paid attention in some of his classes, Lee would have known about Lot's wife and how inadvisable it was to turn around.

He saw the man come swirling out the shadows, a short length of scaffolding balanced in his hand. He almost danced past Dylan, swinging the bar in a short arc and connecting with the other's knee. The clatter of metal as Sloane dropped the tube almost covered the scream, but not quite.

Lee almost ran, but having seen the way this person moved, he decided he wouldn't stand a chance in a flat out race. As Nick came towards him, he pulled off his gloves and put them back in his pocket, then stretched out his arm and gathered Lee into him, not quite hugging him, but pulling him along beside him. The boy nearly yelped with terror.

Nick could feel the lad quivering beneath his hand, which was hardly surprising. He patted Lee's shoulder.

'Two or three things here, Lee. People like him…' Sloane jerked his head back in the general direction of Dylan. 'People like him are bad news, right?' Lee nodded, not trusting himself to speak. 'Stay away. Steer clear. Two: If you want money, get a fucking job at Asda, it's safer. Three: Don't talk to anybody about me.' He stopped and whirled Lee round, grabbing his elbows and holding him at arm's length, staring into his eyes. Lee dropped his gaze. The grey eyes he had stared into momentarily were the emptiest things he had ever seen. Cold and bleak, hard and merciless. He nodded, feeling the grip on his arms loosen and drop away. He stood stock still, fully expecting to get hit or kicked into unconsciousness. Instead, he heard the grate of a cigarette lighter and saw a lit cigarette appear under his nose. He took it quickly, not wanting to touch the hand that offered it to him, and drew the smoke deep into his lungs. He calmed almost instantly.

Nick walked across to a nearby stack of boxes and sat down, gesturing for Lee to come and join him. They sat smoking for a while, watching the smoke drift up and away in the clear night sky.

'You still at Freeways?' The question took Lee by surprise. He shook his head and tried to speak, but his voice clogged in his throat. He coughed.

'No… no I'm in supported lodgings in Torquay.' Nick nodded.

'Did you know Terry Faulds?' Lee felt the terror crashing over him again, turning his gut to ice. He wanted to puke. Nick felt rather than saw the reaction.

'Calm down, fella. I'm just interested in why anybody would want to do that to a lad like Terry. Did he know our friend there?' He pointed vaguely back at Dylan, who was struggling to stand up.

Lee shook his head, not sure what this man wanted from him.

'I think Terry used to smoke a bit of weed, you know? But his thing was cars. He sold a couple to a bloke in Barton once.'

'Okay.' Nick stood up. 'I know the man. I'll have a word with him. Thanks.' He started to walk away, then turned back. 'Lee, I was serious, yeah? Stay away from cunts like him. You'll end up… well, stay away.'

Lee was still scared, probably more scared than he had ever been, yet he felt something about this strange cold man, something that whispered to him, told him he could say what he was feeling.

'Get a job?' He muttered, and the act of speaking gave him a small rush of confidence. 'Get a job!? Think I haven't tried? I only have to put my address on the application form and I'm as good as forgotten. You got no idea what it's like, being...'

Sloane shook his head and wagged a finger at Lee, trying to think of how to explain to this hope-less youngster that it could be all right, if he'd stop being his own worst enemy.

'Lee, I'm not your fucking social worker, I don't hand out life advice for the down and self-pitying... but I'll tell you this much, the answer's in your own hands, the solution's right there. What did you put on application forms? You put the name Freeways, right?' Lee nodded. 'Just stick down the number of the house. People in town know about Freeways, but how many of them know that it's 224 Dartmouth Road, eh?' He watched Lee's face melt into that familiar expression of realisation, puzzlement and embarrassment that the answer could be so simple.

'Who d'you work for then?' The fact that the stranger was actually human had given Lee back some of his usual cockiness. It fled as Sloane took a step in his direction.

'Ferdy Epstein's not someone you need to get involved with, so just stick to Asda for the moment, right? And feel sad for yourself if you want, yeah? But don't be sorry, it weakens you and you need to be stronger than most, kid. A lot stronger.'

They stared at each other for a moment. Lee stretched out his hand.

'Thanks.'

The stranger's mouth stretched into what looked like a quick smile, then he turned and walked back down the yard. Lee watched him until he was gone, amazed that he managed to say the things he had. He turned to see what Dylan was up to.

He was hobbling and hopping towards him, clutching his arm and crying in agony. He barely glanced at Lee as he went past, he was so intent on getting to the hospital.

Lee sat down on the crate again and leant back against the wall of the boat-shed. His heart was still hammering in his chest, doing its damnedest to crack his ribs and get out. What a night; what a fucking night! He shook his head in disbelief and vowed he'd never do anything like that again.

How long he sat there, he wasn't sure, but eventually, he stood up and headed back to town, wondering how he was going to get back into Torquay. He had no idea of the time, but it couldn't be early.

As he neared the hole in the fencing at the side of the gates to the boatyard, a voice said,

'Lee? What are you doing here at this time of night?'

~~~

Beyond the fence that ran parallel to the boatyard, Creep walked silently along the path, watching Lee heading towards the gate. What a night! Unbelievable! Creep smiled to himself, happy to have been witness to Dylan the Dealer's demise. He bobbed his head in time to the definite beat that that phrase had; Dylan the Dealer's demise, da-da, Dylan the Dealer's demise. He almost laughed.

He paused, suddenly aware of movement up ahead. He ducked down and scuttled to the side, dipping behind a swathe of nettles. Glancing to his right, he saw Lee approaching the gates. He ducked down even further, fear of discovery leaking from his forehead and stinging his eyes. He put his arms over his head and closed his eyes. He thought he heard a voice; it sounded as if it knew Lee. Screwing his courage up to fever pitch, he waddled forward, trying to peer between the bushes and the buildings. He saw two figures heading up the hill that led to the back road giving access to the posh houses up the lane.

He stood up, breathing a sigh of relief. He hadn't been caught and Lee was all right.

It was good that he'd met someone he knew.
~~~

CHAPTER EIGHTEEN

2007

Flute felt as if he was buried in glue. Every action and thought seemed slow, laborious, exhausting. His head was stuffed with candy-floss. He ached constantly and was on the verge of tears or fury the entire time. There were no half measures, emotionally speaking. Even Bill Rockingham, the only man who had an inkling of what Flute was feeling, tried over and over again to get him to go home, take sick leave and recover, and got short shrift.

Flute had known that this week was not going to be the easiest of his life, but even he had not expected the violence and depth of his reaction to Tom's anniversary.

Wednesday had, perversely, been the easiest to cope with. He and Rockingham, Rockingham's wife and couple of close friends had gone to Hound Tor, Tom's favourite spot on Dartmoor and the place where his ashes had been scattered, and laid a wreath overlooking the valley between Hound and Saddle Tors. No overt outpourings of grief, just a quiet remembrance and a silence that allowed them all to think of Tom as he had been; as he would now always be. Death permitted immortality for those left behind.

But the empty space that had appeared in Flute's life after Tom had gone suddenly opened out into a roaring chasm, echoing the grief and longing that Flute felt every minute of every day, but amplifying it a thousand fold.

He had thought, hoped, that this feeling had been successfully battened down, but the storm of remembrance had ripped free the ropes that held everything in check. Even when talking to Cavannaugh about the Faulds murder, he found his thoughts shearing away, recalling the smallest of things about Tom and their life together.

He was functioning, but only just.

Lying on his desk were reams of paper and he had an almost irresistible urge to scoop them all up and crush them into a ball. Throw them out of the window, let the breeze take them and his sorrow, and scatter them forever. Let someone else cope with it all.

He stared blankly at a sheaf of notes and let his finger flick the corner of the bundle. He found a certain comfort in the idiotic, repetitive action. He wondered vaguely if Terry Faulds had suffered at the hands of the killer as much as he was suffering now. In the depths of his subconscious, he recognised the crassness of this thought, but was unable to break free from it. The poor kid had been beaten, scored and tortured before he'd had his throat cut. The forensic psychologist said it was similar to other cases on record where the perpetrator had seemed to be purging himself by proxy, perhaps persuading himself that he was forgiving the victim for some imagined crime. The word that had actually been used was sin. 'Some imagined sin.'

In amongst the turmoil that was Flute's mind, he recognised that the probable key to the murder was the shoes. Those damn shoes. Why? Why put them on the kid post-mortem? Who knew what went on in the head of a madman? The psychologist could offer no real insight, just vague possibilities.

Flute sighed heavily and stood up, making a concerted effort to drag himself back to the real world and get on with something. Anything. He went to the coffee machine; it was a start. As he waited for the perverse monstrosity to try and get his order right - it had a habit of giving the customer what it wanted, not what had actually been ordered - Cavannaugh came crashing out of the office where he had been checking and chasing records of any similar crimes.

'I think,' he said, holding out a print-off from the computer, 'that we just may have something.' He thought for a moment, before holding the sheets out to Flute, then qualified. 'No. We've definitely got something!'

Without looking at the proffered sheets, Flute took his coffee, grunted and went back to his desk. Cavannaugh's shoulders slumped and he sighed; he had no notion what was eating his boss, but he had felt sure that this would go some way to cheering him up. He trailed behind Flute, noticing that the usually crisp and well turned out inspector was looking dishevelled; even his hair, normally immaculately groomed, was dull and sticking out at angles.

Flute collapsed into his chair and held out his hand, sipping the coffee and grimacing.

'What's the story?' He glanced at the sheets and tossed them onto the desk. Cavannaugh opened his mouth, puzzled by Flute's attitude, but decided it was better not to say anything and just answer the question. Before he could pass on what he had found, Flute said,

'Bear with me Derek, humour me, okay? It's a personal thing.' Flute calling him by his first name was strange enough, but hearing the normally taciturn man admit to having a personal life was even odder. Cavannaugh nodded, not quite sure how to handle the situation. He decided it was best to carry on and keep a weathered eye on things.

'Because we've got nothing to go on,' he started, pulling up a chair on the other side of the desk and sitting down, 'I had a look around unsolved murders of kids about the same age as Terry. It's depressing how many there are. However, Staffordshire came up with something interesting. Back in 1979 there were two unsolved killings, one at the start of the year, one at the end. Both victims were seventeen years old and living in a children's home... er...' he checked his notes, '... a place called The Lawns. Both kids had their throats cut and were found wearing brand new shoes. Oxford brogues. Black.' He paused, waiting for Flute to say something, but he appeared to show not a flicker of interest. 'So, they had pretty much what we have now. Nothing. And, unfortunately, it stayed that way. They had never found who had killed the kids.'

'What about the home? Was that investigated? We've got a huge operation going on here at the moment, haven't we? Historical abuse and so on?'

Cavannaugh gave an inward sigh of relief. This was more like it. He nodded, perhaps a little too vigorously.

'Oh yeah. Operation Cromwell they call it. I'm getting one of their boys to have a ferret about a bit, see what we can see. But I can tell you this, Sir. The year before the murders in Staffordshire, The Lawns was closed down. Nothing ever came of the investigations then, but rumour was rife. The chappie I talked to up there tells me that they've got an investigation going on, along the same lines as Cromwell. He's getting back to me.'

Flute smoothed his hair back behind his ears and sat back in the chair.

Although pale and drawn, his eyes had suddenly become a bit brighter; he seemed more of this world than he had ten minutes before.

'Well, we can use all the help we can get on this, Sergeant. Were there ever any other killings of this type afterwards?'

'Not of children, Sir, no. But, again, the copper I spoke to, who was a young blue cap back then, remembers the killings and about six, seven months later a woman who had worked at The Lawns was murdered. She would have been in her late sixties, he said. Been poisoned. Crick, he said her name was. Edith Crick.'

Flute drummed his fingers on the desk, then held out his hand.

'Let me have a look at that. In the meantime, get back in touch with your new best friend and pick his brains some more. Anything we can get might be of use.'

Cavannaugh took himself off, leaving Flute to peruse the new information. He gleaned nothing else from what was written, but somewhere in there, something nagged at him. He didn't think it was anything overwhelmingly important, but something…

There was a knock on the door and Bill Rockingham came in, carrying a clear plastic evidence folder, looking serious. He gave Flute a hard stare before saying anything. Satisfied that Flute was at least paying attention, he waved the folder.

'This arrived in the post, addressed to the Investigating Officer, Terry Faulds. So the gloves went on before it was opened.' Flute held out his hand.

'Excellent.' He looked at the contents and his heart sank. 'Oh bugger.'

'Thought you might have a reaction like that. But it was kind of inevitable that the time wasters and nutters would come crawling out of the woodwork. However, I think this might be the real McCoy.'

Flute looked at the carefully cut out and pasted letters on the page in the folder but drew comfort from one small thing. The sender had signed it by hand.

'Well if this is genuine, we have the signature.' He turned the folder over to look at the envelope on the other side. 'Exeter post mark. Why can't we have local sorting offices anymore, Bill?' Rockingham gave him a beats me look. 'Has anyone else seen this?'

'The civvy clerk gave it straight to me and now you've got it.'

'Good. I want to be able to use the name he's given us as some sort of check, always assuming it's genuine.'

'Well, I can't say, I'm no expert, but whoever put this together has mentioned a couple of things that haven't been released, as far as I know. That's what made me think it might be the real thing.'

Flute looked again at the letter and re-read it. Somehow or another, his patch had acquired a bona fide psycho. The letter was short and not so sweet, composed of letters clipped from various newspapers and magazines. Flute allowed himself a grim chuckle; the writer was nothing if not a traditionalist. But why bother signing it by hand? Whoever wrote it must have known that they would, in all probability, be identified by the handwriting. Maybe there was more than a glimmer of truth in the old idea that people who committed such crimes actually wanted to be caught.

'Thanks Bill.' He handed the folder back to the sergeant. 'Let the fingerprint lads have their moment with this. Can you get me a couple of copies made please?'

'Not a problem.' Rockingham turned to go, but thought better of it. 'Everything okay, Monty?' Flute flapped a hand in the air, as if wafting away an annoying insect.

'Fine Bill… no, really. Been a bit wobbly, but it's getting better, slowly. Thanks for asking.'

'Good, good… I'll get those copies up to you as soon as I can.'

Flute watched him go and sat back, head supported by his linked fingers. Well my friend, he thought, I think… hope… you've just let us in. We're coming for you, Cupid, we're coming for you.

CHAPTER NINETEEN

2007

Lee felt the chill and heard the water, slapping and gurgling at the shore. Dank, green darkness filled his head and from those foetid shadows, the memories came tumbling out, cackling like madmen, clawing at his sanity. Every memory was there, fully formed. He knew.

He opened his eyes and tried to open his mouth to scream; there was something blocking him, stopping him from drawing a deep breath and giving vent to the panic and terror that bloomed in his chest, smothering him.

Lee tried to raise his arms to rip away whatever it was that sat over his mouth, but he couldn't move them. All he could do was wriggle.

The darkness in which he found himself felt thick and bloated, feeding on what little light leaked through to this prison. He could see walls, and the floor above which he was suspended, and, if he craned his head back, a timber framed roof and tiles clinging to the beams. And he could hear the water, still dripping and slurping, whispering wetly to his raw and stretched imagination.

He wriggled more and found himself swinging round. He was in a blind panic and could hear himself whimpering and gurgling against whatever was clamped to his face, shutting out the ability to draw a deep breath. He snorted through his nose, sniffing back the snot and tears that clung to him.

The water in front of him roiled like a living beast, undulating slimily, slapping tiny tongues against the wooden pilings. He could just see the outline of a rowing boat tied to the wooden wall.

How long he hung, swaying and spinning, he didn't know, but eventually, as his heart stopped hammering in his ears, he calmed enough to try and take in his surroundings.

It was a boathouse and it dragged a faint memory to the surface. He'd seen something like this... he thought of Kev and Jasmine and Krissy. They'd been out walking. They'd been bored and decided to walk along the river from Eastown, hoping to get to Dartmouth.

His breathing became deeper as he calmed, lulled by this memory. His eyes flickered and he concentrated. There was a row of roofs above the reeds on the opposite bank. He remembered Jas making some comment about them being only big enough for dwarves. They'd walked on and eventually had got bored with their adventure and turned round. The roofs had got taller in the time they had been away.

Kev, being the nerd he was, went 'WOW!' and explained that they must raise and lower with the tide, so the boats inside could get out.

Lee's eyes jumped open. He wriggled a little and managed to swing himself round to see the boat. The gap through which it would get to the river was too low. He looked around, craning his neck to see.

He was hanging from a beam, on the end of a rope attached to some sort of pulley contraption. But the part of the building in which he hung seemed solid enough. How the fuck did this work?

He bent his inconsiderable mental abilities to trying to figure out how the boat got out of the boathouse... anything so as not to have think about what he was doing in here...of who had brought him here in the first place.

As he twisted and struggled, he rotated and saw the door at the back of the boathouse open. The figure standing there made him redouble his efforts, trying to tear himself free of the ropes.

He didn't even mind that his bladder had let go.

~~~

The night air felt good, unsullied on It's flesh... Cupid slapped the stupid face. It had a name now, use it!

The night air felt good on Cupid's flesh, the flesh of giving and of pleasure and of freedom. And not just Cupid's freedom, oh dear me no! Of the Chosen's freedom too.

Cupid flexed bare feet inside the soft leather of the old Oxford brogues. It was only right and natural that they, too, should be present. The admonishment had been severe the last time Daddy had missed the freeing of the spirit. But not this time.

Cupid looked at the reflection in the window and smiled. Coy and shy. Perfect. Absolutely perfect. Picking up the woven shopping basket,
~~~

Cupid set off down the sloping garden to the boathouse. The tide would be at its ideal height by the time this night's work was done.

~~~

The door swung shut behind the monstrous apparition that Lee had glimpsed. He screwed his eyes shut, but the chimera was branded on his eyelids: the flabby nakedness, the blonde, curly wig, the sickeningly vibrant make-up smeared across the grinning face. And on its chest was daubed a heart, red, ripe and almost throbbingly real.

Utter, all consuming terror closed the boy's throat as he watched the figure pull away the gingham napkin that covered the basket it was carrying and lay the contents out on a nearby table. He couldn't tear his eyes away from the knife. What little light there was seemed to slide with seductive intent along its length.

Cupid looked up at the boy and smiled his most comforting smile.

Lee cringed as this phantasm leered at him, licking its lips and waggling its tongue, making obscene slurping noises.

Cupid came and stood beneath him, checking the ropes that bound him and touched his legs reassuringly.

Lee felt the tug as the bindings were pulled and shaken, and he felt the fingers sliding up his legs, squeezing and pinching, testing, as if he were buying a slab of meat.

'Now,' the nightmare crooned. Lee craned forward, trying to see what he was doing. 'Be calm and co-operative. We won't be here long and then you'll be free.'

Cupid went to the side wall where the rope that held Lee up in the air was attached, and unwound it, letting the boy down… down… down, until the tips of his toes were scant inches above the floor.

'We will be as we were when we arrived in this world,' Cupid said, almost singing the words as he pulled the clothes from Lee's body, ripping them out from behind the ropes, folding them and laying them on the table.

Cupid kissed his thigh and let his hands run over Lee's stomach.

'Before freedom, before everything, comes admonishment.' He picked up what Lee recognised as a curry comb. He'd used one at the stables. Cupid held it up to his own cheek. As he spoke, his eyes wandered from Lee to the table and back again. 'Then comes chastisement, then forgiveness…' His spare hand danced across the leather strap and the leather worker's needle; he caressed the blade of
~~~

the knife with his thumb whilst his fingertips flitted over the ball of twine and the brightly coloured plastic straws, resting finally on the box of matches and the candles. '… then, after so much love, there will be freedom.'

He picked up the twine.

CHAPTER TWENTY

2007

Everything was silver and gold, flashed with a rainbow and rolled in wonder: the light through the mist that trailed round the trees; the water off which the light reflected; the leaves of the bushes and the blades of grass. A phantom fox stopped halfway across the meadow, paw raised, ears up, watching and listening. A crow gave a raucous cry and, somewhere on the river, a duck set up a commotion as it crashed free of the undergrowth and skittered through the mist, looking for whatever it was ducks looked for on an early summer's morning.

The fox, satisfied that there was nothing unusual happening in his kingdom, lowered his shoulders and trotted away through the long grass, disappearing into a stand of elder, ash and young sycamore.

Although still early, the air was warm and sounds drifted across the river from the village. The church spire rose serenely above the mist and an early morning dog barked excitedly. Somewhere, hidden amongst the rolling hills, a tractor coughed and rumbled its way along a hidden lane.

Had anyone else been strolling along the river path at this early hour, they would have heard the sound of music. A high, lilting, sweeping pipe that spoke of sadness and joy, love and laughter, all encompassed in the simple, flowing notes.

Alexander Cowparsley - his choice of name, not his parents' - strolled in a dream through the grass, playing his penny whistle and revelling in the peace and solitude he always found along this stretch of the river. The sun, new risen and warm on his face, threw spears of light from the water and small explosions of gold from the dew on the grass. Everything was shiny and new, when viewed through Alexander's half-closed eyes. His parents often told him that this was his problem, living in a half-world where everything was wonderful and nobody disliked anybody else. Alexander often wondered why it couldn't be like he saw it, but he was perfectly prepared to live and let live.

He was a well-known figure round town, carrying his huge back-pack, adorned with an avalanche of carrier bags that held his world. He was a multi-coloured snail, hauling his life on his back.

Alexander finished the tune he was playing and slid the whistle back in to his raincoat pocket. He looked up and down the meadow. Even for this quiet place there seemed to be very little activity; he usually saw at least two or three people walking their dogs. Still, not to worry.

He shrugged the pack from his back and carried it to the base of a tree near the river. He stripped off his coat and shoes and socks, planning to have a dip, washing himself and his clothes in the process. It was going to be another warm day, and he could spread himself out on the grass to dry.

He floated on his back, feeling the warmth seeping through his eyelids and sensing the diamonds glittering all around him. There was a fresh, green tint to everything; it lay upon his face and warmed his stomach, giving him a peace that was complete.

He felt his dreads being caressed by the grass that over-hung the bank, and the leaves and branches of the tree above cast gentle shadows across his face. He opened his eyes and looked up.

The gamekeeper, checking the pheasants in the woods above the river, heard the screams and thought the world was ending.

CHAPTER TWENTY ONE

2007

Bill Rockingham took the steps up from the interview rooms two at a time, glad to be away from the sobbing and pleading Alexander Cowparsley. He held three brown paper sacks full of clothing that were bound for forensics. As he made his way to the front desk, Flute called to him.

'Bill! Can I have a quick word please?'

Rockingham stepped inside and Flute waved him into a chair. He dropped the paper bags by the wall and sat down. Flute nodded at them.

'Has he said anything coherent yet?'

'Not a sausage. The duty solicitor's on her way but I don't think she's going to be any help. The bloke really has no idea what sort of a mess he's in.'

'They were Terry's then?'

Rockingham shook his head and scratched his chin.

'The bloke's coat and shoes were by the tree with his other belongings. His clothes were soaked and I don't think they're going to be much use to forensics. No, the shoes, trainers, had Terry's name drawn in biro on the tongues; Terry on the left, Faulds on the right.'

Flute sighed. A part of him wanted to get this thing done and dusted - a small part - and Cowparsley was, at the moment, their only real suspect. But the larger part of him knew that this was going nowhere.

'Is he just being clever?'

Rockingham barked a harsh laugh. 'He's just addled, Monty. Completely shot. I think that whatever small amount of him that used to live in the real world went on holiday when he saw the body hanging in the tree. I've put in a request for the police psychologist to call in as soon as he can, but I reckon we're on a hiding to nothing here.'

'Yeah, yeah… bugger!' Flute banged half-heartedly on his desk and flopped back in his chair, staring off into the middle distance.

Round and round in circles, going over the same ground. Nobody had come up with anything, well, very little anyway. They had a connection to the killings back in the '70's, then everything went cold until Terry Faulds' body appeared.

Cavannaugh was still exploring what went on at The Lawns all those years ago, and that was the problem; they were so desperate to find something that would help their investigations that he was worried they would be led down a dead-end by some tenuous piece of information that, in the cold light of day, had no real bearing on it at all.

'What about the body, Bill? Anything new?'

'Sod all. The black Oxfords were almost exactly the same as those found on the first victim. He died in pretty much the same sort of way, but the forensic psychologist says that the killer is methodical, almost ritualistic. The torture isn't frenzied, it's purposeful. As was said, it's as if there's a purging going on. That's about it.'

Flute gave a small, resigned laugh.

'Thanks Bill. Let me know when the duty arrives, I'll go down with her and see what we can glean from that poor bugger.'

As Rockingham collected his evidence sacks and left, Cavannaugh tapped on the door and stepped in. He was smiling. Flute raised an eyebrow.

'Are you the bearer of glad tidings? I certainly hope so, I could use some good news.'

'Well, yes and no. Could be something, might be nothing, but it bears checking out.'

He sat down, checking an empty coffee cup on the desk. 'Do you want the whole thing or just the last tit-bit?'

'Tell me all.'

'The Lawns. Set up in the early sixties as an independent charity for children who couldn't be looked after by their parents, for whatever the reason; they were dead or inside or abusive. Colonel Charles Milford and an army colleague, Major Henderson Dickens, were the founders. The investigating team up in Staffordshire have got reams of stuff about this place. They had a housekeeper, Edith Crick, Dickens' sister…'

'She was the one that got…'

'Poisoned, correct. They were, it has recently emerged, a right charming trio. In a nutshell, multiple abuse. Nasty, nasty stuff. Milford and Dickens had their little favourites and, whilst it seems that Crick wasn't directly involved, she was complicit. The whole sorry mess came to light about seven years ago…'

'And it's still being investigated!?' Flute was incredulous.

'It's a real can of worms, Sir. One of the ex-residents topped himself, but left a great long tract, detailing what had happened to him. And that was the trigger that fired the gun. Systematic, long-term sexual abuse on a horrendous scale.

'Unfortunately, both Milford and Dickens are dead. They retired from The Lawns about the same time that Crick was killed and both died of old age, a couple of years apart, in the late eighties.'

'What about the kids? Where are they?'

'Scattered to the four corners. The guys doing the digging have come across at least twelve suicides. Many of the old residents have changed their names, but some have come forward. Others have said, basically, what's the point? The abusers are all dead. Any staff members who were around knew nothing, all the abuse took place in Milford's private flat at The Lawns.'

'Why didn't the victims speak out at the time?'

'Too scared. Milford and Dickens ran the place almost like a military training camp. Very strict, stiff punishments for rule breaking. Those kids were utterly terrified, all the time. Milford and Dickens had their special favourites over the years, as I said; the ones they saved the really choice stuff for. Some of the people who have come forward, around the early to mid-sixties this seems to have happened, are telling tales of some kids, saying that they were being adopted by our pair. The team are seeking that information out.

'Here's one of the things that really did it for me. Several of the victims have told of some of the rituals that occurred at The Lawns involving some weird pseudo-military shenanigans that involved nakedness, obviously, and wearing odd items of clothing, including… black oxford brogues.'

'Bingo! Well found, that man, well found.' Flute rubbed his hands together delightedly. At last, something that might lead somewhere. 'You said one of the things that did it for you?'

'Indeed. Milford, Dickens and Crick made an awful lot of money from their enterprise at The Lawns, and there's a special team dedicated to finding out what happened to it. Much of it was invested and will probably never be seen again. But some of it, apparently a lot of Milford's cash, was put into property. All over England... and one house in particular, right here in town.'

CHAPTER TWENTY TWO

2007

Things in the Shadrack household were fast getting out of hand. Brian found himself standing in the hallway, with Aileen on one side, demanding that he do something about David's language and general attitude, and David standing by the front door, yelling the odds about his rights and what a crap life he'd had and asking why Warren had stolen his jacket. Brian now had some small idea what it was like to be tethered between two chariots pulling in opposite directions.

He stood, head in hand, listening to the cacophony blending into a shrill hectoring that was indecipherable. He lifted eyes and gazed at the ceiling, extending his hands in the general direction of the two warring parties, trying to push silence at them. It didn't work. Taking a deep breath, he decided to grab the bull by the horns.

'All right, enough.'

The noise continued, Aileen moving on to the general state of David's room, and the untidy culprit, having had no luck with shouting, proceeding to grab coats from the hooks by the door and fling them to the ground.

'I said…' Brian drew an ever deeper breath. '… ENOUGH!!'

The silence was deafening. Hooray, he thought. He quickly turned to David, pointing, and said, 'Pick up the coats, hang them up and get into the lounge… NO! I will come and talk to you there.' He looked round at Aileen, tilting his head slightly and raising an eyebrow.

She in turn gave him the famous pursed lips look. After so many years together, this visual shorthand came in quite handy, although Brian knew, as sure as he knew the sun would rise tomorrow, that there would be a 'discussion' with Aileen later.

David gave the coats a cursory kick and stamped off into the lounge, glaring at the television as if Graham Norton and his guests were the cause of all his troubles. He grabbed a cushion and hugged it protectively, muttering under his breath.

Brian tried to stroll, in a nonchalant yet firm way, into the room, to give an impression of being in control. He felt a complete fraud. He wasn't, in point of fact, angry with David; the whole situation had grown out of all proportion and it was obvious that David was feeling insecure, because his reaction had been totally over the top. However, Brian was absolutely livid with Warren, who had been told in no uncertain terms by David that he couldn't borrow David's Hard Rock jacket, yet, here they were, an hour later, with the jacket and Warren gone, and the house in turmoil. Brian was just glad that Brent was having a sleep-over at a friend's that evening.

Brian took a beer from the small fridge, opened it and turned to face David, offering him the bottle - strictly against the rules, but it sometimes worked as a peace offering. If he'd smoked, he would have offered the lad a cigarette too.

'Listen, David, we need to…'

'Yeah, yeah, whatever. Say your piece and let me go to bed… fucking stupid…' His voice trailed off to incoherent expletives. Brian sat in the armchair opposite him, nursing the beer bottle and looking at the floor.

'Okay. Okay, I will say my piece and I hope that after I've said it, you might try and talk to me like a person and not something that you'd just scraped off the bottom of your shoe.' He waved the bottle slightly to silence David's response and looked up. 'No… you told me to say my piece, so now you listen.

'What Warren did was wrong and believe you me, he will be apologising and making some kind of amends, on that you have my word, but your reaction was, to put it mildly, way over the top. Way over. I'm not going to try and pretend that I know what you're going through, how you're feeling, but I do try and understand… we all do. But your…'

'No you don't. You don't try at all to understand… least ways, Warren doesn't. He just doesn't want me here, it's that simple. You got rules and regulations that are s'posed to be for everybody, but it's me that gets all the conditions, all the you-can-do-this-but-only-if-you-do-that bullshit. You can't understand what it feels like, you…'

'All right, all right, granted, we can't fully understand, but at least let us try, hey? Talk to us David, don't bottle it all up and then let it all come fizzing to the surface like this. We're not mind readers, Aileen and me, but we want to try and help if we can. Okay? And do me a favour, yes? Watch your language.'

'What!? Warren swears like a trooper! See? See what I mean about one rule for me and…'

'I know… hang on, hang on! Whoa! I know Warren f's and blinds, but tell me, when was the last time you heard him swear in the house? Honestly now, when?' Brian waited. 'Right. Outside the house, at school, with his mates, when we're not around, I'm not stupid. Neither of us are, we know about kids… apart from anything else, we…'

'Yeah, I know, you were young once too.' Brian looked at David closely and saw a small smile trying to break through. He nodded.

'Sorry, corny example… but the thing is, it's true. It's what you guys forget… stop! By you guys, I mean kids of your age generally, not just kids in care, okay? You guys forget that we were your age once, and it wasn't that long ago, let me tell you.' He took a sip from his beer and waved the bottle at David. 'Sure you won't? No? Fine. So, let me deal with Warren and you deal with trying to remember that you can talk to us, fair? Go on then, get to bed if you want…'

David stood up, looked vaguely about him and sat down again.

'It's just that, well, when…' He scratched his head, then accepted the proffered beer. Brian went to the fridge and got another. He had a feeling that it might turn into a bit of a session.

~~~

Flute stood by the car, staring at the house. It sat back in the trees and he could see no lights, yet he had the feeling that they were being watched. Cavannaugh appeared at his elbow.

'All set?'

'Yes Sir. We've got a couple of uniforms round the back and two more waiting for the word if we need any help at the front of the house.' He peered into the shadows. 'Think we might be in luck?'

Flute drummed his fingers on the roof of the car then straightened up, pulling his jacket forward and shrugging more comfortably into the shoulders.

'Only one way to find out. Come on, let's see if this is where the story ends.'

He walked across the road purposefully, hearing Cavannaugh's
~~~

footsteps following. Flute waved to the constable further down the street, indicating that he should draw closer.

Finding the house had been a fairly easy task. Milford had left various parts of his estate, and this house, to a G. Ballantyne.

If Ballantyne was Cupid, then they were in luck, but somehow Flute didn't think they could be that lucky. Something wasn't sitting quite right. They had managed to find the firm of solicitors who had handled Milford's estate, but there was no one in the company now who had been around when the will was executed and the papers had all been archived. It would take a considerable amount of time, so they had been told, to ferret them out - always assuming that they hadn't been lost or destroyed.

What puzzled Flute was the fact that the house had been left to 'G' Ballantyne. No first name, just the initial. He had asked the solicitor about that. He could almost see him shrug over the telephone.

As they drew closer to the front door, Flute could see a faint blur of light at the back of the house, like somebody had left a door open slightly. He pushed the doorbell and knocked loudly.

After a moment or two, the light blossomed and a voice, older than time itself, croaked querulously.

'What do you want? It's too late for me to be opening the door.'

Cavannaugh saw his boss's shoulders slump.

'Get on the blower, Sergeant. We'll need a WPC I think.'

~~~

The explosive oranges and purples of the evening were smeared across the horizon; finger painting of God. The traffic on the Ashburton road was light and the smells of the countryside, green and vibrant, washed over their faces as they drove past the police station, making for The Kings Head. Flute had decided that it was time to repair to the little-used, secondary office. It was not something he did very often, but he felt the current situation demanded a little liquid relief.

Cavannaugh, sitting in the passenger seat, stared ahead with a feigned passivity, frankly bemused by this small, but nonetheless significant, event. He had been working with Flute for several years and, although the man was demanding, he was a good copper. Closed on a personal level, but that, as far as Cavannaugh was concerned, was a small thing. He had worked with other senior officers who were only too willing to tell you their life stories at the drop of a hat and spent more time in the
~~~

boozer than on an investigation. Flute, whilst not the complete opposite, was less inclined to chat and more inclined to talk about the issue at hand; usually in the office. Which is what made this excursion to the Kings Head all the more strange. He had never known Flute to go there whilst on an active case. He'd never known him to go there, period. He gave a mental shrug and sat back, deciding to see what the next hour or so brought forth; although he could see, from the set of his boss's shoulders and the grip he had on the steering wheel, that the man driving was far from happy.

Flute's concentration was wavering. The previous week or so had almost drained him to the dregs. The storm that had been threatening to tear him apart was still there, rumbling on the horizon. Thus far he had managed to hold it in check and himself together. But it was becoming ever more difficult since he had visited the scene where Lee Hensley had been found, hanging in the tree. The tree. That was the key, that was what had brought everything to a head.

It was the same damn tree from which Tom had hanged himself. The only person that knew, other than Flute, was Bill Rockingham. Flute was lucky to have such a friend as Bill. But oh my God, not even he realised just how close Flute had come to losing it completely.

Yet despite all this, Flute could not let this case slip from his grasp; he had to resolve it. The powers above were already breathing down his neck, demanding progress. The press were now starting to take an unhealthy interest in proceedings. The story, which had been front page for a few days, had been put on a back burner. Then Lee Hensley had been found. Now the big boys, the nationals, were sniffing about. The Western Morning News had covered it sporadically, but only this morning, the editor had been on the phone, digging.

Flute and Cavannaugh settled themselves at a picnic table on the balcony at the front of the pub, watching the cars flash by and the cows grazing in the field across the road. On the far side of the field, they could just see the late walkers and bike riders threading their way down the footpath from the Domington Estate. A dog barked somewhere in the village behind the hill into which the pub was nestled.

Flute raised his glass slightly in Cavannaugh's direction.

'Cheers Derek.' They both took long swallows and sighed. 'What're your thoughts?'

Cavannaugh blew through pursed lips and put his glass down.

‘That we’re on a hiding to nothing at the moment, Sir. We’ve got connections to the murders in Staffordshire and their investigations into The Lawns. We’ve got the shoes. We’ve got two bodies. We’ve got Cowparsley. The best we have is a letter from this Cupid character, who is, apparently, the killer. No finger prints, no discernible DNA, zip. Seems like an awful lot of something that amounts to nothing.’

Flute nodded his agreement.

‘Very succinct and very true, I’m sorry to say’

He paused, toying with the pint in front of him. Cavannaugh waited, knowing that the real reason for their coming to the pub was about to be revealed.

‘I know this is a little strange, within the normal scheme of things, Derek, but I needed to have a word with you away from the confines of the other place. We… there are going to be, I think, some unpleasant repercussions from all this, and I wanted to give you the chance to distance yourself, if you want.’ He looked at Cavannaugh.

For the first time, Cavannaugh actually looked at his boss. His eyes, normally bright and sharp, full of life, were dull and tired. He saw a man who was in the midst of a crisis. Professional or personal, he wasn’t sure, but the strain of everything showed clearly on his face. He was grey and drawn.

‘I’m sorry Sir, but… am I being thick? I don’t quite understand where you’re coming from with all this.’

Sometimes, just sometimes, Flute had been thinking lately, you take the blinkers off; the blinkers you didn’t even realise you’d been wearing. And it comes as a shock. You care for people, you love someone, you do anything and everything you can for them and, if you’re lucky, they reciprocate. Only those close to you matter, everyone and everything else is peripheral; they’re sometimes important, but not anything particularly to worry about. You turn on the tap, water comes out; you switch on the TV, you see the news; you open the freezer and, if you’ve remembered to shop, there’s your dinner. Things… are. With your blinkers on, you take them for granted.

Take off the blinkers. What about the people who turn on the taps to get the water to your tap? The programme makers? The girl at the check-out? Peripherals. He looked at Cavannaugh, and wondered how long he had been assuming that the man would be there, doing his bidding and getting results for him?

It had come as a shock to realise that, without Cavannaugh, Flute would be floundering, flapping around like a fish out of water. This man, and Bill Rockingham, in a more direct way, had been the anchor that had kept him from running aground in the storm that had been his life for the last month or so.

It hadn't been a road to Damascus, no epiphany but more a slow realisation that Cavannaugh, amongst other things, had become a given in his life. How often do you say thanks to the guy that stacks the shelves?

Flute swirled the beer round his glass and drained it.

'Thanks for all your help in the past, Derek. But this little nut we have to crack is one of those that might take a sledge hammer rather than a nice, delicate set of silver-plated ticklers. The papers are starting to get a grip of what's been happening, and upstairs are beginning to grumble. I've had the ACC on the phone, after the Chief Inspector had had a word, and it's starting to feel that, although they mouth all the right phrases, they're already starting to look for a scapegoat.'

He sighed, chewing his bottom lip and staring off into the middle distance.

'You know about me, don't you?' He waited, watching the slightly bemused look on Cavannaugh's face smooth into realisation. More credit to the man; the lack of embarrassment was refreshing. Cavannaugh nodded, having an awful feeling that he knew where this was heading. He took the bull by the horns.

'You mean the fact that you're gay?' Flute nodded. 'Does this actually have any bearing on the way we're working the case?'

Flute laughed.

'Thanks for that, Derek. No, no it doesn't, but...' he shrugged. 'Sitting here like this makes me wonder if I'm being heavily paranoid and I've thought about it, but I don't think so.

'The ACC has already wondered if I need to 'get away' to 're-charge my batteries.' I could give him the benefit of the doubt, I suppose, and say that he is concerned for one of his senior officers and I could, quite happily, get sick leave. Thing is Derek, I don't need it and, more importantly, I don't want it! Did you read The Western Morning News yesterday?'

Cavannaugh felt a small, cold hand grip the back of his neck; he knew exactly which passage Flute was referring too. He could have quoted it almost word for word.

'In charge of the investigation is Detective Chief Inspector Montgomery Flute, 51, the forces' first openly gay senior officer.'

Cavannaugh took an angry swig at his beer. Now he did know where they were going. Flute gave a small smile.

'Obviously you did.'

'They can't take you off the investigation just because…'

'No, no, no, I'm sure they wouldn't… they couldn't, not in so many words. But this investigation involves kids and the press are starting to give it more than a cursory glance. Murder, children and gay coppers… it's not a happy mix for them. You know as well as I do how many different ways there are to get moved.'

'That is just so much bullshit!! Just because you're gay doesn't make you a paedophile or likely to… to hit on the kids or anything else for that matter! Jesus!'

Flute raised a calming hand. He was perversely pleased by Cavannaugh's reaction. He'd rarely seen his sergeant so fired up.

'All I'm saying is, Derek, that I have a nasty feeling that this might start to get personal, from my point of view, and what you don't need is to be… tainted?… stained?… by anything that might happen. You could end up being the white t-shirt in the wash with a red sweat-shirt, yes?'

Cavannaugh stared long and hard into the depths of his beer, trying to divine some meaning there. He snorted.

'If that's the case, then I end up pink. Sort of appropriate really.' He smiled. 'Want a refill?'

Flute nodded. Just how often did he say thanks to the bloke that stacked the shelves?

Not often enough.

~~~

Cupid stormed. Cupid raged. He lost control completely. The boat house was a wreck. Utterly destroyed.

The boy was not the boy; his chosen acolyte, his chosen love.

They had tried to trick him. They had fooled him.

They needed reminding just who he was, what his mission was, and that they could not stand in his way, would not stop him with their petty, devious little tricks.

Cupid wept with frustrated rage. This would take time to rectify. But when he had the real boy here, he would have to be so caring, so loving,
~~~

as to stun the world with his passion and sensitivity.

Cupid sat with his feet dangling in the rising water, splashing with tiny, ferocious kicks and running his fingers idly across the blood-slicked boards.

They would know that their underhand conniving had caused great suffering… and not only his. He looked across the boathouse, to where the boy lay.

Part one tomorrow, he thought, and allowed himself a smile. Parts two, three and four later.

They would suffer too. Oh yes. They would understand.

CHAPTER TWENTY THREE

2007

Ferdy Epstein had never had children and he wasn't sure if that was a good or a bad thing. It was good inasmuch as it kept his wife happy, she'd decided long ago that childbirth would be an unnecessary complication in her ordered, happy and expensive lifestyle. That, coupled with the fact that it was painful, messy and involved commitment, made it an almost forgone conclusion that the Epsteins would be without progeny.

Ferdy, on the other hand, sometimes wondered. In the quiet moments of his day, when he sat in the office staring at the walls and smoking, he wondered. He would often drive through Torquay, along the front, past the theatre; see the families walking in the sunshine, dodging the seagulls, playing on the beach, and think about being a father. How it would have felt. How different everything might have been if they had had children.

His associates would have had a good laugh at that. Ferdy Epstein, a Dad?! Fuck off! But still, he wondered. If Ferdy could be said to have a weakness, then contemplation and a vivid imagination in certain areas would be it. But as with most things that Ferdy did, even when imagining and wondering, he knew he was doing it and recognised the fact that it could be construed as a weakness; and in his line of work, that was something that he couldn't afford. But as long he kept it in check, there was no harm.

There was a difference between wondering and doing, wondering and allowing the dream to cloud your judgement. Sentimentality was something of which Ferdy could not be accused.

He sat in the office now, watching the bar area via the CCTV, and asked himself how he would deal with things if the man he was watching had been his son. He wasn't of course, but it was an interesting proposition.

Nick Sloane folded the newspaper and threw it across the table in disgust. There was nothing on the front pages of any of the newspapers but the Cupid killings. Even the local free rag had the story mixed in with the adverts for handymen and lonely hearts. It wasn't that they shouldn't report it, but the way they told the story made his gorge rise. The whole sensationalist thing; the screaming, banner headlines; the stupid, cheap puns on Cupid and his arrows; the complete lack of thought to the family of the lad who had been murdered. And giving the sick, fucking arsehole who had killed these kids the air of publicity to breathe was the thing that stuck in Nick's throat more than anything.

In one of the national papers, they had actually done a mock up of what they thought the letter this Cupid had sent to the police actually looked like! Cut out letters and all. Jesus, they were as twisted as the man himself.

The first body part had appeared four days before, along the river where the other two lads had been discovered. The police, led by the indomitable Monty Flute, had then decided to put regular foot patrols out along the paths. Stable door, Monty, thought Nick, stable door. Did they honestly think that the killer was going to go back there now?

On the following two days, more pieces appeared round the town and yesterday, the police had found a parcel on their front doorstep! It had been the poor little sod's head. On their doorstep, for Christ's sake!

The lad had been identified as Warren Shadrack, a local boy who played for the local football team, went to school in the town and was, to all intents and purposes, someone who had been in the wrong place at the wrong time.

Sloane reached across for the Morning News. These guys, at least, had tried to report the whole thing with a modicum of sensitivity. Factual and outraged at the same time. He scanned the story again, wondering why the hell he was so angry.

He did what he did for a crust and never wondered about the morality of it, unless it was in an abstract, detached sort of way, yet this… this had really got to him. He could read stories about hundreds getting washed away in the tsunami, kids starving to death or getting murdered by gun-toting fanatics in some far-off wilderness, old couples getting shot in Cornwall by idiot, drunken opportunist thieves, and it didn't stir anything in him other than a mild interest and a small thought that, perhaps, he should care more. But this? It really, really made him angry.

The newspaper had given brief details of how the youngster had died as well as who he was and the fact that his parents were foster carers. Sloane flicked the paper out and laid it flat on the table. He hadn't noticed that bit before. He read the paragraph more closely. Freeways was mentioned. The previous two victims had been past residents at the home and the boy's family were foster carers. He wondered. The police would have made the connection, he knew Flute of old; surely he wouldn't have missed that… would he?

Nick pushed the paper away in disgust, telling himself to stop being a dickhead. This had nothing to do with him. Stay away from it. He had other things to occupy his time, including the reason for Ferdy calling him this morning.

He heard the doors to the foyer wheeze open and close. He could see Ferdy's oily little form sliding across the dance floor like some ghostly figure from the age of swing. The metal cleats on his heels clicked and echoed as he strolled towards Nick in the half light.

'Nick! My boy! How are you? Keeping well, I hope?'

He poured himself into the seat opposite Sloane, and turned the newspaper to face him with the tip of his finger. He sighed, and even that sounded as if he had been sitting in the office rehearsing it, along with the sad little lowering of the shoulders and slow shake of the head.

'Dear God, what is this world coming too, eh Nicky? What?'

He pushed the offending article away with the same fingertip. Epstein watched the half-closed eyes which stared across the table at him, that saw nothing but focused on something; the hunched shoulders and the bouncing, impatient leg. Nick's fuck-off-and-get-on-with-it stance. Ferdy clapped his hands - let's get down to business! - and said,

'So. You want coffee? No? Right then, here's the thing. Remember the little problem we had with… what was his name?… that Dylan character? Well, it seems he hasn't actually taken on board the lesson you so kindly gave him.'

Nick sighed and collapsed back into his chair. Business as usual then. Suddenly, he wanted to be out of the club and back in the fresh air. He saw the headlines and smelled Ferdy's overpowering cologne and felt his stomach churning uncontrollably.

'What's it to be then?' Nick said.

'He needs disappearing. I've heard that he's getting good rates from Polo, out of Plymouth, and the last thing I want is that scummy, fat fucker getting a foot in the door on my patch.' He pointed at the News. 'If our friend goes walkabout, I think the good men of the local constabulary are going to be too busy to worry about him going night-night. Besides, there's the kids involved and I know he's been flogging gear in that direction. Don't want them digging around us with that shit storm for company, do we?'

He pushed the heavy gold identity bracelet up and down his wrist, a sure sign that he was in two minds as to what to do next.

'Come on Ferdy, spit it out. I want to get out of here.'

Epstein clasped his hands together, almost as if he were praying, and bent across them as he lowered them into his lap. He fixed Sloane with a steely, steady gaze. This was his this-is-serious mode. A sight not often seen.

'I'm worried. Nick. Seriously. We can't afford to have the blue shite wandering round our patch. Any sort of connection, any sort at all, and we'll find ourselves in solitary getting a beating from the guards who are s'posed to be keeping us safe from the dandy boys in the main nick.'

'What? You want me to go Poirot and find this fucking nutter?'

Epstein shook his head vigorously.

'Jesus, no! I want you to keep your ear to the ground, see if you hear anything out there. We've got ways of getting stuff to the filth if we need, and it won't compromise us.' He started to fiddle with his jewellery again. There was more. 'The best thing we could do… and I think this is viable… is to go to the horse's mouth as it were. Someone who knows a bit about this sort of thing. And…'

'You can fuck right off, Epstein! I told you years ago that I'd do most things, deal with most of your associates, but there is no way, no way on God's green earth that I'm getting anywhere near him. When I get to meet him, it'll be his last day breathing.'

Epstein coughed and sat back. Predictable reaction. Even he disliked dealing with Tantalus, but by Christ, he was a good customer. But Epstein had to play it very, very carefully. He couldn't afford to upset Tantalus, but, equally, he couldn't risk alienating Nick. And above all, he had to protect his business and himself. Epstein knew that if he could find some way of getting to the maniac who was killing these kids, he would have Nick do everybody a favour. Altruism wasn't in Epstein's make-up, but in this case he would make an exception, if it were humanly possible. Nick needed to get involved, and the only way he could see was to have him talk to Tantalus - that perverted piece of shit was almost certain to have something to give, because, in his line of business this sort of thing, this Cupid, was definitely unwanted.

'Okay, okay! It was just a thought. Keep the ears open though, eh Nicky boy? We might be able to do ourselves some good and the filth as well. Don't forget our friend Dylan though.' He pushed an envelope across the table. 'Call this a bonus.' He stood up, shooting his cuffs and straightening his tie. 'Come in over the weekend Nick, we got some amazing dancers. Nice girls, you'd like 'em.'

Ferdy strolled away, clicking confidently, calling an amiable greeting to the barman who had just arrived to bottle up.

Sloane picked up the envelope and slid his finger under the flap. Feeling the weight of the contents, he realised just how worried Ferdy was. This had to be five grand if it was a hundred. He looked at the bundle and saw a piece of paper folded beneath the band that held the notes together. On it was an address and a telephone number. Christ! Epstein never gave up.

He put the information into his inside jacket pocket. You never knew. He might even give Tantalus a call one day… but it wouldn't be to ask him any questions.

~~~

Creep had not emerged from his pallet hideaway for nearly three days, and he was ill. He'd been surviving on rain water, and precious little of that, and a few scraps he had managed to forage from the bins nearby.

When he heard that Lee Hensley had been popped, he nearly shit himself. He'd seen him walk away from the boatyard with… and then he turned up dead. Creep couldn't even let himself think the person's name, never mind say it out loud. He knew that if he said it, if he thought it, if he pictured the person, then somehow, he'd come for him. Find him. Kill him. It wasn't much of a life, but it was the only one he had.

Creep bunched himself into the corner of the confined space between the stack of pallets, shivering and almost unconscious. It was getting dark. It was the worst time for him; the time when the noises started; the time when he needed to sleep, but couldn't, because all he could see was
~~~

Lee's body, hanging in the tree by the river and all he could hear was a soft, whispery voice, calling him, telling him that he was already dead. Creep knew he was dying. Felt worse than death itself. He'd been scared before; when you were like him and some of the other kids he knew, it was almost a way of life, but this? This was pure. This was distilled, unadulterated terror. He almost longed for the days when he lived with his old man. At least then he knew what to expect.

Creep wasn't dying, although that was a possibility. But he was going slowly and quietly mad.

~~~

'A mistake?! A mistake?' Flute threw the report onto his desk in bemused wonderment. 'This kid is snatched from the town centre, tortured…' he consulted the report again. '…'in the most brutal and horrific way that I have ever experienced' … those are the pathologist's words, not mine… tortured, hacked up like a side of beef and dumped from here to the middle of next week, and now the psychologist is telling us that, although this is Cupid, it was a mistake? Does the man read the paperwork we generate… does he read the fucking papers!!? We know it was a mistake… bloody Cupid told us so himself! But we're to blame for that, according to him.'

Flute saw Assistant Chief Constable Airley and DCI Bob Rooke, a great slab of a copper that would find it hard to be inconspicuous anywhere, slip into the back of the room. He knew what was coming. Airley had already offered to get in touch with the Staffordshire investigation in the hope of speeding things up and now he was here in person. They'd had no joy with the solicitors who had handled the Milford estate and Flute was banging his head against the brick wall at the end of this blind alley into which the whole of the Cupid investigation had turned.

He nodded a greeting to Airley and Rooke, dismissed the assembled officers and called Cavannaugh over. The officers filed quietly out of the room, avoiding the gaze of Airley and Rooke, as if they might turn to stone if they looked into their eyes; Rooke was ugly enough to be a blood relative of Medusa.

Cavannaugh appeared at Flute's elbow before the dynamic duo by the door could get across to them.

'Derek, just keep at it, okay? I think this little committee of two might be the bad news I've been expecting.'
~~~

'Not to worry, Mr. Flute. I'll keep you in touch if it goes that way. Good luck.'

He turned away to find the ACC and Rooke bearing down on them. He nodded politely and made a hasty exit. He didn't envy Flute the next twenty minutes or so.

The two men waited until Cavannaugh had closed the door, then pulled a couple of chairs up to the desk. Flute nodded at Rooke.

'Hello Bob. You well? Mr. Airley, good to see you. Thanks for the offer of assistance.'

Airley swept his cap from his head and laid it fastidiously on the desk, making sure the peak was front and centre. Rooke dipped his head once in Flute's direction and rumbled a greeting.

'Hello Monty.'

He looked as if he wanted to say more, but Airley cleared his throat, sat back, crossed his legs and said,

'Well, Mr. Flute, we appear to have a somewhat difficult situation on our hands, do we not?'

Flute made the assumption that the question was rhetorical and waited for what else was to come. He didn't have long to wait.

'Three murders, one maniac whom we cannot identify, despite our…' he flicked invisible dust from his trousers, '… best efforts and a media that is, to put it mildly, baying for somebody's blood. Preferably the killer's, but I think we all realise that, with our poor showing thus far, ours would do; or, more specifically, yours.'

The strange, pale green eyes surveyed Flute passively, waiting for a response.

'Bit of a fix, Monty,' intoned Rooke, pulling a purple handkerchief the size of a tent from his trouser pocket and blowing his nose. Starlings launched themselves from nearby trees in fright. 'The press are having a bloody field day… and they seem to have latched onto you and…'

'I know Bob, I read the rags. All I can say is…'

Airley raised his hand, waving it impatiently.

'The thing is, Mr. Flute, not only is this damaging you…' This was spat out quickly, in a get-it-over-and-done-with fashion; Flute knew Airley found him distasteful. '… but it is having a hugely detrimental effect on the investigation and the force as a whole. The public, whilst understanding that your… they realise that being a homosexual does not equate with child molestation, but they seem to be losing…'

'I'll step down and let Mr. Rooke take over. You only had to ask.'

Flute watched with mild satisfaction as Airley squirmed and tried to look anywhere but at Flute himself. He saw Bob Rooke give a little shrug and mouth 'sorry' at him.

'Bob, if you can, use Cavannaugh, he's right up with it and he's a damn good copper.' Flute stood up. 'I'll be taking some sick leave, if that's acceptable Sir?'

Airley clenched his teeth, preparing himself to mouth the platitudes that were required of him.

'Please realise that this had nothing whatsoever to do with... with... the thing is, we need the public to see that we listen to their concerns, and, let me say, these concerns are not just arriving via the media. We've had numerous telephone calls from members of the public about this.' He carefully didn't specify what the 'this', that the public were so concerned about, might actually be. 'Mr. Rooke will be taking charge of the investigation, effective as of now. I take it you will give him your fullest co-operation.'

It wasn't a question as such, and Flute saw Rooke bury his face in the purple patch in embarrassment.

'Goes without saying, Sir.' Flute faced Rooke and smiled. 'We can head off to my office and I'll hand over everything, but, with all that's been happening, might I suggest that you do keep Cavannaugh as your number two? He's been here since the off and he's invaluable.'

Airley made to say something, but Rooke beat him to the punch.

'It'd be good to tap into his knowledge, Monty. My Sergeant's off on a course and I'll need somebody who knows what's what.'

Airley stood up briskly and picked up his cap, brushing specks of dust from its glistening peak.

'Good, good. How long a period of leave do you require, Mr. Flute?'

'I think... I think as long as it takes, Mr. Airley.'

Bob Rooke ducked his head to smother a smile and coughed.

'Very well.' Airley's back stiffened and his lips all but disappeared in a thin, mean slash. 'Mr. Rooke, please keep in touch, we need to move this fiasco on as quickly as possible.'

He twisted his head as if to ease tension, turned and walked from the room without looking at Flute.

'Sorry about that, Monty. I wanted to come over and have a chat, one to one, but fart-face decided he wanted to be...'

‘In at the kill?’ They laughed nervously. ‘Not to worry, Bob. I come across that sort of attitude almost every day. You get used to it. Come on, let’s get some coffee and I’ll bring you up to speed. Not that there’s a huge amount to show.’

CHAPTER TWENTY FOUR

Flute drove past Freeways on his way back to the house. There was a patrol car there most of the time, or a beat copper, watching and waiting. Some of the kids were sitting on the wall at the front of the house, chatting to the officer on duty. They were laughing. He wondered how well they understood the situation they were in, whether they actually realised that they too were potential victims, or if they just thought it was a bit of a joke.

He had spoken with Deidre Cochrane, the manager, on several occasions, and she had told him that the youngsters were well aware of everything, but kids, any kids, had the remarkable ability to phase out things like this. And most of the ones who lived at Freeways relished all the attention they were getting. They were important - and that made them feel good.

When he had chatted to some of them about Lee Hensley, he had marvelled at their acceptance of something so horrendous, so final. They had been upset, that much had been obvious, but he had seen in their eyes a depth of sorrow that went beyond the death of Lee, a sorrow born of something that he would never be able to fully comprehend.

None of the kids at Freeways were angels, most of them were known to the police in the town, but, all the same, having read some of their histories, he had to wonder what would happen in the future for these children. For there was no doubt in his mind that that was what they were, when all was said and done: children who had seen more and suffered more in their short lives than he could ever imagine.

Freeways was inhabited by girls, bar one lad, and thus far, Cupid had only been going for boys. Checks were run on all the staff, past and present; a few gaps in history, but that was something everyone had;

otherwise, nothing. They knew they had somebody stalking kids in care and, it seemed, lads from Freeways in particular. There was a link to the operation in Staffordshire; all they had to do was find it. It seemed to Flute that they had a whole field full of haystacks and a particularly small needle to find.

He didn't envy Bob Rooke at all.

~~~

Kevin Poundsberry sat on the wall surrounded by people, including, of all things, a copper!! Tamsin and Pauline were being really friendly, and even Jas had stopped pounding him. Result! That was her most favourite thing to do, it seemed to Kevin. She would appear behind him and thump him several times, hard, shouting,

'Pound the Poundsberry, pound the Poundsberry.' That was generally the signal for everyone to join in. It hurt, but he liked it when the others let him get involved. Sweet. He also realised that there was something else happening; he wasn't that involved. Jas and Krissy had been appearing and disappearing most of the morning, sometimes huddling deep in conversation by the front door, then going inside. Krissy would come and sit on the wall for a while, and he noticed her give Tamsin or Pauline a little smile or a nod. Then she'd go and Jas would join them.

He listened to Pauline, chatting about Snow Patrol and flirting, in an amateurish way, with the policeman. He saw Jas and Krissy coming out the house, followed by Deidre, who was waving her arms about and demanding to know where the girls were going.

And Kevin knew why Deidre was agitated. Jas was carrying her Shopping Bag. Jas' Shopping Bag was legendary at Freeways. Whenever it was over Jas' shoulder, she was going shopping. But all the kids knew it meant that there'd be a few freebies floating round the house that evening.

Kevin noticed something that he wondered if Deidre had seen. The bag was full already, which was, as Kevin knew, very unusual.

'We're going out for a picnic, all right?!' Jas swung round to face Deidre. 'Me 'n' Krissy… 'n' anyone else who wants to come.' She glanced round at the others, and winked quickly. 'We ain't going to town, so you don't have to worry that I'll get nicked. Now get off me bloody back!'

She flounced away, shadowed closely by Krissy. They were both smirking.
~~~

There! He'd been right. They were up to something. He hoped that he'd be allowed to tag along. He fancied a picnic.

Deidre Cochrane threw her hands up in despair. She also knew that they were planning something, and the look on their faces told her, better than the written word, that it wasn't anything to do with picnics. Yet the Shopping Bag had something in it, so maybe it wasn't an outing designed for thievery. And, if she was perfectly honest with herself, it would be good to get rid of them for the afternoon. She had so much paperwork to do and not enough staff to cover the house properly. Mo Palfrey was on holiday, Simon had called in with a pulled muscle and two of the others were off sick. She'd had to spend a fortune on relief workers this week. Her budget was shot to pieces already.

'Just stay out of trouble then… and don't be back late. We need you here before dark.'

The laughter by the wall faltered for a moment. All of the kids turned and nodded solemnly. They knew. The constable put in a word or two as well.

'Yeah guys. Back by nine at the latest. We will come looking for you else. Okay?'

The girls huddled for a moment, then set off down the road, with Kevin trailing along behind at a respectful distance.

'Where d'you think you're going, Ponce-Berry?'

Kevin stopped slowly, dragging his feet, the smile on his face crumbling away to his usual expression - confused, worried and not a little sad. Jas poked him in the chest with one sharp, carefully painted nail.

'You been invited then? Did I say you could come? You, you're always following us around like a bad smell.'

'Yeah, stinky,' agreed Krissy, giving Jas a quick look, to make sure she had said the right thing.

'Poundsberry the Pong, that's you.' She laughed, looking at the other girls, inviting them to join in. Daring them not to. Kevin felt the darts of their humour stinging his eyes. He had probably never heard of the expression 'Every Dog Has Its Day', or 'Flash of Inspiration', but somewhere in Kevin's head, a connection was made. Totally subconscious, utterly unplanned.

'I know what you're doing…' He saw Jas shoot Krissy an evil look, saw Krissy shaking her head in denial. '… and, and, I can just as easy go tell the copper too, as well as Deidre. So… so I'm coming, all right? You ain't going to stop me, neither.'

He was panting, sweating with fear and delight. He'd pulled one over on Jas! Sweet-est!!

Jas gritted her teeth and stalked off down the road.

'Yeah well, whatever. No skin off my nose, Pongo.'

The other girls laughed nervously, and Krissy scampered along beside Jas, whispering fiercely in her ear, promising her that she hadn't told Kev what they were going to do. Kevin floated along in their wake, hardly believing his luck. He was part of something. It didn't matter what, he was with the crew and they were doing something. Together.

The night before, Jas had been making her way back, by a roundabout route, from Cider City. She'd made herself a few quid, had a drink or two and kept most of the blokes on her side, which was nice. She was, in an abstract sort of a way, looking forward to getting back to Freeways, having a shower and telling Krissy all about her night. Especially the bit about Beano. He was gorgeous - and she knew that Krissy had a thing for him, and that her exploits would drive Krissy fucking insane!

She also knew that if any of the staff found out that she had left the house, alone, they'd go completely ape-shit and ground her for the rest of her life. Well, fuck 'em. She knew that the crazy bloke only liked boys and there was no way that she looked anything like a fella.

As she weaved her way down the footpath by the river and the cooler night air started to squeeze up the backs of her arms and across her bare midriff and the shadows got deeper, the fact that she was alone began to sink in. The cider started to wear off just enough to remember that HE used to like lads too. And girls. In fact, pretty much anything that he could stick his dick into. Or hurt. Or both.

That memory sent a cascade of adrenaline crashing through her system and got her scurrying into the bushes, across the wall and on to the dimly lit industrial estate.

She stood for a moment, breathing rapidly, as if she had just run from Cider City, not strolled, and listened. Just a soft breeze, wafting the distant smell of diesel and the sound of traffic, moved the leaves very gently.

Jas shook her head, straightened her shoulders and counted to three, getting ready to start walking, head held high, full of confidence. No one would mess with her!

The groan nearly made her scream. She felt her bladder squirt as she spun round and round, looking for whoever had made the noise. There was nothing. A fox screamed, and this time, so did Jas.

She had started to shout threats then, promising whoever it was that she would rip their fucking eyes out with her nails if they tried anything. She moved back towards one of the units, planning to take cover in the shadow of the roof overhang, then leg it back to the main road.

She crouched for a moment at the corner of the building, watching the quadrant in front of her, trying to peer into the other shadows, seeing if anyone was watching.

There was another, fainter, groan, and it sounded as if it was coming from behind her. Not possible. All there was anywhere near her was a stack of pallets. Hunkered down, back to the unit door, she could smell her own piss and taste her own terror. That made her angry; furious. She had sworn to herself, after it all happened, that nobody, no fucker would ever make her feel like that again.

She got into a crouch, reached up under her skirt and pulled the g-string off. It actually felt a lot more comfortable. She hated the bloody things, but they drove the lads crazy. Stuffing the scrap of cloth into her clutch bag, Jas listened carefully, looking around for something she could use as a club. Another groan. Weaker it seemed, almost as if the groaner was giving up.

'Who's there?' She hissed. 'You'd better show yourself, or I'm going to rip your bollocks off if I get hold of you.'

Nothing for what seemed like an age, then,

'Jas?'

Soft, almost a sigh, but definitely her name.

'All fucking right!' She screamed. 'Where the fuck are you?'

Fury and fear propelled her out into the light, turning slowly, looking for the owner of the voice.

'Jas… Jas… 's mee… 's Creep…' The black plastic bags that were wrapped round the pile of pallets behind her rustled and flew apart as she spun round to see a figure fall through the gap. In the pale orange light, she could just make out Creep's deathly pale face. 'S'only me… 's only ol' Creep…'

It was all he could manage before he passed out.

Jas had managed to drag him back into the makeshift shelter, gagging at the stink and feeling the start of what was going to be a massive bloody hangover.

Caring was not something that came naturally to Jasmine Colleridge, which, given her history, was not surprising. But as she pulled Creep back into the shelter of the pallets, she could feel how thin his arms were and his ribs felt like fragile sticks, even through the thick coat he was wearing. His breath was coming in short, shallow gasps and that breath was sour, rank. She kicked all manner of half-seen detritus, trying to clear a space where she could stretch Creep out, then cover him with something. It was obvious he was very sick, but she knew, having had chats with Creep over the last couple of years, that the very last thing he would have wanted was to go to the hospital.

Jas knew a little of Creep's story and it was enough for her to remember that his abuser had been a doctor.

She patted the pockets of her lightweight body warmer and found the tin of cider she had been saving for when she was home and in bed and chatting to Krissy. She knew instinctively that Creep was dehydrated.

Been there, done that.

She wasn't sure how much use a tin of cider would be in helping Creep; she seemed to remember, from one of the few classes she had ever attended, that booze wasn't something that helped with lack of water. The opposite in fact - but it was all she had.

Creep groaned again and tried to sit up. He was mumbling and seemed to be trying to brush something away from his face. Jas had seen some of the kids do this at Freeways, as they came up from a bad dream. Slap away the nightmares. Hit them… and the fucker that caused them.

'Jas? Jas?! You still here, Jas?'

He coughed dryly, drawing his knees up to his chest and grasping them together, each hand holding the other wrist.

'I'm here, Creep. Here…' She handed him the cider. 'Try a drop a' this, it might help.'

She popped the ring pull and handed the can to him. His skin felt hot and dry. He coughed again, a deep, rib-rattling hack, then passed wind. The stink was foul.

'Sorry,' he mumbled, taking a swig at the can. '… when is it?'

'When's what, mate?'

Jas sat down, leaning against the pallets and trying to grab a little fresh air through the gap in the plastic sheeting.

'Day… what day is it? Now… what day?'

'When d'you last eat anything or have a drink then? You look rough as rats mate.'

'Can't go out… mustn't… can't… he'll get me… he'll do me. Stay away Jas… leave me to it.' He took another long pull at the can. 'Tired… thanks for…' He waved the can weakly.

'… got any… you alone?!! No one else is there? You alone?'

He tried to push himself forward, get to the entrance, but Jas leaned forward and gently pushed him back.

'Just me Creep, just me. What you been up to? Who's after you?'

'No… just… nothing, nothing… thanks for this. Got anything to eat? Any scoff?'

Creep emptied the cider and tossed the can into the corner. As he lay down, sounding drowsy, he started to cry. No tears, he had no water to spare, but his body convulsed and his voice shook uncontrollably.

'Scary me, scary me,' he muttered. 'Better here… won't see… got any scoff mate? Better… I'm a… dead now… dead…'

He slept.

Jas sat in the corner, knees drawn up in a mirror image of Creep's earlier position. She just stared at him, feeling useless and frightened and angry. She would bring food tomorrow, and water.

The five kids looked like any group making their way to the river on an early summer's evening for a picnic. Anyone caring to look closely though would have noticed that, unlike youngsters off to have a good time, there was no laughter and very little chatter.

They crossed the school playing field, Jas having decided that it would be safer to approach the industrial estate from the country end of the footpath, rather than the town side. She told Kevin to keep an eye on their backs, in case anyone was following them. He nodded, not daring to ask why, because he assumed that he was supposed to know already.

The previous evening's encounter had shocked Jas more than she would have admitted, but she was determined to help Creep. The only other person in the group who knew the real reason for their excursion was Krissy. She thought Creep deserved his name, didn't like him, mainly because he smelled, but she wouldn't have missed out on this for anything. Besides, Jas had told her she was coming.

Once they had slithered down the grassy bank to the trees at the edge of the path, Jas turned to them and motioned that they should sit. She told them what had happened the previous evening.

'So we're taking Creep some food and drink and if anyone, anyone…' She turned a baleful eye to Kevin. '… yaps to Deidre or any of the staff, I'll fucking do you, okay?'

She waited for agreement. They all nodded. Nobody crossed Jasmine when she was in this sort of a mood.

'Here's what's going to happen. Pongo, you stay here and keep an eye open…' she raised a threatening finger as Kevin opened his mouth to protest. '… Don't. You. Dare. You stay here. We're going onto the path and every so often, one of you'll stop and watch. I'm going to get Creep and bring him back here, into the warm. If you see or hear anything, and I mean anything, you call me, but do it along the line, yeah? Right, let's go.'

The girls trooped off down the path through the trees and Kevin lay back on the bank, staring at the sky. Every so often he would pop his head up above the bank, checking the field beyond. Nothing stirred; no dog walkers, no footballers, no late stragglers from school. A bloke on a bike went drifting by, but Kevin only caught a glimpse of the back of his head as he disappeared along the path under the foliage.

Twenty minutes later, Kevin got his first, up-close-and-personal contact with the fabled Creep. He began to wish he'd stayed at the house.

Jas was supporting him as they came along the path. Krissy was on the other side of Creep, but barely laid a hand on him. Kevin could tell from the look on her face that she was feeling queasy. Tamsin and Pauline were a few feet to the rear, heads together, whispering and glancing at Jas and Creep as if they were something from their worst nightmares.

Jas helped Creep to sit on the bank next to Kevin. She looked across at the lad and smiled… actually smiled! Kevin felt his heart soar. How sweet was that? He said hello to Creep, then shuffled on his behind a little further away. Creep smelt foul.

'Given you the wrong name, haven't I, Pongo?' Jas said, curling her top lip. She opened the Shopping Bag and began laying food and drink out on the grass. 'Come on you lot, sit down and eat something.'

Tamsin and Pauline, who were standing some way off, started to back up slowly.

'We're going to head back to the house, Jas. Hamish said he was going to take us to…'

'Oh go on, fuck off the pair of you. If you can't be bothered to help a mate, then stuff you. But don't expect me to be giving you twos, or anything else, from now on. Go on, fuck off!'

'Screw you too, bitch!' Tamsin said as they walked away.

'If Deidre finds out about this, you're fucking dead!' Jas shouted at their backs.

Creep chuckled weakly and reached for a sandwich.

'Christ Jas, you don't change much do you?'

Krissy sat near Jas' feet, staring nervously at Creep, picking sporadically at a packet of crisps. Kevin just watched, not sure if he should be excited by all of this, or if he should have followed Tamsin and Pauline back to the house.

Creep put away more food in ten minutes than Kevin had ever seen anybody, anywhere ever, eat at one sitting. And a litre of water, and two cans of cider. Then promptly spewed the whole lot back up, having first managed to get to the bushes.

'Eeeuww!' Cried Krissy, flapping her hands and doing her best imitation of an American teen movie star. 'Gross!'

Jas gave her a pitying look, pulled another packet of sandwiches out of the Bag and opened another can of cider. Creep walked slowly and tiredly back to the group and lowered himself to the ground.

'Aah, Jesus, I feel like somebody's stamped on me guts.' He laid back and put his hands behind his head. He seemed relaxed, but Jas saw him glancing left and right, watching, watching, all the time watching.

'Okay.' She stretched out one leg and gave Creep a none-too gentle kick. 'Now you owe us. What've you been up to?'

Creep shook his head and sat up.

'No. Thanks for the food and all, but I'm not getting you involved, yeah? No way.'

'Strikes me we already are, numb-fuck.'

'It's not anything to do with you, all right?' He spun round to face her, eyes blazing, brow creased and teeth bared. 'Thanks for helping, but I'm not saying anything. Maybe he won't come looking, maybe he didn't see me…' Creep was staring at the ground now, working hard to convince himself more than the others. '… maybe… but I can't…'

Jas knew how to get what she wanted from most lads, and Creep was no exception. She laid a hand on his shoulder and squeezed gently.

'Come on Creep… maybe we can help?'

'Oh, leave him alone,' whined Krissy, tearing up a handful of grass and flinging it into the air. 'If he doesn't want to tell us, then leave him… OOOWWW! What the fuck was that for, bitch?!'

She rubbed the top of her arm where the can Jas had thrown had hit her.

'What do you think?' Jas returned her attention to Creep. 'Maybe who didn't see you mate?'

Creep looked up and stared at each of them, shaking his head.

'Maybe… I s'pose you're already… in a way… but… oh shit!! Fuck it!! Listen… I'm not even sure that it was him… him that did it… but, but… oh fuck it. Listen…'

And they did.

They were sworn to secrecy. They argued against it. But in the end, they swore. Because you had stick together, didn't you?

Kevin knew now he should have stayed at the house.

CHAPTER TWENTY FIVE

A week can be a very long time for very many reasons, particularly when you're a teenager. When there is something to look forward to, time drags its heels and clocks meander, teasing. But when there is nothing to anticipate and all you can see on the horizon are the thunder clouds of the same old storm, about which there is nothing perfect, then time can stop. Even seem to be going backwards.

The past week for David Trelawney had been a blur of nothing but tears and anguish. He had been drifting around, doing nothing and feeling that he should be doing something. His care manager was frantically trying to find another placement for him, to remove him to a place of safety, but, even though the boredom and the uncertainty weighed on him, he wasn't sure that he actually wanted to move.

He was in a washing machine of emotion, sloshed back and forward. He wanted to stay and help the Shadracks if he could, but they didn't see him. Brian and Aileen saw nothing, not even Brent, who had been packed off to an aunt's for the duration. They roamed the house, pale and hollow, Brian wandering around picking things up, looking at them, putting them down, Aileen sitting like a ghost in the kitchen with Warren's football jersey clutched to her breast. Everywhere David went, he saw Warren, saw things that reminded him of the night his jacket had gone missing.

Guilt was the thing that most gnawed at David. If he hadn't refused the loan and Warren had gone out earlier, he would still be alive. If David had been more reasonable about so many things, Warren would still be here. It was his fault that Warren was dead. Everything was his fault.

He was in care; his fault. His Mum didn't want to know him; his fault. His Dad couldn't even be bothered to own up to him; his fault. No amount of talking would persuade him otherwise. He might say he understood, say he realised that Warren's death and his being in care were things caused by other people's actions, but really, in his heart of hearts, he knew differently. His fault.

In the twilight, as he wandered along the lane, he could hear the occasional lowing of the cows in the field, and hear the blackbirds chittering out their warning as he strolled by. He had found a stick in the hedgerow and was whipping the heads off dandelions, slowly at first, watching them flip up into the air and tumble gracelessly to the road. Dead beauty now.

He hacked harder and faster, decimating the group at the bottom of the five bar gate where he had stopped. He heard the wind whistling harshly as he brought the stick down on the top of the gate, harder, harder… HARDER! It snapped, twirling away into the field.

He could feel the tightness in his chest, the tears tapping at the back of his eyes and his throat closing over, but he gritted his teeth. He wouldn't give himself the satisfaction, the release, of crying.

Leaning on the gate, he stared down the sloping field, seeing in the distance the clock tower that sat atop the church half-way up the hill in the centre of town. He could just make out the dim glitter of a bend in the river and the small puffs of green that were the trees that marched, in disorderly fashion, away towards Dartmouth.

Everything was empty and quiet. Even the cows had stopped complaining. He kicked the gate and looked up at the sky. Darkness was seeping in from over the hills, pushing the light away. He heard again the policeman at the Shadracks telling him not to go too far and to be back before nightfall.

He snorted. What was there to go back for? Another empty evening; he wasn't even allowed to go and visit his mates at Freeways. He shivered as a cool breeze appeared from nowhere, lifting his hair from his forehead and drying the sweat that lay there.

Throwing the remains of the stick away, he hoisted himself over the gate, deciding to strike out across the field and head back to the house via Yabsley's farm. Maybe he might even run into old man Yabsley, he was always good for a natter and a glass of scrumpy.

The thought of proper company made the walk all the more enjoyable, and he started to notice things; the rabbits, crouched in the longer grass at the edge of the field, nibbling nervously in the last of the daylight; the fleeting shadow of the barn owl, swooping in deadly silence, searching for its prey; the bark of the fox as he called to his mate.

What he didn't see was the darkness peel away from the shadow of the old horse chestnut in the lane and slide over the gate, to disappear in the black hedgerow.

~~~

'Why are you calling? It had better be for a very good reason.'

'He's losing it.'

'Then we terminate our agreement. You deal with him. If anything, and I do mean anything, comes in my direction, if I even think I might be implicated, you know what will happen.'

'The police are sniffing around the…'

'What!?'

'It's okay, it's okay. I just need somewhere to…'

'NO! Get rid of them.'

'These are good. Very good. I just need somewhere to store… to hide…'

'Get. Rid. Of them. If you hide them and they're discovered…'

'You won't help then?'

Silence.

'I'll think of something; you'll love them, I promise. Don't worry, I'll…'

'You've been warned, remember that.'

Click. Dead air.
~~~

CHAPTER TWENTY SIX

As Brian Shadrack weeps into his wife's hair and she stares, stony faced, at the dead TV screen, Cavannaugh and Rooke are frantically correlating information; they feel they are getting close.

As Monty Flute stands at the highest point on Hound Tor, feeling the wind in his face and Tom in his head, Nick Sloane is trawling the bars and pubs of the town, searching.

As Jas, Krissy and Kevin sit in Jas' room, hopelessly going round in circles, trying to decide what they should do, David Trelawney is in darkness, too scared to cry and wishing he had someone to think of and call upon.

As they search for answers in their own way, Cupid laughs. He is immortal, indomitable, infallible. He hears their fear and tastes their tears and it gives him all he needs to know that his mission is divine and he will continue. He will prevail.

~~~

All three sat on Jas' bed, staring out the window, across the garden to the playing field beyond.

'It's the best we can do. We've got to trust someone, and there ain't anybody here for that. So… Kevin, go and tell Creep. You got to get him to do it. Got to!'

'How do we know that David isn't already… y'know?'

Jas slapped the palm of her hand on the window in frustration.

'Just fucking do it Kevin. Just… do it, all right? Get Creep here tonight, outside the office window, and we'll give him anything we find. Just get him here!'

'Yeah, but how…'

She spun round and grabbed him by the hair, pulling him close so that
~~~

her nose was touching his. He yelped.

'Because I heard them talking, okay? I heard the copper telling Deidre that they'd got a letter from this nutter... David's still alive, all right? Now...' she shoved him off the bed and turned back to the window, '... just get Creep here.'

Jas was feeling things that she had never felt before - at least, not nearly so powerfully. She understood death better than most kids of her age; she had seen it and, once, felt its fingertips touching her face and its breath on her eyes. She knew fear and hate and thought she understood love. But, as she sat watching Kevin trotting across the garden, heading off to find Creep, she was starting to see there was more to all these things than just words.

If love was more than a frantic fumble and wet sheets, two tins of cider and an emptiness that echoed with self-doubt, then maybe what she was feeling now was the closest she would ever get to caring for someone. She needed David to survive. If he didn't, then she felt there would never be anything but the sound of her own tears to keep her company.

The talk of death, of not seeing someone ever again, had brought bitter memories crawling back into her head. These others, these stupid children, mocked it. They knew the word but had no understanding of it; of its permanence, its all-encompassing finality. Its nothingness. And she wanted more than that for David and for herself. Deep down, what they were doing, what she was planning, was a selfish act of survival. She needed more than she had, more than what was waiting for her, a few years down the line.

She let the tears tumble down her cheeks, and didn't care if Krissy saw them or not.

~~~

'I think we've got the house!' Cavannaugh pushed past the constable standing in the office doorway, talking to Rooke. 'What do you want to do?'

Rooke stood and waved the PC away, coming round the desk and holding his hand out for the piece of paper that Cavannaugh was waving. He scanned the print rapidly, chewing his bottom lip.

'Right. Do you know where this place is?' Cavannaugh nodded. 'Good. Take two uniforms and a couple of DCs... no, just the DCs, I don't want any suspicions getting raised. Canvas the neighbours, have a
~~~

look around. If anyone's in at the address, you're, I don't know, Jehovah's or something. Got it? If there's nobody there, leave the DCs watching and get a car in place nearby. Constant radio contact, all right?' Again Cavannaugh nodded. 'Nice work, Derek. Where from?'

'The solicitors and the local estate agents. All the paper work was signed by G. Ballantyne, same as in the will. It's our man.'

'Excellent. Go on then, get your team together and…'

'What about the lad, David Trelawney?'

'I've been talking to the psychologist about the letter from Cupid, and he seems to think that, apart from it being genuine, the boy will be kept alive, but the time scale is uncertain. If, when you're at the house, you see anything that indicates Cupid is keeping him there, you go in. We deal with consequences later. I need that lad alive and preferably unharmed. Otherwise, watching and waiting. I dearly want this bloke caught red-handed. I don't want some smart-arse QC getting him off on a technicality.'

'I'll keep in touch and let you know what's happening.'

Cavannaugh trotted from the room, calling out as he caught sight of one of the other officers who was involved with the case. He told him what he wanted and that he would meet them down in the car park in twenty minutes.

'And see if you can get hold of Judy Sparkes. If we're going to be Jehovah's Witnesses, then its better we have a woman with us as well.'

He went back to the office he shared with three other officers and collected his coat, finishing off a lukewarm cup of coffee as well. He stood for a moment, breathing deeply and trying to get his thoughts together. His only regret was that the Boss wasn't there to see the culmination of all their work. He dipped into his jacket pocket and retrieved his mobile phone.

~~~

The clouds chased shadows across the hills, making it seem as if the land was moving. Although the sun was shining, the stiff breeze from the west gave the air a pleasant edge, fresh and reviving.

Flute sat on a rock, staring across the valley towards Hay Tor, watching a group of riders guiding their horses between the rocks that were scattered haphazardly in their path. Behind him, further down the slope, he could just hear a group of youngsters laughing as they tried to play with a Frisbee in the wind. Above his head, a skylark twittered, a
~~~

sound that always put in him in mind of the moors and solitude.

This was the only place where he could think of Tom and be at peace with the memories. Where the guilt weighed less heavily and he could, perhaps, start to believe that there was nothing he could have done to have prevented what had happened. Perhaps.

But Tom had always been very adept at hiding his emotions, what he had been thinking. Any number of people had told Flute that he couldn't have been expected to realise, that he wasn't a mind reader, that Tom had to hold some of the responsibility. And the fact was that if Tom didn't want him to know, he wasn't likely to have found out.

Flute shook his head. This was old ground. He could follow his own footprints, so often had he been over and over it. Yet, no matter how often he walked this way, he could never, ever remember any hint of what Tom was keeping from him. Or was that wishful thinking too?

He supposed, sometimes, that Tom had done what he had out of guilt or shame - he couldn't seriously believe that Tom would have killed himself just because he had been diagnosed HIV positive. Everybody knew that that wasn't the end, not by any stretch of the imagination. But couple that with the reason for it… who knew?

As he reached into his day pack for a bottle of water, his mobile warbled. Should have stayed down in the valley where there was no signal, he thought, sliding the cover up and accepting the call.

'Flute.' He pulled the cap off the water bottle up and took and swig. 'Hello Derek. How's things?'

His stomach clenched slightly as he listened to Cavannaugh and he had to breathe deeply to stop himself gagging. The very thought of going back, of being involved again, at any level, suddenly seemed very scary.

'Good for you, well done. How's Bob Rooke doing?' He nodded and listened with half an ear, finding that he didn't actually care how Rooke was faring. 'Any news of the lad?'

That was what concerned him more. Another kid, another life in jeopardy, the possibility of another statistic that most people would read about, shake their heads and sigh and go back to their lives, convinced that the world had just gone a shade madder.

'Well, good luck. Let me know, if you can, what happens. No, no, I'm fine. Thanks for asking. Yeah, okay, talk to you soon.'

He dropped the phone back in to his bag and stood up. Suddenly, he felt very hungry. He looked down to the car park and decided a sausage roll and a coffee from the Hound of the Basket Meals was just what he needed.

~~~

Nick Sloane sat quietly at a table near the back of The Hornblower, sipping his pint and watching the football whilst keeping an eye on the door. He had spent far too much time scouring the town for Dylan the Dealer, and he was starting to get angry; which wouldn't be a good thing for Dylan when he found him.

Once Nick was on a job, he wanted to get it over and done with as quickly as possible and move on to the next thing. His previous chat with Dylan should have been enough, but the bloke obviously thought that, with the Plymouth boys supplying him, he would be safe. The man was either dead sure of himself or just plain dense. Nick fancied the second option.

He looked at the clock behind the bar and sighed. Half past ten. If his man hadn't arrived by quarter to, he'd call it a day and have to come back tomorrow. Bloody hell, what a waste of an evening.

A bunch of four lads came through the door, ordered their drinks and took a table near the toilets, just across from Nick. He frowned. Friday night, late-ish, and yet these guys, whilst it was obvious that they'd had a few sherberts, seemed remarkably subdued.

One of the lads said something and his mate, a skinny, long-haired individual with bad dress sense and a face you could play join the dots on, banged his pint down and grabbed his wrist.

'Just shut up Tony, yeah? He said he'd be here. He wasn't here at nine so the next one's at quarter to. It'll be cool. Dylan's a good lad, yeah? No worries.'

Nick settled back into his chair. This was more like it. Thing was, if Dylan the Dickhead saw him waiting here, he'd high-tail it before you could say ten quid deal. Nick picked up his pint, checked the time again, and moved down to the bar, making sure that he would be hidden by the door when it opened.

'Give us a large brandy love, please.'

He drained the beer and watched the barmaid banging the optic to get it to work. Last one before business, a small straightener to help him through the arduous business of ticking somebody off, the quiet chat having been unheeded. Nick hoped he wouldn't have to go one stage
~~~

further, as Ferdy had suggested. Disappearing someone was more complex and messy than that fat little twat realised.

The door crashed open and Nick saw Mr. Trendy at the back of the pub stand up and wave. Finishing his brandy, he glanced quickly in that direction and, sure enough, there was the dense one, swaggering with a limp now, heading up to do business. Nick watched for a moment, seeing if the deal would be struck in the pub, but he somehow doubted it. He knew the landlord's reputation for intolerance in that quarter and supposed that the transaction would take place somewhere close by. He stepped back onto Fore Street and took up position in the shadows of an alleyway opposite.

He supposed that he wouldn't have too long to wait and he was right. Ten minutes later, the idiot herded his customers out the door and guided them down the street. Nick followed, pretty sure that they were heading for Cider City, which was a shame because there were usually quite a few people there on a Friday night, which meant that he would have to be a little quieter than he had expected. It also meant that Dylan had learned not to do business in isolated spots.

They headed on to the bridge and, sure enough, disappeared down the steps that led to the island. Nick followed, pulling on his gloves and flexing his hands.

He ducked down the steps quickly. The last thing he needed was Dylan glancing over his shoulder and seeing him. He hopped over the railings and dropped into the shadows, watching the figures weaving down the path that led to the end of island. There was no way off the island other than coming back past Nick, so he found a bench and sat down, looking around and seeing how many of the local residents were home this evening.

There was a couple of youngsters away to his left, sitting on another bench by the river, playing tonsil hockey and he could just make out somebody under a huge old yew tree, curled up and sleeping something off. There may have been others, but if he couldn't see them, chances were they were on the other side of the island, watching the submarines race. God bless sex and its diversionary functionality.

He heard voices and recognised Mr. Trendy extolling the virtues of Dylan's merchandise.

Make the most of it, thought Nick, he won't be in business too much longer my friend. The group strolled by in a huddle, discussing the merits of heading down to the river to drop the tabs or heading back to Tony's place. Nick turned his concentration back to the place from which they had come. Nothing moved. He saw the flare of a match or cigarette lighter off in the distance. So Dylan had finished for the night and was having a blow, was he? Excellent. So much the better for Nick.

Staying in the shadows as much as he could, Nick made his way across the island, round the yew tree, and headed towards Dylan so as to approach him from the grass and not the path. No one steps out into the river, do they?

He saw the dealer sitting with his back resting on a tree, staring across the water towards Quay Marsh and smoking a joint. Nick could smell it as he walked over.

'Hello Dylan.' Dylan was almost on his feet before the words were out of Nick's mouth, but the fist that crashed into the soft spot between his collar bone and neck got him sitting again. Nick hunkered down in front of him, resting his fingertips against the tree and leaning close. He could smell the beer and dope on his breath and see the fear in his dull yellow eyes.

'What is it with guys like you Dylan, eh? Do you not listen when people tell you something or is it that you think you're somehow above all that? Or is it that you think you're immortal, invisible and untouchable? Mmmm?'

Dylan just stared up at him, the joint hanging loosely between his lips, trying to say something.

'What's the matter Dylan? Cat got your tongue?' Nick reached out and pulled the joint from the dealer's mouth, watching the skin stretch and tear where the paper had stuck. 'Ooh, that's going to be sore. Feel that sting? That's the thing that you'll remember as the most pleasant part of this evening. No, really, you will.'

Dylan rolled to one side and started to scuttle away on his hands and knees. He was whimpering and coughing as he went. Nick walked quickly up beside him and brought his foot up into Dylan's gut. He heard the breath whoosh out of him and heard the choking. Nick was on all fours beside him, resting ear to ear, with his left hand curled gently in Dylan's hair.

'What are we going to do with you, eh? You do realise, don't you, that you've been a very silly man?' He gripped his hair more tightly and pushed Dylan's head up and down. 'You can say 'yes' you know.'

'Y... y… yes.'

'Yes what?'

'Yes… I b… b… been very silly.' Nick kept moving his hand, forcing Dylan to keep nodding.

'And how am I going to make sure you listen this time? Am I going to have to break both your legs?' He stopped pushing and let go of the hair. 'Or am I going to put your lights out? Or shall I just tie your hands behind your back and shove you in the river?'

Dylan made a half-hearted attempt to crawl away again, but Nick just laid a hand on his head and tapped.

'Not a good move, matey. Very unwise. And there was I thinking that we'd managed to reach an understanding. Maybe you just can't listen properly. Is that it? Are you just too fucking stupid to understand how close you are to getting offed? Well? Is that it?'

'No… I mean… I mean yes, yes, I'm too stupid… but I am listening. Honest. And, and I'll go away…' He raised his head slightly and tried to look at Nick. His eyes were wide and hopeful, as if he had just come up with the most fantastic scheme for solving all their problems. 'Yeah, yeah, that's the one! I'll go away. You won't never see me again. Honest. Promise…' He saw Nick shaking his head.

'Nice idea, but, you see, I have a problem with believing you, after last time and all. Do you blame me? I mean really, do you blame me? No, I can see that you don't. So I suppose I'm going to have to give you a right ticking off!!'

Dylan closed his eyes and, even though he didn't believe in God, started praying.

Nick pulled off his gloves as he walked slowly back towards the bridge. The night air felt cool and soothing on his forehead, working hard to push away the headache that was starting to rumble at the base of his neck.

He looked across at the couple on the bench, leaning close to each other, talking in hushed tones and each stroking the other's hair. He stopped for a moment, staring. How many years had it been since he'd walked through Cider City? How many years had it been since he'd sat with someone, like those two, and wiled away an hour or two with sweet nothings? He snorted and started walking.

The hand came out of nowhere, grabbing his left wrist, pulling.

Nick's mind became blank. He reacted. He pushed at the assailant, shoving hard. It was the last thing they would expect. Grab somebody, and the automatic reaction is to pull away. Never do that. Push. Best defence is attack.

As he pushed, he heard whoever it was grunt. He moved swiftly. The attacker had grabbed him with his right hand. So as Nick pushed he moved off to the attacker's left, jerking against the other's thumb, twisting round and grabbing the wrist, pulling the arm up round the other's throat.

As he moved, his right hand slipped into his coat pocket and grabbed his knife. A compact little item with a quick release button on the side.

His attacker's arm was up underneath his chin as Nick calmly put the blade against his face.

'You've got about three seconds my friend, then I start cutting.'

CHAPTER TWENTY SEVEN

Sometimes fear is the strongest reason for doing something that you fear. For too long, Creep had been living under the shadow of so many different, terrifying things that he found it hard to decide which he feared the most. Was it the memories of what had happened, both recently and in the past, or was it the fear of what might happen? He couldn't decide, but thought it was a simple, yet complicated, mixture of the two.

When Kevin had appeared at his pallet stack, wide-eyed and almost incoherent, Creep suddenly realised that he, Creep, was the adult that this kid was turning to. The years had piled up behind him and, whilst still living as a child, with the hopes and fears of a child, they had shoved him unceremoniously into early adulthood without so much as a by your leave. And that was probably the most frightening thing to discover about yourself: you're grown-up. Someone else was looking to you to help, where, for all those years, you had been looking for help yourself.

Creep had listened to what Kevin had to say without saying anything himself. He just nodded in all the right places and, when Kevin had stood to go, he had said,

'Yeah, okay, see you later.'

But Creep couldn't do all this by himself, could he? He couldn't possibly stand up and be a support for somebody else when he had still to learn how to stand on his own two feet… could he?

He had gritted his teeth and left the shelter of his pallets, on his own, for the first time since Jas had dragged him to the picnic and probably saved his life. He had to help. He couldn't let his friends down.

So he had wandered, keeping an eye on the clock in the war

memorial, trying to decide what on earth it was that Jas wanted him to do after they had found what they wanted; he comforted himself with the thought that they wouldn't actually find anything, and then he could go back to being the lost and lonely child he had been an hour before.

Watchers become watched.

He had been sitting behind the rubbish truck at the back of the off-licence, leaning against the wall and drinking a beer when he saw a vaguely familiar figure leave the Hornblower across the road and come and stand in the shadows not ten feet from where he sat.

The man had glanced around but had failed to notice Creep, because Creep was good at what he did - be unnoticed.

It was the guy who had so severely battered Dylan the Dealer. Creep's mind chugged into motion, making connections, remembering what had been said by this man when he had warned Lee to stay away from people like Dylan. It had sounded almost as if he cared about what happened to Lee and the kids at Freeways.

And so he watched and waited. He saw Dylan taking a group of men out the pub and off towards Cider City. Creep had a nasty feeling that Dylan was going to get another beating, but he followed.

He saw the man waiting, and when he had disappeared to the far end of the island, Creep had positioned himself by a huge old oak tree. He had no idea what he was going to say to the man, or how he would even approach him, but he had to try. He wasn't strong enough to do all this stuff on his own. He thought he could, he desperately wanted to be able to, but he couldn't. The fear ran too deep.

Two terrors were doing battle inside of Creep and neither was gaining the upper-hand. So he brought a third into play, hoping that they would cancel each other out. As he waited for the man to come back, he realised that his clever ploy hadn't been so clever after all. He now had three demons clumping around inside his head, confusing him more than ever.

The man walked silently, almost as silently as Creep, when he was in real Creep mode, and Creep would have missed his chance completely had he not stopped to watch the young lovers on the bench.

No planning now, just reaction. Just do it and get it over with. Creep didn't even stop to wonder what had happened to Dylan. The adrenaline pumped him up beyond caring. He grabbed the stranger's wrist and, as he was whirled round and felt the knife pressed against his cheek, he suddenly realised what a huge mistake he might have made.

'You've got about three seconds my friend, then I start cutting.'

Creep's throat had closed over completely, he could barely breathe, let alone talk. His left arm flapped uselessly, trying to signal that he wanted to talk.

'Oi! You all right mate?'

Nick saw the man on the bench by the river stand up and look over in their direction. His girlfriend grabbed at his arm.

'Leave it Peter, let it go!'

'That's right Peter.' Nick said, letting go of Creep's wrist and grabbing him by the scruff of the neck. 'Let it go. That's the best advice you'll get all night. Take her home, there's a sensible bloke.'

The girl grabbed her bag from under the bench, and pulled Peter away towards the road. He made a token effort to resist, but it was, even to Nick's eyes, severely half-hearted. Peter had heard something in Nick's voice that had made him wish to be somewhere else, and quickly.

Nick watched them go, still holding tight to Creep's collar, but he could tell from the way his attacker was standing, limp and submissive, that he would have no further trouble from him. He pulled the rag-doll away from the trees and across to the recently vacated bench. Shoving Creep roughly down, Nick placed one foot on the seat and leant on his knee, folding the blade back into its handle and slipping the knife back into his pocket.

'Now then my friend, who in hell are you?'

In the half-light, Nick could see that the lad, barely twenty and smelling centuries older, was plainly terrified, almost catatonic with fear. Curiouser and curiouser, thought Nick, walking round and sitting next to him.

'What's your name?' The boy muttered something and Nick saw a thin line of saliva stringing its way from his mouth. Creep hunched over, hands clasped and shoved between his legs, shaking so hard that Nick could almost hear the teeth rattling in the lad's head.

He put a hand on the boy's shoulder; he yelped and hunched over even more, whimpering.

'Say again?'

'Cr... Creep... they call me Creep.'

Nick patted his shoulder.

'Right, Creep. What's the story my friend? What in the name of

Christ are you doing jumping me like that, eh? You almost got hurt, yeah?'

'No, no, no, don't hurt me... I... I just want to t... t... talk to you. Help.'

'It's all right, it's all right, you don't need help. I'm not going to hurt you.'

Nick was about as puzzled as he had ever been. Strange things happened in his line of work, but this was unprecedented.

'No... n... n... no. I want your help.'

Nick leant back, hands grasping his knees, and looked up at the sky, hoping to find some answers there. He let out a long breath and slapped his thighs, leaning forward, trying to see Creep's face.

'And how do you think I can help you then? Money? Is that it?'

He watched as Creep, hands still clenched between his legs, began to straighten up. The boy wiped the back of his hand across his mouth and nose, sniffing and taking a deep, shuddering breath. He squeezed his eyes closed, pressing his lips together and Nick could see, almost feel, the effort that went into getting himself upright and capable of talking. Creep shook his head and tried to look at Nick, but ended up staring at his feet.

'Not money. No, not money. Help.'

Creep's head was spinning. He was trying so hard to be coherent, tell the story so that this guy could understand just how important this was, not only to Creep, but to Jas and everyone. And David. Most of all, David.

'I saw... I saw you with Dylan.'

Nick felt his heart sink and a strange, empty space appeared in his chest. Bloody hell. He tried to keep his voice level. Now he needed to know just how much this kid had actually seen.

'So is that why you were waiting for me here then? Because you'd seen me and Dylan down there?' He jerked his head in the direction he had come from. Creep shook his head.

'No, no, not tonight. Before. With Lee at the wharf. Remember? I saw you help him, before... before... before he...' The fear of recalling that night sent Creep into another fit of the shivers. His eyes glazed over and Nick could see the tears spilling over and rolling down his cheeks. Nick's brain clicked into overdrive. This was about Lee. The murders. Did this kid think that he had... no, that wasn't possible. He was too scared to have approached him if he thought that Nick was the killer. He wanted help, Nick's help. He began making connections.

'Creep… Creep, listen. It's okay. Just talk to me.'

He waited a moment, hoping that Creep would respond, but he just sat, shaking, which was hardly surprising.

'Okay, okay, listen. I'll ask you a few questions, you answer the best you can. How's that sound?'

Creep nodded. He just sat, staring at the floor, tears pouring down his face. There was no movement now, barely even the sound of him breathing. He was waiting for Nick to get it right.

'So, you saw me… you saw me have a word with Dylan, then talk to Lee, right?' Creep nodded. 'Good. Are you from Freeways? Or rather, were you at Freeways?' Nod. Aaah! Now things were starting to drop into place. 'So you knew Lee. What about the first lad, Terry, did you know him too?' Another nod, more definite. 'So… Christ!! Did you see someone take Lee… after I'd spoken to him?' Vigorous nod. 'Come on Creep, you've got to talk to me… do you know how important this… of course you do, of course you do. Fuck. How can I help?'

He waited, watching the courage get dragged up from somewhere. Watching a kid try to tap reserves that somehow seemed bottomless; there was always enough there for one last effort… or so it seemed. Creep coughed, then said,

'Jas… she's at Freeways… thinks that there's something in the office, hidden, that'll tell us where… where he's taken David. She wants me to be outside the office window to collect whatever they find. They'll just pinch somebody's keys, it happens all the time, and have a root round. I wanted to help.'

He managed to look at Nick, and there was such a depth of sadness and fear in his eyes, that Nick nearly gathered him up and hugged him.

'Who the hell do they think… what do they think they're going to…'

'I told them who I saw meet Lee, after you'd left. I don't think… at least, it's not likely, is it? It's not likely that… that this person would have done anything, but Jas… Jas, she thinks so.'

'So who did you see meet Lee that night?' Creep started to shiver again, shaking his head in quick little jerky movements. 'Hey, hey, hey, it's all right, it's all right Creep. It's just you and me mate, just you and me.' Creep just shook his head again. He wasn't saying anything. 'All right, okay, leave it for the moment. So… the idea is that you want me to come with you to Freeways and get… something that might not even be there to help save this David bloke. Jesus, Creep! Why not just tell the police?'

Nick couldn't believe he was hearing that phrase coming out of his own mouth. Tell the police? He saw Creep turn and look at him with a mixture of disbelief and wondering contempt. Nick held up his hand.

'Yeah yeah, okay, I get the message.'

He scrubbed his face with both hands, thinking that he should just get up and walk away. That would be the sensible thing to do.

'Was this David at Freeways?'

'He was, up to about a month ago. Went to a foster placement… it was the son of Dave's foster parents that got killed. Remember?' Nick nodded. He remembered all right.

'So David's been missing for how long?'

'Dunno… but Jas says he's still alive. She heard the coppers telling Deidre… she's the manager at Freeways… they were telling her that Dave's still alive. That's why she wants to do something… Jas wants to do something, not Deidre… well, Deidre does but not…'

'Bloody hell!' Nick put his arm round Creep's shoulder, feeling a slight resistance, then an almost grateful collapsing into him. 'You've certainly gotten yourselves into something here, haven't you mate? What's David like?'

'He was… he is a really good bloke, you know? Just nice. He had his moments, yeah? But compared to some of the kids at Freeways, he was all right. I liked him.'

Leaning in to Nick's shoulder, Creep felt safer than he had done for he didn't know how long. It was like this man knew what it was like to be where Creep and his mates were. Understood.

'Yeah. I liked old Trelawney. He was all right. That's why we want to do something. He…'

Nick pushed Creep away, harder than he had intended, and grabbed both his shoulders, turning him to look into his face and watch his eyes.

'Who? Who did you like?'

He squeezed Creep, not wanting to scare him - although he had - but needing him to answer, quickly. Creep tried to pull away, fear resurfacing in his eyes. Nick held him firm.

'Creep, please, this is very, very important, yeah? What did you just say?'

'I liked… I… I… liked David; he was all right.'

'The name, Creep. You said his name… what?'

'Tre… David Trelawney. What? What's the matter?'

'Do you know… Jesus!! Do you know, and this might seem like a silly question, but do you know what David's mothers' name is? Eh?'

He watched Creep thinking, he could see him trying hard.

'Please, try to think if David ever said, ever told you.'

'Rose. Her name was Rose.'

The night telescoped, faded, buzzed in his ears. He could hear Creep's voice, reaching him from the other side of the world, echoing in his head like an old memory. He'd lost track, given up, but he'd never stopped thinking about it. About him.

Suddenly, he was seventeen again. He was standing in the doorway of his parent's living room, watching his old man pawing a frightened, dark eyed girl, who had asked for help. And he'd ignored her. Run away.

He was fighting for his life again. He could see his father, spit cascading from his mouth as he lunged at him, knife in hand. He felt the scar beneath his ear throb and felt the jarring impact as he brought the lump of wood crashing down on the back of that hated head. And he was running again. Changing names.

When he had been someone different, in Freeways; when he had been Rob Wilkes (Christ! How long had it been since he had even thought of that name?) and running; when he had become another person, taking the old manager's surname and then using Simon's surname as a sort of silent thank you to the only man who had ever seemed to care, even a little, he had become Nick Sloane. He knew the girl his father had raped had had a child; knew it was a boy; knew his name was David Trelawney. But he had lost track and never found the way again - until now.

What were the chances? It might not be his half-brother, might just be a coincidence, but he didn't think so. His gut told him that this was his brother. And he was in terrible trouble. Time to stop running, he thought. Time to stand still and let the birds come home to roost.

'Are you okay? Hello!! Are you…'

Nick squeezed Creep's shoulders again.

'Eeerr… yeah… yeah, I'm fine.'

Nick leant forward and rested his head in the palms of his hands. He was the one shivering now. He could feel the cold in the pit of his stomach sliding round to caress his spine and the back of his head. Time to stop running. He laughed, a short harsh bark, and slapped his legs.

'Who did you see meet Lee that night, Creep? Who was it?'

He turned to look at the boy, and smiled. That smile scared Creep more than anything else that had happened this evening.

'Please. Who was it?'

'Piggy.'

There, it was out. Done. Creep felt as if he had lost a friend as the fear slewed off him like a snake skin.

'Piggy,' said Nick. 'Piggy… fucking Mo Palfrey.'

'You know him?'

Nick laughed again, standing up and motioning Creep to do the same.

'Oh yes. I know our Piggy… it was me that gave him that name. Me, when I was somebody else; when I was more like you than I feel comfortable with.' He clapped his hands. 'Come on mate. Let's go see if your friends have found anything, yeah?'

CHAPTER TWENTY EIGHT

With a confidence that he certainly didn't feel, and courage screwed up to screaming pitch, Kevin looked Jas straight in the eyes and said,

'YES! Creep'll be here, so just give it a fucking rest, all right?!'

Jas regarded him through half-closed lids and pointed a delicate pink finger nail at his heart. She felt even less confident than Kevin, but was a deal more adept at hiding what she was feeling; years of practice.

'You'd better be telling me the truth, you little twat, or I'll carve my name on your bollocks with this, got it? Right, Krissy, you know what's going to happen don't you?'

Krissy raised a long-suffering look at the ceiling and then went to study her breasts in the mirror.

'Yeah, yeah. I'll pick a row with Tam then you can nick the keys and we'll keep an eye out… why can't I come to the office with you then?' She sighed theatrically. 'D'you think my tits are big enough?'

'Fuck me backwards! You'd better get it right, you silly cow, or I'll…'

'What? What'll you do, fuck face? Carve your name on my bollocks, you bossy minger!? I got a good mind to go and tell Hamish what you're planning, yeah?'

'Good mind, you soft bitch? If you had half a brain, you'd still be a thick cunt! Just do what you're told, yeah? Jesus…' Jas lowered her voice to soft, vicious whisper, '… this ain't about you, you fucking half-wit! It's about David, all right?'

Kevin sat quietly and wiped his sweating palms on the quilt. He hated all this shit; all the shouting and swearing and arguing. He just longed to get on with everybody, go to his tutoring sessions, go to the flicks with Simon, just get on with it.

He hoped all this would be over quickly.

The door at the top of the stairs swished open and they heard Hamish calling them to the staff over-night room to get their hot drinks and biscuits before they settled for the night.

Jas, Krissy and Kevin stood up and looked at each other. Each could see the fear in the others' eyes, could almost read their thoughts, but they said nothing about it; some things you just didn't talk about, unless it was one to one, in the depths of night, when the dreams and memories melted together to nightmares and you needed to whisper your darkest fears to somebody, anybody.

Jas grabbed Krissy's left breast, hooking her fingers beneath the wire of her bra, and pulled her close, breathing in her face. Krissy squirmed and gritted her teeth, determined not to cry out, feeling Jas' thumb nail screwing into her nipple.

'Just do it and don't fuck about, all right?' Jas scraped down with her nail again and let Krissy go. 'Kevin, go and knock on Pauline's door, you know what to say, yeah?'

He nodded and trotted away, shouting to Hamish that he wanted four sugars in his coffee. He needed to go to the bathroom badly, but he knew he had to do what Jas had told him. She was really scary when she got that look on her face; it reminded him of his Gran, when she'd had a few too many sherries and got the belt out.

Jas walked into the night room and sat on the bed, watching Hamish laying out the biscuits and the mugs, putting the report sheets on the bedside table and getting his book out of his overnight bag.

'What you reading now?' Jas asked nonchalantly, laying across the bed, making sure that enough cleavage was on view. Hamish didn't turn round.

'It's about the ancient Egyptians… and Jas? Get off the bed please, there are enough chairs in here for you to sit on, okay?' He walked out the room without even looking at her and called down the stairs to Yvonne, the other staff member who was sleeping in. 'Von!! Bring up some sugar please!'

Jas got up from the bed and smoothed her skirt, glancing in the mirror over the sink, making sure she was noticeable. She had a quick practice smile, checking her eyes to see that they were suitably smoky. Not that Hamish would notice; she reckoned that most of the men who worked here were gay anyway.

Jas chewed her bottom lip, starting to feel nervous. Nicking the keys and leading the staff on a wild goose chase was fine, when it happened off the cuff. It didn't really matter whether they got the keys back in five minutes or fifty. But tonight, it was desperately important that Kev and Krissy kept it going for as long as possible and that Hamish and Von didn't suspect that they were chasing smoke, that the kids didn't actually have the keys because she would be down in the office.

She could feel the skin on the backs of her arms and legs prickling and she felt hot and cold at the same time. Like, sometimes, when she lay in her room, lights out and TV on mute, listening to HIM whispering to her again and again… and doing things.

She dug her nails into the palms of her hands. It helped, but she was still feeling floaty. Sliding her left hand up her right sleeve, she pressed her little finger nail into the soft flesh of her upper arm and raked it down hard. That worked; the pain shocked her back to normality.

Hamish came back into the room, tossed his keys onto the bed and sat, pulling the report sheets from the bedside table to start writing. Jas said,

'Hamish, I need to do some washing, can you open the laundry please?'

Hamish sighed and looked at her in that way he had - fed up and about to give her a lecture, but knowing, in the end, that he'd open the laundry, just to get them all settled and the house quiet.

'Jas, you've had all day to get your washing done, haven't you? I know Simon talked to you this morning, but you, apparently, had better things to do… remember? This is ridiculous! It's…' He checked his watch. '… it's nearly midnight, and you want to start washing your things now!? Really, it's too…'

Jas fought hard to control her temper. Of all nights, this was the one where Hamish went against form and actually used the 'N' word. She couldn't believe it! They were fucked before they even got started.

'Hamish, please…? It's kind of…'

'Sorry Jas, no, not this time. It's too late and you had the chance this morning. You'll have to do it tomorrow, okay?'

The 'N' word: No. Jas tried to marshal her thoughts and come up with a convincing argument to persuade Hamish, but nothing came to her… apart from her volatility and that was what saved the plan. To have argued would have led nowhere.

To have tried to persuade would have been fruitless - Jas never persuades or argues rationally, she screams. She shouts and kicks and uses some of the language that Hamish hadn't heard since he left the Navy. All Jas had to do to get the plan moving and back on track, was be her usual, charming self. Von arrived with the sugar just as Jas launched into one.

'Oh great! Give someone a bit of power and they start fucking with your head! All I want is to run me knickers through a cool wash, for fuck's sake! I'm not asking you to give me money, you tight Scottish twat!! It's not as if you're paying for the fucking 'leccy bill, is it, eh?'

Von deposited the sugar on the table and came and stood between them, resting a hand on Jas' shoulder and asking Hamish, with a look, what the hell was going on.

'Jas… JAS! Shut up a moment, please. Now, why do you need to do this now?' Jas folded her arms and gave Von a look and jerked her head at Hamish.

Von smiled.

'Okay, I think I get it…'

'Hoo-fucking-ray! See, tight arse? It takes a woman to understand another woman! Twat.'

Von mouthed the word 'period' at Hamish and held her hand out for the laundry room key. Hamish unclipped the key from his bunch.

'Why didn't you say something, Jas? I'm not completely ignorant, you know.'

'Yeah right! Like I'm going tell you I'm on the blob and that I need to wash 'em out!? Fuck off. Just open the door, yeah?'

She looked down and started examining her nails, hoping that Kev or Krissy would hurry the fuck up and start doing what they were supposed to do. Almost on cue, there was an almighty scream from the far end of the corridor and the slamming of doors.

'Give that back, you cow!! My Mum gave me that!!'

Jas did her best not to smile. Excellent. Krissy had nicked Tamsin's Bagpuss - she couldn't have chosen a better target herself. Then Pauline started yelling at Kevin. Christ knew what he'd done to kick her off, but she sounded like she was fit to kill.

Hamish looked at Von, and they both pushed off out the door, Hamish leaving his keys on the bed where he had thrown them.

'Von,' he called, 'Check Pauline, I'll go and see what Tamsin's up to.'

Jas winked at herself in the mirror, scooped the keys from the bed and headed downstairs.

It took a moment or two to find the right one, but she was soon in the office, leaning her back against the door and listening to the commotion upstairs. Banging the switch by the door down, the room flickered into life.

Filing cabinets, with all the notes on the residents, were lined up against the left hand wall and at the far end was the odds and sods cupboard. The windows were immediately facing the door and the four communal desks were in the middle of the room. Off to the right were the things that Jas wanted to get into - the staff lockers, where they kept all their paperwork and personal stuff.

She had no idea what she was looking for, but it would be in Piggy's locker, that much she was sure. She tiptoed across the room, although, with noise emanating from upstairs, she could have had a rave down here and nobody would have heard.

The lockers were large, floor-to-ceiling cupboards, two layers high and tall enough to hang coats in. There were sixteen of them, and all in need of a coat of paint. The top row were held shut with a variety of small padlocks, easy enough to break open.

Some of the lower cupboards had no doors at all and were stacked with piles of old files and books and handouts that had been put there to read at some point in the future.

The place was a mess.

Piggy's locker was the third one in from the left, and had the same, small padlock as the others. Jas gave the handle a swift tug, to see how hard it would be to bust open. She smiled - piece of piss.

Trotting over to the odds and sods cupboard, which was always unlocked, she rummaged in an old tin that held all sorts of useful things, including a screwdriver.

Mo Palfrey was a tidy man and liked everything in its place. A spare coat was hung on a hanger and pair of trainers and a pair of wellies were pushed to the back of the space. There was pile of text books stacked next to the shoes, along with a couple of files.

Jas pulled those out and leafed through them. County handouts on child abuse courses, report writing courses, core skills - nothing of any interest or help to her.

In a small satchel-like briefcase, she found a couple of old diaries that had an address printed on the inside cover in Palfrey's neat script. She put one of them on the desk behind her. Now they knew where he lived.

She checked the pockets of the coat, picked up the books and, holding them by the spine, gave them a shake, like she'd seen on the telly, when the police search a place. Nothing. Not even a dirty postcard.

She was starting to panic a little now. She looked at the clock above the filing cabinets; ten minutes, she'd been down here ten fucking minutes and found nothing! She went back to the carrier bag, flicking more thoroughly through the files and sheaves of paper. Christ! There had to be something!

Creep had seen the bastard leading Lee away. Seen him. There had to be something, had to be.

Not once since she had hatched the scheme to search the offices and Piggy's locker had she considered the notion that, if Piggy was the killer, why would he keep anything connected to the killings in his locker? What if there was nothing? What if she was wrong? What, what, what… what if it wasn't him? Fuck, it had to be, just had to be.

She closed her eyes and rested her forehead against the locker next to Palfrey's, knocking her head against it in frustration. She could feel the tears gathering beneath her eyelids, pricking her, reminding her of David and what this was all about.

She punched the open door, making her knuckles throb. The pain from the punch and the stinging from the scratch beneath her arm made her all the more determined to keep looking.

Stepping back, she perched herself on the edge of one of the desks, looking at the bank of lockers. There was no point in breaking open any of the others, it was Piggy that she was interested in, not Hamish or Von or Simon. The lockers with no doors on beckoned, but what was the point of looking there? If he didn't keep anything in his own, locked locker why would…?

She froze. A memory, one that she would have rather forgotten, swam lazily to the surface of her consciousness.

In the bad old days, when HE had controlled her life, checking everything, searching her room, never allowing her any privacy, she had been invited to a party by one of her school friends. The letter had arrived while HE had been out, otherwise she would never had known anything about it, until it was too late.

She knew she couldn't hide it anywhere - HE knew all the likely places and the thought of him finding something hidden from him, something deliberately concealed, had made her feel sick.

So she had just put the letter on top of her desk and left it there, covered by school work and books. Several times, HE had rummaged through her things, but had never thought to look where everything lay in view. It had been her one triumph in those years - until Kitty, whose party it was, had phoned and asked him to pass a message on, telling her that the party had moved to the following weekend.

Of course, Jas had already concocted a cover story, so that she could get out. In the solitude of the office, with the muted thumping of the riot in progress overhead, she felt her heart close tight and her stomach roll over slowly. But she had kept it from him. And she could have succeeded, but for dumb, blind chance.

She dropped to her knees and started to pull all the piles of paper and files out of the open locker, stacking the papers that were merely stapled to one side and piling the ring binders to the other. A light haze of dust wafted round her head and she felt her hopes disappearing into the air with slowly swirling motes.

She pushed the stack of files over in frustration. They slid in an untidy heap, and she saw the edge of a photograph slide from the inside of a file from the centre of the stack.

She caught its edge between her shaking finger and thumb… pulled it free… turned it over… and wished that she'd left well alone.

It was a boy. Naked, dead and bloody.

Oh Christ! Oh shit!! What now? What should she do? Fuck… she pulled the binder out of the mess and lifted it onto the table, smoothing its surface with shaking fingers, trying to decide what to do.

Open it? Give it to Creep? Go and get Hamish? Closing her eyes, she lifted the cover, feeling the pages tumble through her fingers, hearing the soft chatter of plastic pockets hitting the back of the file. She threw open the folder and opened her eyes.

For a moment, she couldn't figure out what it was she was looking at. Two pages, inside plastic sleeves, all with four photos on a page. All of mutilation and horror. She slammed the book closed.

A rattle on the window made her scream and jam her fist in her mouth. A pale, ghostly face floated there, mouthing words she couldn't hear. Creep waved and beckoned her over, motioning her to open the window.

The relief she felt at seeing a familiar face made her feel faint. She sat down on a nearby chair, resting her elbows on her knees and cradling her head in her hands. Creep tapped at the window again. She peered at him between splayed fingers, feeling sick and scared. He beckoned her again, using both hands, flapping them urgently.

She grabbed the folder and the diary and tried to stand, but her legs refused to hold her steady. She staggered into the lockers and eventually bounced her way to the window. Forcing the sash open, she pushed the file and diary out to Creep.

'You found something?' Jas barely had the strength to reply, she just waggled her head. 'What… in his locker?'

'Just get away, Creep and…' She caught a movement behind him and saw a stranger standing in the shadows, watching them. 'Who the fuck's that?!'

Creep glanced over his shoulder.

'That? That's the man who's going help us get David back… he's cool, Jas. He's one of us.'

As she began to calm down, she felt the urgency resurface, and she looked at the time. Jesus! Twenty minutes! She felt as if she should argue with Creep, demand to know what the fuck he thought he was doing, bringing a stranger in on their plans. But she just couldn't muster the strength, couldn't be bothered.

'Just meet me in Buzz first thing tomorrow, with that…' Her hand hovered nervously above the folder, loathe to come in contact with it again. '… and don't you dare fucking lose those, all right?'

She peered quickly through the gloom at the man. He hadn't moved, but even as she looked, he took a step forward, pulling gloves on as he did so, and pulled the file from Creep's hands.

'Don't worry, we'll take good care of these… and the owner. Jas… Jas?' Nick didn't wait for a reply. 'Just stay here and we'll deal with this, okay? You've done more than enough.'

For once, Jas just stared and accepted what Nick was saying. It actually felt good to have someone take control. She might feel differently in the cold light of day, but, for the moment, she was more than happy to relinquish the responsibility.

She started to close the window. It had suddenly grown too quiet upstairs.

'I gotta go…I think Kevin and Krissy just run out of steam. Creep?'

He turned back.

'Who is he?' She nodded at Nick's back, hunched over the folder, examining its contents in the light spilling from the office.

'He's Dave's brother, yeah? How cool is that?' He waved and turned away. 'See you tomorrow.'

CHAPTER TWENTY NINE

Bob Rooke stood inside the front door of the police station, listening to the clamour from without, shaking with rage. The entire car park and most of the road outside was clogged with reporters, TV OB vans and gawking onlookers - the sort of people who caused traffic jams on motorways when they slowed down to rubberneck an accident. Rooke looked over at Bill Rockingham, standing behind the desk, raised his hands and let them drop to his sides.

'Can we not get them cleared out of the car park Sergeant?'

'Apparently, the public have a right to know what's going on, which means, as far as I can gather, they have a right to do what the hell they like and stop us doing our job! I've got a hand delivered letter here for you, Sir. It was pinned to the door sometime last night.' He held out the envelope.

'What is it?' Rooke took the letter. It just had the name 'Flute' written on it. 'Flute? Not looked then?'

The sergeant shook his head.

'Thought it best not to. Knew you'd be in and as you're handling all Monty's... Inspector Flute's investigations now...' He let the sentence drift as Rooke tore open the envelope and peered inside.

'Get me some gloves, quickly.'

Rooke blinked the sweat out of his eyes. Rockingham put a pair of latex gloves on the counter as Rooke laid the letter down and took off his coat.

'Where's Cavannaugh?'

'Upstairs checking-in with the surveillance boys at the house.'

'Right.'

Rooke pulled on the gloves and dipped his thumb and forefinger into the opening. He pulled out a single sheet of paper, folded in half. In the middle of the note, he could see two photographs. Laying the letter on the counter, he opened it and saw Flute's name and an address. The next line was covered by the pictures. He pushed them to one side.

'This is where you'll find him. Get there before I do.'

Rooke flipped the photos over with the tip of a pen that was lying on the counter. Rockingham closed his eyes and turned away.

'Dear God,' he whispered.

Rooke put his hand over his mouth, drawing in great lungfuls of air, concentrating on not being sick. From behind his hand, he said,

'Please tell me that the CCTV was fired up last night…' He looked in the sergeant's direction and saw him shake his head. 'Oh bollocks.' He stared at a point somewhere behind Rockingham's left ear for what seemed an age.

'Right.' He banged the counter. 'Get Cavannaugh down here, he's off to check this place out. It's not the address we're covering. Oh Christ, don't tell me we've been watching the wrong bloody house, please!!' He whistled between his teeth, tapping his fingers on the wall, mind racing. 'I'll be in my office. I've got to have a word with Airey. Tell Cavannaugh to see me when he gets here… and stick these bastard things in a sealed bag.'

He stamped off down the corridor, dragging his raincoat behind him, shoulders stooped. When this is all over, he thought, I'm retiring. Enough is enough.

~~~

Nick sat in the supermarket café, staring into his coffee. A bacon sandwich lay ignored and half-eaten on a plate nearby. The flies were grateful.

What a mess. What a God-awful, bloody mess. He'd had no sleep; having dropped Creep off after they had left Freeways, he'd headed home to look at the file. He doubted he could have found sleep, even if he'd wanted to. The images were scrapping and scratching away inside his head, refusing to let go, appearing in his mind's eye like an out of control slide show.

When he'd been at Freeways, he'd never liked Mo Palfrey. The man was officious and unrelentingly authoritarian. Never laughed, rarely smiled, unless it had been at somebody else's misfortune, and had never had a good word to say about anything or anybody.
~~~

But this?! This sort of sadism, this cruelty was even beyond the comprehension of Nick Sloane - and he'd seen and done things in his life that would be considered brutal. And Piggy had all this, all these kids, at his fingertips. Piggy's own personal larder.

Nick had spent what remained of the night pacing around his flat, laying plans, discarding them, rethinking, trying to see what the outcome would be. He not only had to stop this maniac but guard his own safety as well. He could see, only too easily, how simple it would be if he was caught, for the police to have him tied in as an accomplice. He'd never breathe free air again.

He looked at his watch. Eight forty five. He finished the rest of his coffee without even tasting it and stood up. He had agreed to drop Creep at Buzz this morning, to try and way-lay Jas. She was, Creep insisted, going to turn up there and demand to be involved. He would try and make sure that she stayed in town.

'Make sure she does,' Nick said, leaning across the passenger seat as Creep hopped out. 'The last thing I need is to have to worry about some mad little cow screaming around while I'm up at the house. Be at the market square about four thirty. It should be all over by then.'

Creep waved acknowledgement as he hurried across the road and disappeared into the wine/coffee bar that was Buzz.

Nick drove round the one way system and headed for the war memorial. It was a ten minute walk to the house, if he managed to find a parking space.

He had a plan, if you could call it that, but he hoped the police would have beaten him to it... although he doubted it. Police and competence were two words that rarely appeared in the same sentence in his humble opinion. But he really wanted to have a quiet word with Mo-fucking-Palfrey.

He eventually parked close to the boatyard and strolled up the footpath, onto the narrow lane, where an old mill now rotted in splendid isolation, the stream that had once tumbled down to give it life long dry. The roof was pretty much gone, just a few mouldering beams hanging on to the second floor walls, but those walls, although old, were strong. Great grey and silver slabs of granite, held together by drying yellow loam. He peered through the empty windows and looked through the door, up to the sky above. It was just a shell, but the solid stone stairs still ran round the walls to a point about fifty feet above him, where a little granite shelf sat, a place for the crows and jays to perch.

The house Nick needed to reach was up a dirt road to the left of the mill, but to approach that way left too much to chance. He needed, should it be necessary, the element of surprise. A patch of scrub to the right of the mill let on to a strip of woodland, choked with thorns and dead, elderberry-clad trees. He knew the way through to the field beyond, where he could make his way to the track in relative safety.

Pausing momentarily in the mill's gaping doorway, listening to the rooks flap away, he suddenly realised he had another brother to think about and hoped he could do a better job of looking after David than he had with Tim. He felt the old, familiar anger rising inside him.

He shook himself like a wet dog, flinging the memories away, then squeezed through the undergrowth, feeling the nine millimetre Beretta beneath his arm press against his chest. He patted his pocket - the cylindrical suppressor was still there. Here goes nothing, he thought, as the cool, damp air closed round him.

Nick pushed his way through the woodland, aiming for the field he knew ran parallel to the track. If memory served, he should emerge fairly close to the house but still have enough cover to get where he needed to be. His years of identifying brothels and drug-houses in seemingly innocuous surroundings would stand him in good stead; he would know.

He nearly tripped over the remains of an old barbed-wire fence as the green gaggle gave way to open meadow. Stopping under the shade of a may tree, he looking right, up the steeply sloping field towards another hedge, behind which, he knew, ran the lane that he'd recently left. The meadow was, from his vantage point, long and narrow, so when he looked down the hill to the left, the track and the house beyond were visible. About thirty yards along the left hand hedge, a new gate had been installed that allowed the owner access from the lane.

A car's engine revved in the distance. Nick crouched down and leant back against the tree, watching the lane. It seemed to be getting closer but the sound was not that of a driver with purpose, with somewhere to go. He saw the silver shape gliding along the lane, slowly flickering between the trees and bushes. He could just glimpse the driver, leaning over the steering wheel, peering at the houses as he drove. This was a man looking for something.

As it approached the house in which Nick was interested, the car almost came to a stop, then, as if the driver realised that he should be just casually wandering by, it picked up speed and disappeared from sight. Nick waited, knowing that there was nothing at the top of the lane but a footpath that led to a small village, about five miles away, and that his mystery caller would be heading back in a minute or two. Not that it was any real mystery to Nick. They might as well have come by in a patrol car, it was so obvious.

Ten minutes passed and the car had still not come back down the lane. Nick was starting to get anxious. He needed to get over the road and have a look round. He had to know if Cupid was there; or if not there in person that this was the place where he would eventually bring David.

A movement at the other end of the meadow caught his eye - there was something, or somebody, moving through the trees. Nick allowed himself a small smile. Maybe the local boys in blue had bucked their ideas up after all. Had to be a local lad, nobody else would have thought of using the old trail back to here.

As he watched, the figure stepped from the cover of the trees and strolled across the field. Nick shook his head in disbelief and revised his recently formed opinion of the local constabulary. What a dickhead! It might have been half way believable if the guy had been dressed in suitable gear for crashing around in the undergrowth, but he was wearing a suit, for Christ's sake!

The man wandered across the grass until he drew level with the gate, then stopped, hands on hips, and stared over at the house.

Nick was starting to get seriously worried now. If this was the place, and fucking Cupid decided to pitch up, there was this stupid prat, with filth written all over him in large, fluorescent letters, standing in the middle of a field, watching!

It was as if the Gods of Sod and Comedy had decided to get together and have a good laugh at Nick's expense, for, no sooner had he thought about Cupid arriving, than he heard another car coming down the lane. And this one definitely knew where it was going.

PC Plod obviously heard it too, and skipped down the hill, just making it to the cover of the hedge when a battered old Sierra came barrelling down the lane and turned into the drive of the house they had been watching. Nick couldn't get a clear view of the driver and the car was lost to view as it followed the drive round to the front of the house, disappearing behind a large rhododendron tree. He heard a car door slam.

He sighed and pulled the Beretta from its holster. The weight of it in his hand made him realise that this was now back to business. He'd spent too long meandering through memories and dreams, when he should have been taking care of the thing he had come here for.

The man down by the gate was walking carefully forward, watching the gate to the house and fumbling with something on his belt. Nick realised that the fool was reaching for a radio. Jesus! That was the very last thing he needed: thirty odd heavy handed coppers prancing about before they knew whether or not the new arrival was actually Cupid.

Derek Cavannaugh, whilst a good, solid copper, had never been involved in anything like this investigation before. He was cursing himself for an idiot, trying to prise out his radio which had become caught in his pocket lining, when he felt something cold and hard press in to the soft spot just below his right ear. A voice said,

'Slowly, very slowly, take your hand out your pocket, put it and its companion behind your head and lie down. Face in the dirt.'

Cavannaugh made to turn round, but the jab from what he was sure was a gun made him think better of it.

'Sensible man. Down you go.' He lay down.

There was silence for a long moment, and Cavannaugh tilted his head slightly, to try and get a glimpse of his assailant. All he could see were a pair of muddy trainers.

Urgency fluttered at the back of Nick's mind; time was of the essence now. He leant down and clipped the prostrate man round the head. Lights out.

The blood was up and he could feel it pumping and thumping in his ears. He hopped over the gate, having first tied the copper's hands and feet with his own tie and belt. Everything was clear. The day was now preternaturally bright, everything enhanced, loud in sound and colour. He was aware of every little stone beneath his feet as he hurried across the lane and onto the gravel drive. He stopped, scanning the upstairs window that he could see over the bushes. A figure flitted across the room. Nick ducked back, hugging the greenery and walking on the grass, heading towards the front of the house.

The gun was hanging loosely at his side, the grip cool in his sweating hand. He peered quickly round a rose bush. The bloody front door was wide open.

He waited. Wait. He had no idea of the layout inside the house. Scenarios popped into his head. He didn't want a confrontation in a place he didn't know, that was confined, possibly a… possibly a what? Oh, get the fuck on with it. Nick closed his eyes and switched off the warning bells.

He sucked in a huge gulp of air, straightened up and ran across the drive, hopping over the front doorstep, and sliding to a halt in an ornate Edwardian hallway.

Silence; broken only by the majestic, resonant ticking of a grandfather clock that stood at the foot of the stairs. Nick cocked his head to one side, listening. Nothing. The place seemed deserted.

With economic stealth, Nick went from room to room on the ground floor. The whole place seemed to be a conundrum of styles, from solid oak grace to the metallic minimalism of the kitchen. The garden, viewed from the kitchen, was a mini-Versailles that sloped away towards the river.

He listened. Nothing. The place was as quiet as a grave. He hoped to God it wasn't.

The grandfather clock in the hall chimed a sonorous quarter; too long. He glanced up at the ceiling, drew a breath and headed up the stairs.

Of the four doors on the landing, only one was closed. Nick paused; bathroom, box-room and spare bedroom. All unremarkable, all empty. Had it been otherwise, he would have known. He'd often wondered how silence could be deafening, yet standing here, in front of that closed door, he finally understood. Fuck it, the time for caution was over. He kicked open the last door and went into the room low, arm out straight, gun poised. And if ever he had had any doubt that this was the place Cupid called home, it was gone in an instant.

In the centre of the far wall was a highly wrought and flamboyant four-poster bed, hung with white lace curtains decorated with pink flowers. The walls were papered with delicate, pale yellow flock and the light fittings were ornate, gold cast cherubs holding the candle-shaped bulbs. The wall to his right was covered in pictures, a mish-mash of styles and periods, but all of them depicting the different interpretations and incarnations of Cupid.

The wall behind the door had a gallery of a different mien. It was covered in picture frames, the cheap, glass variety that just clipped to a piece of board, and they were all crammed with photographs. Some frames just had one picture, others had so many it was hard to distinguish where one started and the others finished. But they all had one in thing in common; they displayed, for whoever was lying on the bed, Cupid's handiwork in all its fierce and brutal glory.

The clock chimed another quarter and added a flourish for the half hour. Too long. Far too long to be wandering around; but this room… this room held a grim fascination for Nick. It was as if a mad child had been let loose to bring to life his every whim and fantasy. The ceiling was alive with models, hung from cotton, of Cupid. Cupid laughing; Cupid drawing his bow; Cupid peering over the shoulder of a wise old man and Cupid grasping the breast of a coy maiden. In the far corner stood a table that had once been a dressing table. The mirror had been removed and the supports draped with the same lace that swathed the bed. There were small photographs arranged on the surface, a wooden box and a forest of thin, pink candles.

Nick moved across the room, ostensibly to look out of the bay window, also draped with lace, but he was drawn by the shrine, for that was undoubtedly what it was.

Four small photographs stood guard round a central frame. The first of the two on the left showed a small group of children, solemn and unsmiling, standing shoulder to shoulder on what appeared to be a large lawn. Two boys and a girl dressed in early sixties clothes. It was cheerless and faded. The second showed an elderly woman with tightly bunched hair and a mean, thin mouth.

Of the two on the right, the first was of a man of soldierly appearance, with shiny, slicked back hair, soft mouth and face but eyes hard as stone and as cold. The second picture was a long shot of a large house, probably Victorian, with wild ivy splashed across its frontage and an air of sadness, of chilly and morose melancholy.

Nick only needed to look at the main photograph to have his feelings confirmed as to the sanity of the worshipper at this temple of psychosis.

It was a head and shoulders portrait of a man, probably in his late fifties or early sixties, white-haired and dour. But the picture had been drawn upon, having had a crayon wig scribbled round its head like a mad halo of yellow. The lips had been heavily coloured red, a great cupid's bow, a Monroe-esque mouth of creepily erotic proportions, the colour matching the circular daubs that adorned the man's cheeks. The eyes were burned holes, singed brown by flame and age.

He hesitated before lifting the lid on the delicately carved wooden box that sat before the largest photo and between the smaller four. He felt as if he was trapped in a weird and nightmarish reality show that modelled itself on all the worst old B horror films he had ever seen, but one that also paid more than a little respect to the really scary ones too. No ten thousand pound prize for the winner though. He lifted the lid.

He wasn't sure whether to feel relieved or disappointed. No grisly trophies, as far as he could tell, just three small glass bottles, the old, five sided variety, with waxed cork in the neck. He wasn't sure what they had once contained, but whatever it had been had dried and gone almost black. Lying in front of the bottles on the faded red velvet lining were three keys and what looked like three small, yellowing nodules - they looked suspiciously like baby teeth to Nick. He slipped the keys into his pocket and closed the lid, thought for a moment, then removed the bottles as well.

Nick felt his hands shaking, the gun tapping feebly on his thigh. He eased the curtains apart and scoured the garden below. There was only one place that he hadn't searched. Just as he dropped the drapes back into place, he caught a movement between the trees, hardly more than an impression, but he was round the end of the bed taking the stairs two at a time before the curtains had settled.

He nearly fell flat on his face in his hurry to get outside, as he tripped over a line of shoes placed neatly at the foot of the bed. Four pairs of black Oxford brogues.

~~~

Creep peered between the branches of the rhododendron tree in the front garden, smelling the exhaust fumes from the engine and watching the front door, hoping that Nick would come back soon, bringing David with him.

Despite Creep's unique scent, Jas clung to his arm, resting her head on his shoulder and trying to breathe through her mouth. They had arrived at the gate just in time to see Nick disappear through the front door, gun held loosely at his side. For probably the first time in her life, Jas wished she had done as she had been asked; stay at Buzz and wait. With Creep. Now she knew, with an awful clarity, that they were bottom-lip deep in the shit, waiting for the Devil to go water-skiing.

They had heard a clock in the house chime twice, and not long after it had finished for the third time, Creep thought he heard a car backfire
~~~

somewhere in the distance.

Jas' nails dug into his arm, startled by the noise in an otherwise peaceful place.

'What was that?' Creep eased her claw from his arm.

'Car backfiring,' he said.

But somehow, he knew it wasn't.

~~~

Nick pulled open the back door and raced across the lawn, heading for the gap in the trees where the path sloped away to the river. He slid to a halt at the top of the hill, staring down into the green and gold tunnel, scouring the borders for any sign of movement. A magpie crashed from the canopy and swooped past his head, calling loudly. One for sorrow he thought, moving forward and starting down the path.

Someone had taken a great deal of time constructing the steps that he eventually came to. They were carefully let into the hillside and a robust, rustic handrail threaded its way alongside. Down he went, two or three at a time, the feeling growing on him that he had fucked about in the house for too long with each step he took.

The tunnel opened out onto a small patio butted up against a large, wooden boathouse that appeared to be floating on the high tide. He could just make out the river over the roof, glittering green and blue in the sunlight as it twisted away towards the town. Several small boats and a team of rowers were out enjoying the best of the day.

The boathouse was made of overlapping weathered planks supporting an old, red-tiled roof. The faded green door was closed.

The jamb splintered as he kicked it open and leapt through. As the door swung back towards him, he gave it another shove with his shoulder before he came to a halt inside the boathouse, turning to face the way he had come.

His world exploded around him as something very hard and heavy caught him on the back of the head. He was pitched forward, landing on all fours, feeling the nausea churning and watching the purple dots popping before his eyes.

Years of self-preservation saved his life. Almost immediately he felt the decking beneath his hands and knees, he threw himself forward, turning to try and face his attacker as he did so.

His raised arm caught the full extent of the next blow, which, had it connected with its intended target, would have splattered his brains all
~~~

over the walls.

He felt the bones in his forearm snap and his finger convulsed on the trigger. The roar of the discharge made his ears ring and he was vaguely aware of a figure staggering back, hands clapped to his head.

Pain screamed along his arm and shoulder as the gun clattered to the floor. He managed to retrieve it with his good hand, shaking his head, trying to clear his vision. He saw Mo Palfrey, discarded oar at his feet, leaning against the wall. The water reflected on the lenses of his glasses, giving him the appearance of having two silver coins for eyes.

Nick saw him grimace, shake his head and then look at him. Palfrey snarled something and pushed away from the wall, heading for the door. He aimed a kick at Nick's gun, missing the weapon but connecting with his wrist. Then he was gone.

Nick tried to stand, but his legs refused to function properly, dumping him back on his behind. His arm throbbed and his head took up the rhythm, allowing the darkness to sneak up on him.

Don't pass out, he thought, DO NOT pass out. He managed to draw his knees up and tip his head between them, gagging as he drew a deep breath and letting it leak out through his nose slowly.

His hearing was gradually returning; he could hear the water sucking at the landing platform and the boathouse creaking. Pulling his knees under him, he moved forward and managed to kneel without tumbling onto his face.

He rested his behind on his heels, easing his head back, eyes closed, stretching the muscles in his shoulders and neck. His head bumped into something that moved, broke contact, then thumped him again.

He opened his eyes and stared straight into the dead face of a boy, swinging from the beam above his head.

They stared at each other and Nick felt his gorge rising as he watched the body spin slowly round.

He staggered to his feet, trying to get to the door and sunlight and sanity. It was his fury that pushed him out onto the patio, kicking wildly at the door. His arm flopped uselessly at his side, but the pain from that just drove him to wilder, more painful, acts of passion.

A hand grabbed his coat and pulled him round. He let out a scream of rage that would have curdled the blood of any battle-hardened soldier, bringing his good arm up, cocking the gun and ramming it in the face of whoever it was had dared to get in his way.

'You're a fucking dead man!! You're fucking DEAD! Get away... move away...'

Voices came swimming eerily through the white noise and the black rage that had carried him away. He screwed his eyes shut and felt his teeth grind together as he fought for control.

'Nick! Nick... it's me... it's Creep. Nick? Can you hear me...? '

'Is he all right now?'

The sound of a female voice punched through the confusion. Nick staggered back a step or two and opened his eyes.

Creep and Jas were huddled together a couple of feet in front of him, staring at him in wonder and fear. Nick slowly lowered his arm and eased the hammer back down to rest. He concentrated on getting his breathing under control and trying not to grab the pair of them and bang their stupid heads together.

'What... what the fuck are you doing here?!' He waved the gun around to stop them answering, but saw them recoil at the sight of it. 'Never mind... never mind. Where did he...'

Creep gently eased Jas from around his neck and pointed up the steps.

'He ran by us on the lawn... I chased him a bit, but...'

'I stopped him.' Jas said, stepping closer to Nick, peering at his face with a puzzled look that bordered on... Nick shook his head again - he could have sworn that she was almost smiling. 'It might only be old Piggy, but he's got past you, hasn't he?'

'Past, but not away.' His broken arm was tugging at him now, grinding broken glass into his shoulder. 'Creep, call the old bill and wait in the house. Don't touch anything...' he moved up the steps, '... and do NOT go in the boathouse, right?' He turned to look at the pair of them, two kids, looking completely lost and forlorn. 'Right?' They both nodded and Nick took off up the steps.

He stopped at the fountain and splashed cool water on his face, wiping it over his head and letting it run down the back of his neck. He heard Jas scream - he should have dragged them up here with him. They'll learn.

He jogged up the side of the house and out to the front gate. The car was still in the drive, engine ticking over. Running across the lane, as fast as the pain in his arm would allow, he looked over the gate, scanning the field. Which way had he gone? He saw Cavannaugh lying on his back in the grass, just starting to come round, groaning and shaking his head.

Nick tumbled over the gate, giving his arm a healthy crack, and went to kneel beside the groggy policeman. He shook him and pulled him into a sitting position, struggling to undo the tie that held Cavannaugh's wrists together.

'Where's that bloody radio of yours?' Cavannaugh blinked and swayed in Nick's insubstantial grip.

'Pocket,' he mumbled.

'Get some people over to the house, the kids need help. I'm going to find our friend.' Cavannaugh managed to stop himself from falling on to his back completely and turned to call after Nick as he laboured up the hill to the lane at the top of the field.

'Who… who's our friend?' Cavannaugh said. Nick wondered at the general intelligence of people in the police force.

'Who do you think, numb nuts? Who the fuck do you think?'

CHAPTER THIRTY

'I don't care how you're feeling! You've been smacked round the head and unconscious! You are going to out-patients Derek, even if I have to knock you out again to get you there!' Bill Rockingham put both hands on Cavannaugh's shoulders and pushed him back into the seat. 'I'll call a car.'

'Bill, will you please stop being an old woman? I've had worse bangs playing rugby and still managed to get to the pub after! Please, just let me sit here and get on with what I've got to do, okay? I promise if I start feeling groggy or sleepy, you'll be the first to know.'

Rockingham slapped the smiling man's chair in frustration and went back to his front desk; it was easier dealing with the press than a stubborn DS.

The sun had already disappeared behind the trees in the car park outside the station, and the security lights cast a harsh blue glow over the assembled members of the media.

They bunched together in small clans, TV, radio, local press, with the national big hitters standing aloof from the rest of the hoipolloi. Wreaths of cigarette smoke curled above their heads and the low hum of conversation mingled with the noise of passing cars.

The general opinion amongst the world-weary, seen-it-all-before reporters was that the local boys in blue hadn't got a cat in hell's chance of catching the killer, they needed the expertise and resources of the Met or one of the other big forces... forgetting, in their cynicism, that the Devon and Cornwall force was one of the largest, best resourced in the country.

Rumour was rife between the clans. All they knew for a fact was that another body had been found and that it was not David Trelawney, the lad who had been taken two days before. Some could state, categorically, that the police had Cupid in the cells; others, that some of the kids from David's old residential unit had caught Cupid red-handed; others knew, absolutely knew (we've got a bloke passing stuff to us from inside!), that one of the local investigators had been shot and was on the critical list. Some of the stories had been started deliberately to try and put the competition off and others were the victims of Chinese Whispers. Turn a radio on and you can listen to what's being said quite happily, but add the TV and the stereo to the equation and you get a cacophony and nothing reliable. Just a mess.

A tall, windswept figure eased his way through the throng, hands jammed into the pockets of his anorak, head hunched low into his shoulders, watching his boots as he weaved his way between the vultures.

A hand tugged at his sleeve and he turned to see a familiar face from the local rag. He gave the man a wry look.

'Keep it quiet, Jason. I don't know anything.'

'Just wanted to ask you how you were, Mr. Flute. Worried about you, we all are.'

'Yes? Really...well that's gratifying to know Jason, it certainly is. Makes me feel appreciated.' He jerked his sleeve from the other's hand. 'But I still don't know anything. Excuse me, I've an appointment to keep.' He lied. 'And Jason? Ssh. Keep your voice down, or I might consider resurrecting that DD charge.' Flute smiled like a spider might smile at a fly in its web and walked away, heading down the side of the station to the door where the transports collected overnight prisoners.

He pushed the button and waited.

The door opened a crack and an unsmiling face glared out.

'Bugger off back round the front... oh! Hello Mr. Flute, wasn't expecting to see you out here.'

Flute pushed the door open and stepped inside, unzipping his coat and looking round.

'Didn't expect to be here, Constable Reeves, didn't expect to be here. Is Sergeant Rockingham upstairs?'

The constable nodded, shut the door and led Flute back through the dank holding area and into the brightly lit stairwell that led up to the main station. As they walked up, Flute asked for a coffee and headed down the corridor to the reception area. He could hear Bill Rockingham shouting the odds at some poor unfortunate at the other end of a telephone.

They shook hands.

'Thanks for the call, Bill. How is he?'

Rockingham chuckled. 'He's picked up a few of your bad habits Monty. Stubborn as a mule, won't go home and mad as a dog that's had its bone nicked and its arse kicked.' Flute tilted his head, questioning. The sergeant hooked a thumb over his shoulder. 'In the back office.'

'Rooke?'

Rockingham puffed out his cheeks and exhaled through compressed lips. He shook his head.

'Off at Middlemoor, having a word with Airey.'

'Aaah… pity. So now the ACC has two sacrificial lambs?'

'Seems that way.'

Flute pulled his coat off and stepped through the gap in the front desk, throwing it on a nearby chair.

'So, what's been happening then?'

Rockingham pushed open the door that led to the back office.

'He's the man to ask.'

Flute looked in and saw Cavannaugh standing in front of the wall, staring at a group of pictures and names pinned there, all connected with lines of different colours. A white board stood off to one side with notes scribbled on it. The desk was awash with paperwork, pizza boxes and other evidence of long days and even longer nights.

A patch of padded lint, held on with micropore, decorated a spot just below Cavannaugh's right ear. He was chewing the tip of a biro and patting the patch thoughtfully.

'Evening Sergeant.' Flute said, pulling a chair up to the desk and sitting down. 'How's the noggin?'

Cavannaugh swung round at the sound of his old boss' voice, grimacing as his head reminded him to move a little more slowly. He smiled, pleased but weary. It looked to Flute as if he hadn't slept in days.

'Sore. Very sore.'

'Aaah, you should have listened to Doctor Rockingham when you had the chance. What's the story then?'

Cavannaugh perched himself on the edge of the desk. Still the same old Flute - short on the niceties, quick on picking up where he left off.

'Back with us then Sir?'

Flute shook his head.

'No, no, no, no, no, just a courtesy call really. Bill gave me a buzz and told me what had happened to you. Thought I'd drop by.'

'Think you'll get the call fairly soon then?' They looked at one another for what seemed like an eternity, then Cavannaugh pushed a pile of papers across the desk to Flute. 'This is a summary of where we are at the moment.'

Flute sat forward and started to read.

~~~

'Your signal's weak. Where are you?'

'Never mind where I am. The house has been found.'

'What!?!'

'Found. They…'

'They? Any more good news?'

'Keep your sarcasm to yourself! I had no time to clear the boathouse.'

'Police?'

'No, I don't think so, no, thank God. A man, never seen him before, and a couple of the lost souls from the home.'

'Lost sou..? Keep your pious ramblings for those who actually care! How did they find it?'

'A file. One in the home, hidden in an old locker. The kids…'

'You are a fool of the first water! An imbecile! What in God's name… never mind. Don't call me again. This number will be lost. We are no longer in business. But trust to this, Palfrey; if I get caught up in your mess, you will regret it for as long you live, which, you can also trust, will not be very long.'

~~~

Kevin Poundsberry sat huddled in an armchair in the TV lounge, staring morosely at the dusty screen and wishing he was anywhere else but here. He could feel the copper's eyes boring into the top of his head and hear Deidre Cochrane's breath wheezing in and out. If Jas had been here right now, he would have killed her.

'So,' the officer said, leaning forward, 'You caused the ruckus while Jasmine took the keys and broke into the office, right?'

'She had the keys! How could she break in?'

'Your smart mouth..!' The detective gripped the arm of the chair and lowered his voice. 'You are in a great deal of trouble here, young man.

Word of advice? Just answer the questions so we can get on with our job and you can… you can go back to doing whatever it is you do. So?'

Deidre cleared her throat and sat forward, doing her best to stop grabbing Kevin by the scruff of his neck and shaking the truth out of him.

'Kevin, where has Jas gone now? We know she was here last night, that much is obvious, but where is she now? You must try to understand, she could be in a huge amount of danger. Please sweetheart, tell the officer what he needs to know.'

Kev squeezed his eyes shut and burrowed deeper into the chair. How could he tell? Only snitches snitch. Slime bags. Jas'd rip his balls off if he told. And what about the others? What about David? Creep?

Kev, and most of the others at Freeways, had had to rely on themselves for most of their young lives, their trust in anybody over the age of eighteen or nineteen virtually non-existent.

Sometimes, to the adults that worked with these damaged children, it seemed that they had managed to reach them, form some sort of trusting relationship. It may have been tenuous, built on sand, but, given the time and love, it could grow, really work.

Truth was that the 'trust' was, in many cases, just a veneer, a badly applied camouflage that, if scratched away, would reveal the beast coiling just beneath the surface; the monster that was eating away at the kids - fear, fury, betrayal - whispering that only they could help themselves. Why trust the very people who had been the cause of all their misery in the first place?

'If… if I tell, can I…'

'We don't do deals, sonny Jim. Just…'

'Please…' Deidre held up her hand, silencing the detective. '… please, let him have his say. What Kevin? If what?'

'If I tell, will you stop the others pounding on me?' He looked at them both, eyes red-rimmed from trying not to cry, pleading with them to say what he wanted to hear.

Deidre felt her heart crumble. That was it? Dear God, what were they doing to these kids? She nodded, not trusting herself to say too much. She patted the back of Kevin's hand and managed to say,

'Of course.'

Kevin stared at her for an age; you could almost hear the argument he was having with himself rumbling around in his head. He sniffed.

'Jas 'n' me went to find Creep…'

'Creep? That's a new name,' the officer said.

'Edward Peterson.' Deidre said, feeling on safer ground. 'They call him Creep. He used to be a resident here.'

The detective nodded and took out his pen and pad. This was more like it; now they were getting somewhere.

~~~

How Creep had managed to get Jas out of the boathouse after Nick had disappeared up the stairs was still a mystery to him and would, almost certainly, always be so. Much of what had happened afterwards was a bizarre blur, just like some of the more frightening trips that he'd experienced when he had briefly done LSD.

He had tried to stop Jas going into the boathouse, but that was like trying to stop a wrecking ball once it had started its downward swing. She had punched and clawed, hissing incoherently and pulled him with her as she kicked open the door.

The only thing Creep remembered clearly was Jas' scream and looking up at the body, swinging there like great red Christmas decoration. That, and the smell. Like the metalwork shop where he had once had the misfortune to work.

The next thing he remembered with any real clarity was lying in the field opposite the house, staring at the sky, with his arm wrapped round Jas' heaving shoulders as she sobbed. He thought he could recall seeing a man walking down the lane to town, weaving as he went as if he was drunk, but he couldn't be sure.

He had no idea how long they had lain there, confused, frightened and wondering what the hell to do next, but they had started to move when they heard the police sirens wailing in the distance. Creep had grabbed Jas' wrist, pulling her to her feet, and started to drag her across the field, towards the end through which Cavannaugh had come.

Jas had offered no real resistance. Creep glanced back as they reached the hedge row and saw vacant eyes and a slack mouth. It was like dragging a rag doll behind him. Raggedy Annie, the doll his sister had clung to a lifetime ago as the Social had come barging through their front door with the police and dragged them away, all to the memorable accompaniment of their mother screaming, his Gran sitting in the kitchen smiling and their father lying on his back in the hallway, cuddling the bottle and the carving knife, singing 'Mull of Kintyre' and
~~~

telling them that he'd see them soon. The memory of his smile still made Creep want to piss himself. Not with laughter though.

He pushed Jas ahead of him, trying his best to clear a path through the tangle, and then carefully sat down so that she could lean against a tree. He kept up a running commentary all the time, telling her it would be all right, that they'd find somewhere soon, that Nick or Simon would come looking for them and that they would help. Whether he had believed any of it himself he couldn't remember; it had all happened what seemed like days ago, but in reality had been less than an hour and a half.

As they sat, Creep watched Jas' face. Her eyes were closed and she seemed to be sleeping now, but it wasn't restful; she muttered and cringed as he held her. Creep wondered idly if any of the kids who had ever been in care got a good night's sleep.

He had listened to the police arrive, toying with the idea of finding somewhere safer to hide, but, when he finally decided to move, Jas had been asleep; so they remained in their modest little bivouac, Jas muttering through her dreams and Creep staring at the leaves and waiting for the police to find them.

He heard the police leaving around the same time that Jas awoke with a cry.

'Leave me alone…' She sat still for a second, seeing nothing but the ragged edge of what she had been dreaming about, watching it disappear through the trees until it was safe. She gradually became aware of Creep sitting next to her. She gave him a tentative smile and said,

'It wasn't David.' Creep was unsure if this was a question and decided to shrug. He was not going to admit to Jas that he had been too scared to give the body anything more than a cursory glance.

'It wasn't.' Her voice was firmer this time, stronger, as she became more alert. 'No. It wasn't.' She took in her surroundings. 'How'd we get here then? Oh Christ, look at the state of me…' She held her arms up, looking down at her grass stained top and jeans, shaking her arms to dislodge the bits of grass and nettles that hung there.

'Sorry… thanks.'

Creep blinked at her rapidly, and found something more interesting to look at on the sole of his boot. He could handle Jas in full flight… just. But this was a little scary, Jas being almost normal. They sat in silence, each pondering what had happened to them in the course of the last couple of days. There was no need for words and even if there had been, neither would have been able to express exactly what is was they were feeling.

'What we going t'do?'

She looked up and hooked Creep's gaze, drawing him in with a slightly knitted brow and a smudge of dirt on her chin.

'Well…' He hesitated, unsure of what Jas' reaction would be when he told of the plan he had come up with, such as it was. 'I thought, that if we stayed on the lanes… I know 'em quite well…that if we stayed on the lanes, we could… it's a bit of hike though, doing it that way, yeah..?… yeah… if we stayed on the lanes we could go to Torquay. I think we might get some help from somebody there. Dunno. Might call the cops, might not. Depends. But I thought…'

'Creep.'

'… that if we stayed in the lanes, we'd…'

'CREEP?!' He flinched away at her raised voice. 'Sorry, sorry. Who? Who's going to help us and not call the pigs, eh?' He was even more worried about her reaction now. He knew what she thought about their secret, potential, saviour.

'Marie'll help us… I think. She was the best I could come up with. She's okay Jas, honest. I stayed there once…' His voice trailed off, waiting for the eruption. Jas just stared at the ground and sighed.

'Fuck… old Mother Sluttybikes.' She looked up. 'Haven't got a lot of choice, have we? Can't say we didn't try though, eh Creep?' The tears spilled over her eyelids. 'Can't say that, can they? Even though we didn't find David, they can't say we didn't…'

Creep held her tight and cried along with her.

CHAPTER THIRTY ONE

By the time Nick got to the top of the field, the sweat was pouring down his back and he could feel his consciousness coming and going in waves. Everything was as loud as a rock concert and as bright as an operating theatre. He could hear the blood pounding in his head and his arm was ablaze. In amongst the outrage he felt at seeing a man like Mo Palfrey committing such horrendous acts was a fury at being blindsided by him as well. It added insult to injury and he was unwavering in his determination to find the little shit and make him suffer as much as the kids he had betrayed. To that end alone, he had to stay on his feet.

Nick pushed through the thin line of bushes that hid the field from the top road. It was deserted. He had to use his left hand to get him over the fence whilst trying to make sure that he didn't bash his right; no mean feat for somebody who used to wonder what use his left hand was, considering he barely used it.

Think Nick, think! Where would you go if you were Palfrey?

I'd need to be safe… nobody knows what's going on, except me and the kids. So where does a fugitive run? He remembered how Palfrey had hidden the file in plain sight, which had been incredibly risky, almost bordering on the cretinous… but had it? An idea started to wriggle about, just below the surface.

He hoped that Creep and Jas had stayed put, waited for the police to turn up, but, remembering how he had felt about the law when he had been at Freeways, he realised that the chances of that happening were slim to non-existent. Which meant that the only people who knew who Cupid was were still the only people who knew. Shit!

He staggered into the road, looking left and right, trying to decide which way to go. Despite the determination that drove him to find

Palfrey, he knew that he had to get his arm fixed. He was damn near useless as he was. The thought of pain relief made him turn down the road and head back towards town.

With difficulty, he shoved the gun back into its shoulder holster, wiped the sweat from his eyes and, taking a deep, deep breath, started to walk. Under normal circumstances, it wasn't that far to the hospital, maybe a mile and a half, two miles, but he was seriously worried that he would pass out before he got even half way.

The road ran straight for a couple of hundred yards before turning right and getting much steeper, heading down past the old mill and back to the river. He decided to take a break... har de har har, break!... at the mill. Things were getting acutely fuzzy round the edges now. He supposed that his arm was a lot more serious than he had first thought.

Nick spent a great deal of time each week in the gym, but he was not just 'gym muscle'. He used his fitness and muscles to ride competitively, mountain biking across the moors, and doing a spot of judo as well. Had he been less fit, he would have been lying in the field, out of it completely, until somebody found him. If they ever did.

As he came round the corner, staring at the lazily swimming hill in front of him, he thought he caught sight of a movement in the waste ground next to the mill. He wiped his hand across his face, clearing the sweat, and concentrated on focusing. He stumbled right and got caught by a clump of elderberry. Ouch.

Closing his eyes he began to shuffle slowly down the hill, using the hedge for support. The singing and buzzing in his ears faded and the faint sound of birdsong penetrated the fog. And something else: a voice.

When Palfrey had originally smashed the old wooden oar onto Nick's arm, the heat of the fight and Nick's wrath had flooded his system with adrenaline; the pain had only started in earnest as he toiled up the field after speaking with Cavannaugh. Adrenaline is the body's natural anaesthetic, and on hearing a voice where he wasn't expecting to hear one, his body released another belt of that wonderful stuff.

Although still woozy, the pain seemed to recede and his head cleared sufficiently to concentrate more fully.

He crept down the lane, drawing closer, straining to hear.

'A man, never seen him before, and a couple of lost souls from the home.'

Nick held his breath. He couldn't be that lucky, could he? He squeezed through the hedge and made his way towards the waste ground through the undergrowth.

'A file; the one in the home, hidden in an old locker. The kids...'

Nick hoped that his approach would be missed, or misinterpreted as natural woodland noise. It seemed that Palfrey was too caught up in his troubles to pay much attention to a bird in the bush. And who the hell was he talking to, anyway? Weren't these fruit cakes supposed to work alone?

He could make out a vague shape through the greenery, pacing back and forward, hand pressed to the side of its head. Sunlight glinted off spectacles. It was Palfrey all right.

There was a cry of pure, unadulterated rage and frustration, and Nick saw Palfrey hurl his mobile against the side of the mill. Temper, temper, he thought, edging closer. What the hell was Palfrey doing hanging around here? Surely he realised that the police would be coming before too long?

I must be psychic, thought Nick, as the sirens sliced the silence and a couple of patrol cars came careering round the bend at the bottom of the hill.

Palfrey darted across the waste ground and pressed himself flat against the wall. God alone knew what was rushing through his head, but Nick thought he could hazard a pretty good guess. Palfrey needed out and away... but that was the easy part, Nick mused, because Palfrey must know, or at least have had a pretty good notion, that the kids would be long gone. He was, after all, a social worker, been around kids for years and knew how they reacted to a police presence. Palfrey could, quite simply, just walk down the hill and not have any notice taken of him. So why wait? Just pure fear, Nick decided. Amazing what a guilty conscience could do for your average psycho.

He watched as Palfrey peeped round the corner of the building, then stepped out and started away down the hill. Nick broke cover and skipped over the open ground to take Palfrey's place against the wall. Having found what he thought to be lost, Nick wasn't about to lose it again.

Nick couldn't quite decide what to do. He couldn't just appear behind Palfrey, there was a definite chance he would be seen and recognised. And if the police saw him, pale, obviously hurt...well, he knew what the consequences would be. He listened to Palfrey's footsteps disappearing down the hill. More sirens. He dared a peep round the building and saw his prey hesitate at the sound of approaching police cars.

Shit! He's coming back! Nick slid quickly along the wall and ducked through the doorway, bobbing down beneath the window and creeping slowly up the old stone stairs to the ledge by the window on the first floor.

He heard Palfrey, breathing heavily, scuttle along the side of the mill. His back appeared in the doorway as he used the narrow, empty space as cover. Nick could see his back and head moving with the unaccustomed exertion. Sweat stained his shirt and he fidgeted nervously from foot to foot, his right hand grasping the rotting door frame, fingers tapping impatiently.

An almost overwhelming desire to draw his gun and put a bullet in the back of that hated head rushed up to grab Nick and shake him. Do it, do it, the voice whispered. Not just for the ones who have gone, do it for you too. For those times he smiled as he put you down. Sneered. Mocked and scorned. Do it for yourself. Go on… you know you want to. Should. Kill the miserable little fucker.

The gun was under his left arm and the only hand he could use was his left. Palfrey would hear him or see him before he got his jacket out of the way.

He looked down at Palfrey. He had stopped moving and was just leaning there, looking out over the waste ground. Nick felt suddenly cold. Unable to move. Had he moved? Did…?

'This must be what they call an impasse.' Even though Nick was watching him, the sound of Palfrey's voice still made him jump. 'Is your gun, even now, pointing at my back? Or is it not?' He sighed. 'Would you rather shoot me in the back, or watch my face? Or shall I… shall I just walk away?' Another sigh.

Sod it, thought Nick, and made a fumble for the gun. It wasn't a bad effort, considering he had to bend his left wrist almost double to get at it, but even as he tried, watching Palfrey all the time, the man took a step back, looked up at Nick and smiled. It was all so familiar.

'I wonder who you are,' he asked mildly and stepped out into the yard.

'PIGGY!!' Nick roared, leaping up a couple of steps and poking his head out the first floor window. 'You stay right the fuck where you are, you bastard!' He couldn't see him.

'Or what, Mr. Man? You'll shoot me?' The arrogant little shit laughed, actually laughed. There was silence. Then,

'How did you know my name?'

It was Nick's turn to smile. Palfrey sounded worried now. Nick leant a little further out of the window and looked down. Their eyes met as Palfrey looked up.

'Remember Rob Wilkes, Piggy? He still reads 'Lord of the Flies' and always thinks of you. How are you?'

He saw recognition dawn on the face below and eased his hand out over the crumbling sill to show Palfrey that the gun was now in operation.

'Well, well. Look how our omissions return to haunt us… you really shouldn't be here you know. A mistake, and see now how we're paying for that indiscretion, that inexpediency.'

That was a surprise. The last thing Nick had expected was something akin to a conversation at a tea party. He had no idea what Palfrey was babbling about, the man was nuts and stalling for time, making Nick all the angrier in the process.

There were a million questions zipping around Nick's head, not least of which was David's whereabouts, but all he could focus on was '… you really shouldn't be here you know.' Palfrey took a step to his right, edging towards the road.

'STAND. Still.' Nick eased the weight on his arm for a second. Palfrey had broken the spell by moving. 'Where's David?'

Nick's main problem, it seemed, was getting his hands on Palfrey. The man was outside and Nick had to get down the stairs, round the corner and hang on to him. He closed his eyes momentarily, cursing Palfrey yet again for his busted arm.

'Oh, I seeee…' Palfrey almost crooned. 'You'd really love to hurt me, wouldn't you Robby? But you can't, can you? Not while you have the questions to which, it seems, I have the only answers! Impasse.' He craned his head back again, looking up at Nick. 'How shall this be resolved, I wonder?'

He leapt off to his right… and stumbled on a small block of granite that had fallen from the upper stories of the mill, landing heavily on his hands and knees. Nick, hampered by his broken arm, had to push himself up to try and bring the gun into play.

The masonry, strong for two hundred years and more, was weak now and one of the blocks upon which Nick had been resting shifted, made a low, protesting, grinding sound, and gracefully tumbled from its resting place, trailing a cloak of debris behind it.

'Oh shit!' Nick gasped.

His weight almost carried him out the window behind the block. Only a superhuman effort, and strong back muscles, saved him. The gun twisted from his hand as he grabbed backwards at the remains of the rotting window frame. He heaved and had himself upright, heart pounding, and leaning gratefully against the wall.

Slowly, he poked his head out and glanced down. Palfrey was lying face down with the granite block, nestled like a second head, by his left shoulder. A small pool of blood seemed to crawl slowly over the dust, creeping round Palfrey's glasses which lay nearby. The sun danced on the cracked lenses, winking mockingly up at Nick.

He carefully walked down the stairs and retrieved his gun, not that he had much need of it now. He thought he would have felt elated at Palfrey's death, but all he felt was the same gnawing, dull anger. Cheated out of the pleasure of watching Piggy die painfully and slowly, and cheated out of finding his brother.

Dropping to one knee next to the body, Nick poked him with the muzzle of the Beretta. Piggy moaned. A small bubble of blood formed over his open mouth and his eyelids flickered. He coughed and cried out softly, a gush of blood soaking the ground.

'Where is he, Piggy?' whispered Nick, his voice a gentle razor. 'Where? '

'K… K… kill me… will… y… y… you?' He sighed and Nick could almost see his spirit rising with that sigh.

He grabbed the back of Palfrey's head, fingers sinking into a soft mush of hair and blood, and lifted. He was grinning viciously, gritting his teeth to stop himself pounding what remained of Palfrey's life out onto the dirt.

'Where, Piggy?'

'Safe…' another cough and more blood, '… and soon… soon to be safer. You're wrong… wrong you know. I'm j… j… just a… a minion.' He gave a weak chuckle.

'Cu… Cu… Cupid lives… you'll never… .nev… er stop… Ooh…' His eyes opened, wide and staring, seeing something that Nick could only guess at. 'Oooh, oh dear… Mary… Mary… help me, help…'

'Now we suddenly have religion, do we?' He squeezed his fingers together, tightening his grip on what remained of the back of Palfrey's head.

'Where… IS…?'

A rush of blood and a frightened, helpless moan. Palfrey twitched hard, once, and his leg kicked convulsively. Gone. Nick smashed the dead, hated face into dirt and wiped his hand on the man's back. Gone. Another one lost. David was as good as dead and there seemed to be nothing that Nick could to do about it.

He stood up, panting, and stared down at the corpse. Laughed. The sudden irony of Palfrey's death, the way he had died, hit him like a blow to the guts. He was chuckling quietly, feeling the hysteria surging up from hidden depths, threatening to drown him. He tapped his right forearm with the snout of the gun and cried out. The pain was a penance for failure, for not doing what he should have done. The laughter died.

Putting the gun back into the holster, he shoved his good hand into his jacket pocket and felt the three small bottles lying there with the keys. Taking one out, he bent down and placed it in Palfrey's curled and slowly stiffening fingers. It seemed like the thing to do.

The sullen, brooding anger began to recede as he stood staring at the body and his thinking mind kicked in as he mulled over the last things Palfrey had said.

David was safe. Cupid lives? David was safe… Cupid lives. What the hell was going on? He needed answers but it seemed that his encyclopaedia had been shut for good.

Go to the library, he thought. And he knew exactly at which fount of knowledge he was going to drink.

CHAPTER THIRTY TWO

Flute sat outside the Warren Inn, staring across the high moor, surrounded by walkers, riders and sundry trippers yet completely alone. He watched lovers sharing a moment of solitude, touching each other in what seemed to be a gentle sort of wonder. He wanted to tell them to make the most of each other; it could all end tomorrow. It could all be snatched away in a pointless second. He wanted to tell them how it had happened to him, but instead he finished his beer, stood up and walked slowly back to his battered old Saab, which looked about the way he felt; ready for the scrap heap.

A group of couples, all in their twenties he supposed, walked by him, heading for the pub, all smiles and plans; hope and happiness. Maybe he was getting too old for all this cruelty, all this love that people wanted to give each other, however it manifested itself. Maybe, when all this was over, he would simply disappear, like the road, over the hill and far away. Maybe.

He had the feeling that things were about to move with a rapidity that all involved in the Cupid investigation would find shocking and surprising. Pieces were falling into place, connections being made; not by luck, as was the case with so many murder inquiries, but by dint of good, solid police work. Ninety five percent legwork, four percent sweat and one percent satisfaction… if the suspect was bagged; if they even had a suspect in the first place.

Flute had remained at the police station with Cavannaugh for most of the day, poring over paperwork, making comparisons, feeling that something was teasing him, dancing at the edge of his vision and remaining tantalisingly just out of reach. Waiting to see who the poor little bugger was that had been strung up in the boathouse. No ceremony, no ritual here, apparently. He had been stripped, hoisted and butchered. Other than the cut that had killed him and a couple of rope burns, there wasn't a mark on him.

Mo Palfrey's body had been found that evening by, of all people, Mike Soloman and Colin. They had eschewed the pleasures of walking by the river since finding the body of the first boy, preferring instead to tramp the woodland paths that ran through the hills at the back of town. What were the chances? Blind bad luck.

The telephone call from Airey had come around the same time, telling him that Rooke had withdrawn and that the chief constable wanted Flute back working.

Not sure what he felt about the whole situation, Flute had agreed to return from leave and pick up the traces. There had been no apology, nothing, just a 'by rote' wish of good luck.

They had a team of four officers digging into anything and everything connected to Freeways, The Lawns, Mo Palfrey, the staff, anything. But there was one thing, above all else, that niggled and gnawed at Flute.

When Derek Cavannaugh had told him who it was who had knocked him out and gone into the house, he had nearly exploded. It opened out a whole new aspect.

Then one of their team had returned from talking to one of the kids involved in the break-in to the offices. Another link had been forged. But that had thrown up another mystery; where was the girl and the lad known as Creep? Were they with Cupid now? They had to assume so, which made everything that much more desperate.

Flute had to make assumptions galore. Had the kids found something? Perhaps. He thought it had to do with the pictures that had arrived at the station with the note that led them to the house.

The boy had been insistent that Jasmine had not told him what she had found in the office, just that it would 'save David and do for Piggy'. A member of the staff team at Freeways turns up dead. He doubted it was an accident - Nick Sloane was involved (another assumption, but it felt right) - yet the initial, on site diagnosis of the coroner's office was just that - accident. Too much of a coincidence, thought Flute. He had to make a tenuous link between the death of Palfrey and the murders.

Had Palfrey stumbled on something? Possibly. Was he involved? Unlikely, he thought, yet the lad at Freeways had insisted that the girl, Jasmine, had been told by Creep that he had seen Palfrey with Lee

Hensley at the boatyard and that she had found something incriminating in the office. And the manager there had admitted that Mo Palfrey wasn't the most popular of the staff team. She had intimated that the exact opposite was true.

And what about that strange little bottle that Palfrey had been holding? The contents had gone for analysis. Another wait, another mystery added to the pile.

Round and around and around we go, he thought, climbing into the car and starting the engine. What needed to happen was for them to find out who this G. Ballantyne person was, what their connection to all this might be. That it stretched in a line from The Lawns to Freeways across the years, Flute had no doubt. But the route it took, how it curled and twisted on its way to his front door, was another matter altogether.

The quickest way back off the moors to town was through Widecombe, turning off near Hay Tor, through Ashburton and so back to the shop. We never close. Flute checked the clock on the dashboard and saw that he had been gone longer than he had planned. Time seemed to drift or snap viciously, depending on his frame of mind. The day had hardly started before it was over. Cavannaugh had told him it was an age thing. For which he'd thanked him and studiously ignored him for an hour.

The press-pack outside the station were in a frenzy, snapping and snarling at each other because they had nobody else on which to vent their irritation. Information and rumour was the very air they breathed and they were choking. The news that Flute was back in charge raised an eyebrow or two but the chief constable had fielded that one adroitly, skirting round previous issues with oblique skill, supporting both Flute and his assistant chief constable at the same time.

Flute seemed to go unnoticed as he steered through the throng and parked at the rear of building. The desk sergeant had obviously seen him arrive and sent someone to open the back door.

A little niggle had been squirming about in his head on the drive back and he went straight to his office and grabbed a couple of files that held the paperwork relating to the inherited houses in town. He needed to nail this, it was really starting to drive him mad; he knew there was something and it was like the most annoying tune in the world, constantly playing in his head. He gave Cavannaugh one of the folders and said,

'Fine toothed comb Derek. There is something in here and I need to know what. I've seen it and it didn't register properly the first time.'

Cavannaugh sighed. He was going cross-eyed trying to put names and dates together; even with the aid of a computer, which had a habit of doing what it wanted to do and not what it was told. It was a laborious, mind-numbingly boring task.

'Any idea what we're looking for?'

Flute gave him an old fashioned raised eyebrow and bent to flipping through photocopies of the papers from the solicitors who had dealt with the houses in the Will.

'It's an anomaly. It's not immediately obvious, yet I must have noticed it when you showed me this lot before. The house itself is patently important, but there's something else. Something else.'

He was muttering away to himself for twenty minutes, first scanning a page quickly for the apparent, then going over it more carefully. He tried staring intently and then letting his eyes just drift, but as time moved on he became more and more annoyed with his own inability to rediscover what he had skimmed, and missed, before.

Without looking up, Flute asked 'Any luck with our search for the elusive G. Ballantyne then, Sergeant?'

Cavannaugh threw his pen across the desk and stretched back in his chair, yawning.

'There are…' he consulted a pad at his elbow, '… thirteen Ballantynes in and around town. And about a hundred or so in the south of the county. That doesn't include variant spellings and similar sounding names.'

Flute grunted - then suddenly, his head shot up and he stared off into space for a second. He grabbed a file and flipped it open, smearing the papers across his desk like pack of cards, tapping the edges urgently. He pulled one piece out, then another and held them up, side by side.

'Idiot.' He spat the word out like a foul taste. 'There it is, you fool.'

He passed the sheets over to Cavannaugh and waited. The sergeant ran his gaze over the print and looked up at Flute questioningly.

'Look at the bottom,' Flute said and saw Cavannaugh start to nod. 'Got it?'

'Bloody hell…'

'And?'

'This is for the house that we've been watching…' he waved one piece. '… this is for the old house at the top of town. Two different signatures. Christ.'

'Look again,' said Flute, leaning forward excitedly.

Cavannaugh shook his head.

'The one for the original house, in the Will, was signed for by a man. That second is a woman's signature. I'd stake my life on it.'

'Christ.'

Flute was up and pacing, firing on all cylinders now.

'Have we got anything at all on the house where you were waylaid? Papers, anything?'

'Some stuff came in early this morning, while you were out.' He rummaged around on a table at the back of the room. 'We found an old 'For Sale' board in the front garden and rang the agents.' He handed Flute the file and watched him shuffle through the sheaf. He pulled a sheet out and Cavannaugh saw his face go blank. He laid the piece of paper next to the other two and sat back.

'Have a look.'

Cavannaugh leant over and felt quite ill at what he saw. Flute nodded.

'G. Ballantyne. Three times, for three separate properties. And three entirely different signatures.'

'Christ.'

CHAPTER THIRTY THREE

'Where the fuck are you?'

'Stood outside Torbay Hospital with my arm in a sling. Thanks for caring.'

'You need to disappear for a while. I want to talk to you. And so do the police.'

Aah, thought Nick. Here we have it, the real reason for Ferdy's concern. The old bill were sniffing around. That explained a lot.

'Which order should I do that in then, Ferdy? Police first, then you, then disappear?'

'Don't be a smart arsed little fuck. Get yourself up to the shops at the top of hill and I'll send someone to collect you. Right?'

'Got to pay someone a visit first, Ferdy, then we can chat away to our hearts' content. I'll call you.'

'Don't you hang up on…'

Nick slid the cover of his mobile shut and dropped it back into his pocket. Ferdy didn't do pink and fluffy, so when his number had flashed on Nick's screen, he had known that it wouldn't be good news. Still, it gave him a small, warm glow to know that he had managed to piss Ferdy off. It made the day seem complete.

He needed to start moving now. Despite what he had said, Ferdy would still be sending one of the other lads up to have a scout round for him. Best be gone by the time he arrived.

Nick toyed with the idea of driving to his next port of call, but decided it would be unwise; he had already chanced his arm - he had a warehouse full of arm and break jokes! - by driving to the hospital from town. Public transport was the way.

As luck would have it, a number twelve laboured up the hill to the turning circle by the main entrance, and Nick hopped aboard, fumbling for change and agreeing with the driver that, yes, indeed, it was a nasty break and that, no, he wouldn't be at Wimbledon this year. How they laughed.

Sitting on the back seat, staring out of the window, Nick realised why he rarely used buses or trains. Even though the upholstery was clean and the floor relatively free of litter, there was still something almost sad about an empty bus. Like a ghost town on wheels, where the spirits scrawled messages to the living on the windows and the backs of seats, crying out their mournful desperation in prose that would have made Shakespeare weep and a navvy blush. The smell didn't help much, either.

Nick knew where he was heading, having checked the address in his A to Z in the car. Plush, hillside suburbia, between Torquay and Babbacombe; tree lined gentility that harboured a canker.

The door slid open and Nick stepped out onto the pavement, breathing in the fresh air, trying to dispel the faint nausea that had started to rumble in his stomach and under his chin. He checked the address on the piece of paper that Ferdy had given him… what?… three, four days ago? He'd never expected to use it, at least, not in this context. When you swim in shit, don't expect to come up smelling of roses.

Nick strolled up the hill trying to look as if he belonged. He knew the area and most of these Victorian piles, once ornate and reeking of money, had been converted into flats long ago. A few, however, remained intact. Like this one. He glanced at the piece of paper. Bingo.

Set back off road, partially hidden by not too carefully maintained shrubbery, it had an air of comfortable circumstance, not too wealthy, not too shabby either, just…ordinary. There was absolutely nothing to indicate that this house was the home to… he hesitated. Evil was not a word he used casually. But evil was the word that fitted best.

Not your shambling monster, mad scientist type of evil, but Evil… in its truest sense. It was sadly fortuitous that all this had led him to meet with somebody he had long intended to have a quiet word with.

He consulted the paper again, looking about, knowing that anyone watching would dismiss him as somebody searching for an address. He walked on, round the corner, noting the well concealed cameras that were hung on the walls. He turned and headed back to the front entrance. Here we go again.

Old stone pillars stood sentinel at the gravel drive. Nothing stirred. Everything was normal, pure and simple. Nick looked at the name plate screwed to the pillars; Olympus House. How apt. He dry swallowed a couple of aspirin and walked confidently up the drive.

He felt anything but confident as he lifted the lion's head knocker on the front door. He waited, keeping close to the door to minimise any hidden camera's view of his face. Footsteps. Relax… relax… the door opened to reveal a casually dressed, smiling man.

'Yes? Can I help?' Nick returned the smile.

'I'm sorry, but is this the Campbell Clinic?' He moved his arm in the sling slightly. 'I have an appointment.' The man shook his head, still smiling.

'No. No, you must have the wrong address. I'm afraid I've never heard of the… what, Campbell Clinic?'

'Oh dear, that's a pity. I have an appointment with Dr. Tantalus…' Nick exploded forward, jabbing at the man's throat with stiffened fingers, watching the flash of surprise, fear and anger light up his face, '… and you really are in the soup!'

The man went down like the proverbial sack of spuds, retching and clutching his throat. Nick stepped in, slammed the door and dragged him away, checking his immediate surroundings. Plush. Expensive. Fucking typical, he imagined.

The doorman was turning a distinctly odd colour. Nick gave him a swift and, he hoped, helpful kick in the back then knelt by his side, still watching and assessing. Four doors, ornate staircase, occasional furniture, obscene backlit window at the head of the stairs. The man coughed and choked; Nick rammed his elbow into the soft flesh above his crotch.

'Shut the fuck up… I'm trying to listen.'

He grabbed the man's little finger and gave it a twist.

'Where is he?' Twist. 'I can do this nine more times, matey boy. Where is he?' Snap. Nick slapped his hand over the man's face, cutting off the screech. 'Let's try again. Where is he?'

'Out.' It was barely a whisper.

'I'll wait. Just show me where.'

Nick hauled his reluctant host up and pushed him towards a door.

'Here?' The man nodded. Nick squeezed a nerve in his neck and down he went for the second time, now out cold.

The room reflected the grandiose taste of its owner. Not dissimilar to Cupid's garden, it was Louis Quinze with extras: glitz, gold-leaf and iffy glamour. Nick helped himself to a drink from a cut-glass decanter, a nice Cognac by the nose, and walked quickly round the room, looking for a clue. Everything here had the air of originality. He felt his nose wrinkle with distaste, knowing how all this had been paid for and feeling his anger rising again.

Hello, that looks dodgy, he thought, moving to a table in the window that held a nasty looking clock under a glass dome. Nothing very French or original about that one. No. There you go; camera.

He chided himself gently; he really hadn't thought this through, so eager had he been to extract his pound of flesh from Tantalus. Nick stepped back into the reception area and knelt none too gently on his new best friend's chest, who, as luck would have it, was just coming round.

'Where are your playmates, shit-for-brains?'

'Sec… second floor… third door… blue, blue corridor.'

And that had been really hard, hadn't it? Time to go. Cut your losses and fuck off, Nick.

He checked his gun and scooted across the hallway to the front door. He turned and stared up the stairway, shouting,

'Tell Tantalus I'll be in touch again really soon, only next time he will be in and we will have chat.' As he put his hand on the front door latch, still watching the stairs and the other doors, a voice echoed softly from hidden speakers.

'Put the gun away, Mr. Sloane. If you open the door, you're a dead man.'

Now he heard footsteps and coming down the stairs were two of the largest, meanest looking men he had ever seen, and Nick had seen plenty of big, mean and ugly. Bathed in the unnaturally soft light from the stained glass window behind them, they looked like the most repellent contestants in the most bizarre beauty contest ever. They even moved in synchronisation, seeming to float with graceful menace down the final flight, both extending their arms in a seemingly friendly invitation.

'Follow Frank and Bruno…' Frank and Bruno? '… and we shall see what we can achieve with civilised methods of communication.'

Nick shrugged and walked across to stand between the two men. They both towered over him, and as he tried to stop his jaw from hitting the floor at their sheer size, one of them shot his hand out and confiscated Nick's gun. It was done before he could even look down at what had brushed the back of his hand.

This was not the way that he had envisaged this happening. It was a serious underestimation on his part; one he hoped to live to regret. Definitely not good.

Frank, or Bruno, held his uninjured elbow and guided him up the stairs, turning left and heading up to the second floor. They walked down the luxuriously carpeted blue corridor and Bruno, or Frank, tapped respectfully at the second door along. The voice that had issued from the speakers said,

'Enter.'

The room was in twilight. The curtains pulled loosely over the windows were of heavy, patterned French lace, wonderfully intricate, and backed with lighter, more diaphanous nets. The walls and carpet were of light Wedgwood blue and the furniture was the complete opposite of the regal, pompous clutter housed two floors below. Everything was functional chrome and leather. The space was lit by dim halogen lights let into the ceiling, and futuristic uplighters, placed strategically round the walls. The far left hand wall, in fact the entire room, was dominated by a huge canvas that depicted… Nick let his eyes drop to the floor. His minds' camera was recording everything he saw for posterity.

Bruno and Frank left him standing at the door and went across the room to where Tantalus lay face down on a massage table. A thin strip of white towelling lay draped across his behind. Two young girls, probably no more than fifteen, stood either side of the prostrate man, massaging his back and shoulders. At his feet was a young boy, about the same age, tending to his insteps and toes. All were glistening with oil. They were, by anyone's standards, beautiful. They were all naked.

Nick had to concentrate with every ounce of will. Insist that his body stand still, demand his face show no flicker of emotion, insist his gut hold on to the coffee and sandwich he had eaten at the hospital.

The room was pleasantly warm and smelled of lily of the valley, but the ice was forming at the nape of Nick's neck and crackling along his arms. He let the furnace of his horror and revulsion feed the fires of memory so that he would never forget. He looked up, and straight into the pale blue eyes of Tantalus.

'Well, Mr. Sloane. A pleasure? Mmmm…I think so. Mr. Epstein said you might be dropping by for a chat, but I must confess, I thought you might have given me a little fore knowledge of your arrival.'

Chalk one up for Ferdy, thought Nick. He was actually grateful for the diversion of Ferdy's name. It gave him something to focus on, something to channel his rage into.

'Oh! My apologies, Mr. Sloane.' Tantalus snapped his fingers and the children ceased their ministrations and stood still. 'Miranda, get our guest some tea. Jennifer, Joshua, you may return to your rooms. A chair.'

One of the bodyguards glided across the room and brought Nick a chair as Tantalus swung his legs off the table and was immediately swathed in a silk robe that the other bodyguard held for him. He stood watching Nick, as he tied the robe across him and came to stand in front of the massage table.

He was like the outside of his house; ordinary. Non-descript hair colour, styled conservatively, no apparent scars or blemishes; he wore a simple ring on the middle finger of his left hand and had a St. Christopher's medallion hanging on his not overly hairy chest. The only real sign of wealth was a Rolex Oyster on his wrist, and even that was understated.

'What can I do for you, Mr. Sloane?'

He perched on the edge of the table, crossing his ankles and resting his hands on his lap. His head was leaning slightly to one side, inquiring, felicitous.

Nick let his breath out slowly, concentrating so hard that he could hear his heartbeat whooshing in his ears. His teeth ached from being clenched for so long. He relaxed, little by little, as the air leaked from his nose. He waited a beat before inhaling and saying,

'I'm looking for a young boy, David Trelawney? I understand… I've been led to believe that you might be able to help.'

Tantalus nodded, moving his head left and right and closing his eyes momentarily - perhaps, perhaps not. Yet there was something about his eyes, something brighter.

'Well, well… Cupid, is it? He is… how shall I put this without seeming too melodramatic? He is a thorn. Tell me, Mr. Sloane, am I to assume you are my Androcles?'

Nick made his face remain impassive.

'Am I to assume that the reference to Androcles is a veiled threat?'

Tantalus laughed.

'It's refreshing to meet someone with a little knowledge of ancient legend.' He leant forward slightly. 'Do you consider me a lion, Mr. Sloane? If you remove this thorn from my paw… tell me, do I seem the merciful kind? Do you think I would spare you, as the lion spared Androcles?'

It was a game of poker, all straight faces and bluff. Nick copied Tantalus' head movement - perhaps, perhaps not. Tantalus sat back and brought his hands to his mouth, clasped together as if in prayer.

'Good. Good. I think we understand each other, Mr. Sloane. Ah, here is our tea.'

The door opened and the girl Miranda, now robed in imitation of Tantalus, carried a tray over to them. Tantalus moved away, gesturing to the massage table. The girl placed the tray on the table and brushed past Nick as she left.

She was painfully young, yet the scent that trailed in her wake was almost frightening; too old, too knowing, too adult. Nick shuddered.

'Leave it. I hope you don't mind Earl Grey, Mr. Sloane. I find it more subtle than other teas. Refreshing.'

Tantalus poured two cups and handed one to Nick, then walked away and sat on a sofa beneath the gigantic canvas. If the move had been deliberate, it couldn't have been better calculated to unsettle Nick and rattle his concentration.

Tantalus sat back, the tea cup poised at chest height, one hand catching the handle of the cup between finger and thumb, the very image of the cultured gentleman. He paused before lifting it and taking a sip.

'I only know of David Trelawney from the newspapers.'

Nick watched him sip his tea, focusing on his mouth, resting gently on the rim, and seeing the liquid drawn between the teeth like filings to a magnet. He stayed staring at the lips as the cup was placed gently back on the saucer. He saw them move.

'But I can't give you Cupid. I've no idea where he is.'

'I'm not interested in Cupid. I want David.' He decided to try playing a little more poker. 'Cupid is already dead.'

Tantalus blinked once, slowly, and took another sip of tea.

'You don't say?' Nick had to hand it to him, Tantalus was good. 'And how might I believe you, Mr. Sloane? Having never met the man, how am I to believe you?'

'Mo Palfrey is dead.' Nick needed his suspicions confirmed. A part of him hoped that Palfrey had been Cupid, another wished fervently that he hadn't been. If he had been, there was a slim chance that Nick might save David, if he hadn't, well, over and out. Tantalus' reaction was unexpected. He laughed.

'Palfrey was a sad, nasty little man.' Nick bit back a retort and clenched his good fist. 'Drink your tea, Mr. Sloane, it's getting cold. He… let me see… he was a go-between. It's a shame he is, apparently, no longer with us. He was your best hope.'

The silence stretched interminably. Tantalus' cup chinked delicately on the saucer.

'I'm afraid I still have my thorn, Mr. Sloane, and you still have your dilemma.' He waved a hand and beckoned Frank or Bruno over. The bodyguard handed Tantalus a cigar and held a match at its tip. An aromatic cloud billowed into the room and Tantalus sighed appreciatively.

'Cohiba Doble Corona, Mr. Sloane, limited edition. Over five hundred pounds for twenty five of them. Worth it though. If you enjoy something enough, any price is acceptable. Wouldn't you agree?' He rolled the cigar along his finger pads with his thumb, watching the smoke unfold from the tip. 'You must tell Mr. Epstein that approaching me was too obvious and not a little rash. You are the messenger that may well bear the brunt of the ireful recipient of bad news, Mr. Sloane; but that ire can be assuaged, I believe. Remove the thorn without drawing any attention to me, making me roar if you will, and the legend of Androcles will be seen to have an element of truth therein. You must look closer to home, I think, Mr. Sloane. Have you ever read 'Great Expectations'?'

Nick nodded curtly. His eyes kept getting drawn to the painting at Tantalus' back. With that, and the pungent smoke wafting round his head, he was starting to feel decidedly unwell.

'Well then, think of benefactors, think of Magwitch, Mr. Sloane. I could be wrong, of course, but Palfrey and I did converse on occasion, and, as strange as it may seem, and I think you have already thought of this, Cupid is not alone. He is… a strange one. An anomaly. But his kind, I fear, are becoming more common. We must be on our guard Mr. Sloane, lest he and those like him are the downfall of us all.'

He took down a lungful of smoke, leant back and blew it at the ceiling. It flattened out and crawled greedily over the picture, a poisonous fog feeding from a poisonous image.

'Goodbye Mr. Sloane. I trust that this has concluded all our business, mmm? Bruno and Frank will escort you to the door.' He rested back on the sofa and closed his eyes.

Nick rose stiffly from his seat and put the untouched tea back on the tray. As he turned to go, a wail that chilled his marrow rose up somewhere in the house and ran, seeking a sympathetic ear, through the corridors. It died into echoing silence. Nick dropped his chin to his chest. He knew that sound, recognised it and locked it away in his heart, something to ponder in the long dark nights. He looked over to Tantalus, who was on his feet, all pretence stripped away, his lips peeled back over his teeth, which were clamped together like a trap. His eyes blazed as he crushed the cigar in his fist.

'Bring. It. To Me.'

A hand pushed Nick out the door and continued to push him down the corridor, down the stairs, across the hallway and out the front door. Just before the door slammed behind him, he felt someone push his gun into his jacket pocket.

He stood blinking in the sunlight, too stunned to move. His mobile warbled in his pocket. Ignoring it, he walked out to the pavement and tuned back to face the house. A butterfly bounced and drifted across his vision, flashing red before disappearing into a bush.

The house stared back at him, daring him to disbelieve what he had seen, challenging him to remain unchanged. Mocking his weakness and pitying his future.

Nick walked away.

The Fortescue Arms was just down the road.

CHAPTER THIRTY FOUR

Nick vaguely remembered being slung into a car, rolled in between cool sheets and slipping back into oblivion, hotly pursued through the nothingness by voices that told him to wake-the-fuck up and stop trying to be a guardian angel. You're nothing, they crowed, and how can someone without hope ever really help? Someone who's lost can't lead the lost.

Someone was moving round the room, drawing the curtains and letting the painful sunlight stab him fully awake. He smelled rather than saw Ferdy.

'Rise and shine, you fucking toss pot. Coffee's on and there's clean clothes on the chair.'

He showered, keeping his plaster dry, found paracetamol in the bathroom cabinet and headed downstairs. Ferdy watched him as he sat at the breakfast bar, trying to aim the WMD that was a mug of hot coffee at his unresponsive mouth.

'Jesus, what a fucking mess.'

Nick glared balefully at Epstein over the rim of the mug, wondering if he meant him or the situation, and wished him dead in all manner of slow and painful ways. He watched Ferdy watching him for a moment, seeing a complicated rainbow of feelings reflected in the man's face. His body language said that he was pissed off, his face gave off a wry amusement, but his eyes said something a deal more complex.

Nick felt like a teenager facing a bollocking for some ridiculous prank.

'What?! You've never seen somebody with a hangover and busted arm before?' Even to his own ears, he sounded petulant and strident.

'Ooh, pardon me for breathing.' Ferdy toyed with his own coffee cup for a second. 'What the fuck were you thinking of, Nick, eh? It was just as well you went to the Fortescue, isn't it? Bobby knows me and he recognised you. If that sick fuck had decided to follow you and finish what you started, well…what the fuck were you thinking of, you dickhead?'

Nick followed his coffee swirling round in the mug as he rolled it in the palms of his hands. Suddenly, he felt empty. A great, crushing sadness welled up inside of him, threatening to squeeze him into oblivion. He almost wished it would. Ferdy pushed a scrap of paper across the breakfast bar.

'This might help to get you going again,' he said quietly.

Nick's head jerked up. He'd never heard that tone in Ferdy's voice before. Wistful, almost as if he saw in Nick something he had once been, or thought to be. Nick snagged the paper with the tip of his finger and pulled it to him. It was a scrap from an A4 pad, half a sheet, torn in the middle. He could see large block capitals, badly formed, mirrored there. He opened the scrap with a feeling of dread threading its way through his gut.

The printed words were large and childish, but neat. The writer had put a lot of thought, not into the composition, but whether or not to actually deliver the note. The curls and enclosed spaces had been filled in, a thoughtful doodle. Shall I, shan't I?

Hello. Can you help me please? I want to go home.

Love Miranda.

XXX

Nick let the tears slide down his face as he crushed the note into his fist and crammed it into his pocket. Ferdy nodded and looked at an interesting spot on the kitchen wall over Nick's left shoulder.

Nick took a long draught of coffee, staring deep into the bottom of the mug, watching the undissolved sugar slide in pursuit of the liquid. How the hell had she managed to get the note into his pocket? She hadn't been next to him more than a moment or two when she'd brought the tea tray in. He set the mug down gently and wiped his eyes with the heel of his hand.

'Leave it Nick. Don't.' Ferdy was shaking his head, staring intently at Nick, as if by sheer force of will he could change what he knew was going on in Nick's head. 'Nothing you can do, son. We got other things to worry about.'

'Nothing we..? Nothing…' Nick said, very quietly. '… NOTHING WE CAN DO?!'

The mug shattered against the kitchen wall and Nick sat, frozen, staring at the remains dribbling down the wall.

'Have you ever been in that place? Have you got any idea what goes on there? Any? Have you seen the kids he keeps there? That picture? Fucking Jesus, Ferdy…'

'All right, all right…'

'… I heard a kid scream as I was leaving, and there was nothing, nothing I could…'

'… ALL RIGHT!! Shut the fuck up!'

The two men stared at one another, breathing heavily. Ferdy tapped his temple.

'You know your trouble, eh? You think too fucking much, that's what you do, my friend. Too much of this!' He tapped again. 'Me? I'm a business man. I got my morals, but they don't interfere with business, right? I'd off the cunt tomorrow, given half a chance, but I won't. I know that. Somebody will, one day, I know that too, but for now? Right now? We need him, he needs us, yeah? So don't sit there flapping your face and sobbing into your coffee, talk to me. Tell me what's going on. Let's get it sorted, yeah?' He reached across and grabbed Nick's wrist, digging his nails into the flesh and pulling him across the bar. 'Yeah?'

Nick's face remained blank but he nodded in agreement. For the next hour he told Epstein all that had happened. Everything. He told him what he thought and what he believed to be true.

And somehow, it felt better. Ferdy listened, barely interrupting, just smoking and grunting occasionally. Then he told Nick that Flute was back on the case and was looking for him.

Nick nodded.

'No surprise there then. That copper I bopped in the field was his Sergeant.'

'Great.' Ferdy paced round the kitchen, moving things and opening the fridge door, turning the taps on and off, fidgeting. 'Who's this Magwitch character then?'

Nick hadn't expected that. He'd expected Ferdy to start blowing on about getting out there and finding whoever it was and having a quiet word with them and, ultimately, putting them to bed. That, but not a question that gave rise to the suspicion that Ferdy Epstein might actually have a thought process. That was quite scary.

'Never read 'Great Expectations' then?'

'Started watching the old black and white film once… think I fell asleep.'

'Magwitch was the convict that grabs the boy in the graveyard near the start, remember?'

'Dirty old bald bloke, yeah? Okay, got him. What's that got to do with anything?'

Nick sighed. This was like pulling teeth.

'Turns out that this Magwitch gets sent to Australia, convict, and makes his fortune. But he never forgot Pip's kindness. He's the one who was sending Pip money. Helping him.'

'You ever helped a convict?'

'Bloody hell Ferdy, let's not get too literal, eh?'

'Pardon me.'

'No. I don't think he meant that I've had a secret helper all these years.' Nick looked at Ferdy and smiled. 'You're no secret anyway. No, I think… you see, in the book, Pip is convinced that his benefactor is Miss Haversham…'

'Who?'

'Never mind, it's not that important. But it's not, it's Magwitch. The least likely person Pip could have thought of.'

'Aaah!' A light bulb came on over Ferdy's head. 'Like the twist at the end of a thriller then? Got it, got it. Hey! It'd be something if it turned out to be Flute, wouldn't it? That'd take a load off our plates!'

'Oh for Christ's sake…' Nick hopped off the stool and went to switch the kettle on. His head was not only still in shock from the excess alcohol, but also messed up with the note and his recent encounter with Tantalus. Not to mention a close encounter with a wooden oar. He leant back on the work surface and looked across at Ferdy.

'Tell me something. Why Tantalus? Why that name?'

Ferdy had his back to him, but Nick saw him stiffen.

'Nick…' Ferdy turned, ready for an argument, looked at Nick's face and sighed. 'Oh… fuck it! You'll only keep on at me. I'm no scholar, right? But there were rumours, so I looked the name up in a book of Greek mythology. Put the two together and... '

'Get on with it.'

'Nut shell then. A bloke that Tantalus dealt with, before he was Tantalus, obviously, did the dirty and sold some of Tantalus' trade secrets out to the competition. Not a good move. This bloke's daughter disappears. Four days later, a large box of frozen, pre-cooked pies turns up on his doorstep. The note read something like 'Steal from the Gods, be punished.' I dunno. Anyway, there are a couple of versions in this book about Tantalus. One, he stole from the Gods, nectar and rice pudding I think, weird! Anyway, he was punished in hell by the Gods. Another version said his punishment was for slaughtering his own son and serving him up as a meal for the Gods, to get in their good books.

'Oh yeah, and he sent the father a tape of what happened before she died. That's Tantalus for you.'

Nick just stared at him, opened mouthed.

'That's the story Nick. But do you believe in the Greek gods, eh?' He laughed and pointed at the kettle. 'Make the coffee. How's your head?'

'Clearing.'

His hand felt the note in his pocket. His head was full of David and Creep and Jas; his heart was so full of horror, hate and fear that there was no room for anything else. This was going to end and he was the one, he decided, that would shut the lid and throw Pandora's Box back into the sea. He knew that much mythology.

Nick's mobile gave off its annoyingly chirpy little warning that somebody desired conversation. He looked at the screen. Withheld number. Under normal circumstances, he would have ignored it, but he waved at Ferdy and said,

'I'm putting it on speaker, okay. Got a pen? Good. Write anything of importance down.' Nick slid the cover up. 'Yes?'

There was silence, but not total. Nick could hear traffic in the distance and muted voices, possibly from a television. The voice, when it spoke, was muffled. Whoever it was had put something over the mouthpiece and was also trying to change timbre of their voice. A bad American accent buzzed from the speaker.

'You want him, you come and get him. Then forget everything. That's the deal. Wharf, three o'clock tomorrow morning. Be careful my friend, you're holding a stick sharpened at both ends.' A moment's silence, then, 'I'm part of you… fancy thinking the beast was something you could hunt and kill!'

The whine of a disconnected line.

Nick closed the phone and put it slowly back into his pocket. He looked at Ferdy, who spread his hands in front of him, imploring, questioning - what, who?

'You heard. We're being played like a bloody harp, Ferdy, plucked into the middle of next week. I can smell Tantalus on this like a fart in a space suit.'

'And? You got what you want Nick, let it go at that. What about the voice? Recognise it? Was it somebody you know?'

Nick huffed and clicked his teeth together, thinking.

'I don't know. Maybe there was something, but I think that's just wish fulfilment. I wanted to recognise it, so I think I do, you know? But still…'

He was motionless, leaning on the bar, arms straight out, watching a fly crawl on a pool of spilt coffee. Then it hit him, why the voice had sounded familiar. But it wasn't the voice.

'Where's my gun, Ferdy?' He raised a warning finger - don't argue! 'Where is it?'

'Upstairs. Spare clips in the usual place. Nick?' Sloane turned in the doorway, impatient to get going. 'Just…just watch it, okay?' To Ferdy, it felt like goodbye.

CHAPTER THIRTY FIVE

They had been in the office all night and most of the day, feeling rather than watching the sun moving across the walls, dragging the shadows around and changing the light. A new whiteboard was stood against the wall and, gradually, a new map had been drawn. Names and dates, places and people, all joined and being drawn together, converging on a spot on the far side of the board where the word 'Cupid' had been written.

Flute and Cavannaugh stood in front of their latest creation, hands on hips, checking and rechecking everything they had written. Cavannaugh sighed heavily.

'Everything fits, I think… but it's… it's…'

'Complicated? Unbelievable? Both? It is that. And it's going to take a deal more leg work and paper shuffling to make it coherent enough to take before a judge, I can tell you.' Flute clapped his hands and rubbed them together vigorously. 'But! But, for the moment, I know we have enough to move on. To arrest them and try to get the fine detail.'

'I see an insanity plea heading in our direction.'

'For one of them, maybe. I think I can live with that.'

Cavannaugh picked up a jug of water and poured himself a plastic cupful.

'What does the psychologist say?'

Flute laughed without humour.

'Oh, I think he's already planning how to spend the money from his bestseller. Books about psychopaths are ten a penny, fictional and non-fictional. Two working together is, apparently, virtually unheard of, but three?'

'And he thinks it's viable?'

'From what he's seen, yes. That being said, he's not so blind as to think that we won't go unchallenged by a defence counsel. There will be a raft of professional opposition, of that we can be sure. But we'll get them.'

'When we find them.'

A uniformed officer knocked on the door.

'Team's ready, Mr. Flute, Sir. Just waiting for you.'

'Get your coat Derek. Let's go and get ourselves a monster or two.'

Two vans full of uniforms, and two unmarked cars swept out of the car park. The press had been told that they would have their moment once the operation had been successfully concluded, but that didn't stop them trying to follow. As the convoy passed over the new bridge, heading for Torquay, several cars appeared behind them, with the press on board, having been notified by their colleagues at the station that there was something happening. Flute had already made sure that a few well positioned motorbikes from Torquay nick would intercept them.

He sat back in the passenger seat, fending off the exhaustion that threatened to engulf him. He just hoped that they would get to the house, another house in the intricate and convoluted paper chase, in time to get David Trelawney and the other two, if they were there, away safely.

He couldn't comprehend the chain that had led three children to this. Maybe, deep down, he didn't want to. It was too frightening. Three children, put into care - when the councils of the day farmed them out cheaply to private agencies - and then left them to the tender ministrations of animals like Milford, Dickens and Crick.

All three adopted by Milford. They had become brothers and a sister. They couldn't even discover what they had been called before they had arrived at The Lawns all those years ago. But they had become the Ballantynes: Graham, Gerald and Gabrielle. Mo Palfrey had been Graham. Was Graham? The whys, the wherefores, the how, would be answered, of that Flute was sure. He was also sure that it would take months and months, if not years, to sort out the trail that they had left behind them until they arrived in his neck of the woods.

The immensity of what had happened, the effects of the ripples from this particular boulder in this precise pond, were incalculable. So many kids. Families. How many would never be named or even discovered? The fact that they had kept moving round the area, selling houses, covering tracks, indicated they knew what they were doing, on one level.

Flute shook his head wearily. Too much to assimilate. Get the other two inside, and start afresh.

He leant forward and tapped the driver's seat.

'Quiet approach please. Tell the others.'

'Sir.'

The vans with the heavy mob inside stopped at the end of the road. The unmarked cars stopped outside the house. Six officers from one van trotted down a back way that led behind the entire row of houses on that side of the street, the others gathered on the corner, waiting for a signal from Flute. He looked at the house; trim, unassuming, safe. That was what so many kids had thought. He raised his hand and waved the group at the end of the road forward. Cavannaugh spoke into his radio.

'Stand-by at the rear.' He looked at Flute questioningly. Flute nodded, once. 'Go go go!!'

The officer with the hand-held battering ram moved swiftly up the path, followed by his colleagues, and had the door open with two swift blows. They crowded through the door, shouting 'Police!' at the tops of their voices, squeezing through the hallway, channelling into the downstairs rooms and through to the back lounge and kitchen.

The team from the back door were already piling up the stairs.

As Flute came in through the front door, he heard a voice at the back of the house shout,

'Crime scene!'

The three uniforms in the room filed out quietly. From upstairs came a different cry. It meant the same thing. There was a loud crash as one of the officers passed out.

'Derek, get the SOCO down here, and an ambulance and the coroner.'

He felt his heart shrivelling in his chest, and a forlorn wind whisked the dried remains away.

Jasmine sat at the kitchen table, chin dropped to her chest, hands resting peacefully on the tablecloth. The chair had been positioned to stop her sliding to the floor. An overturned mug had been left on the table, but Flute had a feeling that it would have something unpleasant left in it for the forensic team. He gently placed the first two fingers of his left hand just below Jas' ear. A small hope, but everyone in the room needed to be sure.

'I know her,' whispered one of the constables in the front door team.

'Cheeky little perisher, always trying to get booze from the offy. Lively. But smiley. Poor little sod…'

'Put a sock in it, Steve,' another said.

Cavannaugh appeared at Flute's elbow and cleared his throat. He looked very pale.

'You need to come up Sir. It's…'

Flute waved him to silence.

'Is it David?'

Cavannaugh shook his head.

'Too old.'

There had been no attempt to cover anything at all in the back bedroom. The boy lay on the bed, hands and legs tied to the four corners. Flute closed his eyes, took a deep breath and looked again. Although the throat had been cut, just like the other victims, there was no pretence at ritual here. It was savagery, not-so-pure and simple. The wound laid him bare from throat to pubic bone and his viscera were trailed round the walls like grotesque decorations. A single, black Oxford brogue had been placed in each hand. A Polaroid photograph was placed carefully in one of them.

Cupid held the boy's head firmly from behind and under the chin, making sure the camera picked up the look on his face. Cupid was kissing his cheek. Flute turned it over. The message read,

'Goodbye! I wish I could say it had been a pleasure! Best to ask Sloane about the boy.

Regards, Cupid.'

With a calmness he didn't feel, Flute placed the picture back in the shoe and turned to Cavannaugh.

'Find Sloane. I don't care what it takes. Roust Epstein, turn Sloane's place over, get him!'

Flute stepped carefully from the room, passing the scene of crime officers on the way.

'Jesus Christ!' One of them whispered.

Flute walked sedately down the stairs, back through the kitchen area, where another SOCO was taking photographs of Jas, and stepped out into the back garden. The warm air and breeze flushed through his system; he bent over a flower trough and puked.

Two hours later, Flute was sitting on the front wall, staring at the glaringly bright, somehow utterly unsuitable flowers in the window boxes. Only a faint shaking of his hand, resting on his knee, gave away his state of mind. Cavannaugh came through the front door and walked across to him. He handed him some papers.

'It's all we could find, but it shows that Gabrielle Ballantyne was Marie Slattersdyke, or the other way round. Nothing to indicate who Cupid might be.'

Flute didn't stop watching the flowers.

'Send Cooper and Daniels back to the station. Get them searching. He's in there somewhere. Find him. Anything on Sloane?'

'Nothing. We've had a look round his place, stem to stern, not a bloody thing. Epstein's being cooperative, in his usual obstructive way, but…'

'JUST…just drag him in on suspicion. It'll give us a bit of time. No. Not interested in his brief, just Epstein. And Sloane.'

Cavannaugh nodded and went back into the house.

The sun, now low behind the houses opposite, flashed its final rays through the branches of a cherry tree standing sentinel on the kerb. Flute looked into its centre, watching the light play on the leaves, seeing lances of gold and green tinged light, hearing the crackle of leaves and the creak of its slender trunk. Just to lie beneath it and sleep. Sleep. He thought of Tom, thought of David Trelawney, of the lad upstairs and the girl in the kitchen.

Jasmine and Creep. He gave a soft laugh. Creep. What a name.

'Not long Tom,' he said softly, still looking up throughout the leaves. 'Not long now.' He pushed himself up and stroked the bark of the tree, knowing full well there were too many unanswered questions to travel that road… and yet, and yet, never had the temptation and the longing been as strong as this. He sighed and went back into the house.

CHAPTER THIRTY SIX

Nick knew it was only a matter of time before Flute came pounding on his door. He was in the process of being stitched up like a WI quilt and knew that if there was the least chance of Ferdy being implicated in anything that might affect his business, then Nick was on his own.

Face it, he thought, you're on your own anyway… always have been. Why think it's going to be any different now?

He had tidied up a few personal loose ends at the flat, then called one of the few people he knew he could trust to look after his car. This mate was as far removed from Nick's life as it was possible to be. As far as the friend was concerned, Nick was off to do the Grand Tour and take in the sights of Florence and Venice. Nick would get in touch when he returned.

On his way back from dropping off the car, he had decided to take a leaf out of Palfrey's book. No point in trying to lie low in any of the usual safe places, there was too much risk of getting caught before his rendezvous with Cupid, so he hid himself in plain sight, spending the day doing the tourist thing: steam train, river boat and bus, the latter of which had deposited him in town, close enough to walk to the boatyard when the time came.

He bought a newspaper and strolled up the hill to Buzz, had a coffee, then strolled further through the narrow streets to the White Horse, right at the top of town. None of them were his usual places of relaxation. Thinking about it, sat at a picnic bench in the garden of the White Horse, he didn't have a regular place to relax. His flat was a place to sleep and store clothes, nothing held him to it; he moved from pub to pub, he had no local as such; he lived to work. Hah! Work. That was due a rethink. Maybe he would head off to Italy. Maybe.

He stayed at the White Horse until almost closing time, chatting to the people who looked as if they were worth talking to, and found that he was actually enjoying himself. A few hairy types with guitars and fiddles turned up about eight thirty and started playing in the back bar. Nick sat quietly in the corner, nursing a Guinness, and listening. It was amazing. So much skill and talent and love of music in such an odd place. The landlord sent across a couple of drinks for them, but that was it. They did it because they loved the music.

The hard part was around closing time. Heading back down through town would be dangerous, there were always at least two foot patrols wandering around by the war memorial. It was where most of the pubs were concentrated. Nick stuck to the back lanes as he headed for the island and Cider City. He'd have to wait there for a few hours then make his way to the boatyard. He needed to have a look round before Cupid turned up, always assuming it was Cupid that would show, not the police.

It was a sultry evening and there was rain in the air, a thunderstorm gathering away out at sea. Clean everything, thought Nick, walking slowly down the path towards the tree at the end of the island where he had left Dylan a few nights before.

Cider City seemed unusually quiet, even for a weekday evening. There wasn't even a small group of the local kids gathered at the large holly tree that formed a natural cave by the leat. Odd.

Sitting down to stare out over the river, he patted his pockets for the umpteenth time, making sure that the two glass bottles and the keys were still there. He had removed his sling earlier in the day, trying to make use of his arm, ease the stiffness that had settled there. It also meant he was less recognisable. He had borrowed a different holster from Ferdy, strapping the gun under his right shoulder, making it easier to get at.

Ready then. He was surprised at how calm he felt. He was ninety five percent certain that he knew who Cupid was, who his other little helper was too. He thought he should have felt more outrage and disappointment, but all he felt was empty. Let's hope it stays that way until I've got David, he thought, tossing little bits of gravel into the river.

He heard voices, checked his watch, and sat still, listening. Kids. Just a few of them, and older than the normal crew. They wandered to the bench at the end of the Island, only a few feet from where Nick sat, concealed by the tree. He heard them talking in low, serious voices. Everything seemed odd this evening. One of them scraped a match on the rough surface of the bench and they fell silent as they sparked up their joints. There was a laugh.

Nick smiled to himself. It was his friend who had come here to buy his gear from Dylan, old pizza face. He drifted a little, giving half an ear to the conversation going on behind him, but not really paying attention. Not, at least, until he heard a name he knew being mentioned.

'… and Fiver lives up the same street, yeah? Says he heard it was deffo Creep they pulled out the gaff.' This was Spot the Moron speaking.

'Bollocks,' one of the others said. 'Fiver's a twat anyway. What's he know?'

'Weeell,' intoned Spot, sagely, 'he's never done me a bad turn, you know?'

The other member of the group spoke up.

'I'd heard something like it too. Only I heard there was two stiffs they pulled. Bird and a bloke'

'See?' Spot said triumphantly. 'Two and two. So who did for Creep then?'

Nick could feel the soil and twigs snagging his fingers as he clawed at the ground where he sat. Surely not? Surely fucking not? He banged his head back against the trunk, his breath coming in ragged, painful gasps, pulled and pushed between his teeth. Jesus, if this was true… he made himself calm down. Concentrate on breathing slowly and deeply. He'd know soon enough.

The pure, undiluted hatred that swilled in his stomach made him float to his feet and walk stiffly from behind the tree, trying not to run, and head back down the path to the main road.

'Whoa ho!' He heard from behind him. 'Had a few too many mate, have we?' They laughed.

Don't come after me, don't come after me, Nick intoned in his head. Don't…don't.

Spot came loping up behind him, dancing round and making childish noises with his mouth.

You bloody had to, didn't you? thought Nick, stopping in his tracks. His hand shot out and grabbed Spot's throat, pushing back and pinning him to a tree.

'You fucking had to, didn't you?' He snarled, squeezing and pushing, feeling the lump in Spot's throat trying to move but getting slowly crushed instead. All he could see was Creep's face, eyes closed, mouth hanging open. Dead.

Spot's mates were behind him, grabbing and pulling, shouting at him. One of them punched him in the ear. Nick staggered back, letting Spot slide to the floor. The punch had cleared his head, although his ear was ringing fit for worship. Spot lay on the floor, wheezing and gasping.

His mates gave him a quick check, then turned their attention back to Nick.

'What's your fucking problem, shit head?' Shouted one, poking his face up to Nick's. 'You are so going to get a slap now.' He pulled his arm back.

Too noisy, far too noisy, was what went through Nick's mind as he brought his head sharply forward and connected with the shouting man's nose. Down he went, blood leaking between his fingers. His mate took a step back.

'Wise move, my friend.' Nick said, rubbing his forehead. 'Just leave it, I'm in no mood, all right?'

He started to walk away, raising his finger warningly as the last man standing started towards him. Fuck it!

Nick turned, pulling the gun from under his jacket as he did so. The hero almost ran into it. His eyes popped and he gave a small, choked cry of surprise.

'It's real. Now fuck off.'

Hero scuttled back to his mates, who hadn't even noticed what had happened; they were too busy helping each other to their feet.

Nick trudged to the bridge, up the slope to the road, and stopped, checking left and right. It was almost deserted. From the steps opposite, a man and his dog appeared. The man nodded a greeting and pulled the enthusiastic animal with him, heading over the bridge towards Eastown.

'C'mon Colin, y'daft bugger!'

Twelve thirty was what the clock on the arch over Fore Street read as Nick made his way out towards the boatyard. He kept checking behind, hoping to God that the three amigos would go home and not try to find him.

He stopped by the newsagent and saw the advert hoarding for the local evening paper. 'Double Teenage Slaying in Torquay!' Oh, shit.

How much use was he? What a mess, what a bloody awful, gold-plated fuck up. Get moving, chimed his inner voice, you're in the main street, you're visible. Move it!

He walked swiftly up the road, crossing over as he approached the pub. Gates barred the road into the yard, but there was a gap to allow pedestrians through because a footpath from the woods behind emerged a little further along. Up beyond the trees, the footpath split in two, one spur leading into the lane near the old mill, the other dropping down into the yard itself.

Not really knowing where he was supposed to actually meet Cupid, Nick sat on an old oil drum that was pushed up against the hedge in the boatyard and waited. The breeze was getting up and the atmosphere was changing, cooler and damper. The halyards on the yachts that had been hauled from the water for repairs chinked and rang discordantly. The sound set his teeth on edge.

It was eerie and lonely and set him to thinking of ghosts. He could almost feel them standing at his shoulder, breathing cold earth into his lungs and waiting; waiting for him to join them.

He pressed the button on the side of his watch. It lit up and showed him that it was nearly quarter to three. His hands were steady, but when he breathed out, his throat shook the air and made his head quiver. He allowed himself to close his eyes, try and centre himself, think of nothing but how he was going to deal with what lay ahead.

A sound from the path behind him made him cock his head and listen. It might have been an animal, but the voice denied that thought. And the voice shocked him to his core.

'I'm sure you don't want to make this transaction unnecessarily long, Mr. Sloane, so just go back to the gate and up the hill to the old mill. We'll wait for you there.'

He said nothing, just stood and headed back to the gate, his head in turmoil. It had been a voice from his past, no doubt, but not the one he had expected. Marie? Marie Slattersdyke!? Jesus. His confusion slowed his pace. Did it actually alter anything? Really?

He decided not and, as he ducked between the gatepost and the hedge, he had decided it made no difference at all. What was done was done. By whom didn't matter. They were dead anyway.

He stopped by the waste ground, looking at the van parked there and seeing no one. Old blue police tape lay on the ground, telling him not to cross the barrier. The passenger door opened and he saw Marie's familiar figure climb out. She stood for a moment, watching him, leaving the door open to allow the cab light to illuminate the scene a little.

'Hello Marie.'

He saw her start and look at him intently. Good. That had rattled her. A small advantage that he might be able to use. Another figure stepped from behind the van and walked to stand behind her. Nick felt himself quail. He had been right. Dear God; but both of them? He swallowed, trying to dampen his horribly dry mouth and throat. He coughed.

'Hello Simon.'

They both let out an audible gasp, the man stepped round Marie and stared at Nick.

'Who the hell are you?'

'You know who I am. Nick Sloane. Maybe…' He let the sentence slide, waiting. Simon Nicholson, his friend, the man from whom he had taken his name, stood staring at him, an awful blankness in his eyes. The eyes of a shark. Nick decided to press his advantage. He had to hope that David was in the van.

'Ah, but you weren't to know, were you Simon? Couldn't possibly have known. You shouldn't use quotes from well-known books when you don't know who's listening, eh?' He took a casual step forward, scuffing at the grass with the toe of his shoe. 'I may be holding a stick that's sharpened at both ends, Simon, but so are you. Did you not think of that? And you were part of me, again, you didn't know it, but I tell you this: I do fancy that I can hunt and kill the beast. Oh yes.' Nick looked up from his scraping, and stared straight into Simon Nicholson's eyes. 'That was the best time Simon, when we watched that film together. The best.' He waved his hands hopelessly at his side. 'Why, Simon? What the hell happened?'

Nicholson took another step forward, head to one side like a puzzled parrot. His brow was knitted, his mouth twisted in an uncertain sneer.

'Rob? Rob Wilkes?!' He glanced back at Marie, who seemed to deflate. 'No. No, it can't be. Rob's long gone. He…'

'He what? Just disappeared off the face of the earth? No, Simon, believe me, Rob Wilkes is here and very much alive. Where's David?'

Nick saw Nicholson's face slacken, then become guarded and

watchful.

'Things have changed though, haven't they… what do I call you? Rob? Mr. Sloane? Or Nick? Good old Nick… HAH! That's a contradiction in terms, isn't it? Good Old Nick? Sorry my friend, deal's off. You know who we are and that's not good for our mission.'

He stared off in to some middle distance, where he could see his goal, shining in the future.

'Oh Rob, Rob. We should have helped you all those years ago, shouldn't we Gabrielle?'

Gabrielle!? Nick held tight to his concentration. This was getting out of hand. He was on the verge of losing any advantage he had gained from the surprise of Simon and Marie recognising him. He saw the woman starting to take a step back. Nicholson hadn't noticed. Nick thought he saw Simon's grip on the present slip from his eyes as he started to try and tell him what he wanted to achieve for all the poor, poor children who had been abandoned and loveless for so long.

'Marie!' Nick called. She stopped, looking between Simon, the van and Nick. 'Marie, why don't you tell Simon what you and Mo were actually doing, eh?'

At the mention of Palfrey's name, Simon stopped mid-sentence and looked round at Marie. Then back at Nick.

'What do you mean?' He asked sharply. Reality check! 'Gabrielle, what's he talking about?'

'You know Tantalus, do you?' Nick said quickly, before the woman could speak. 'You'd probably get on well, but I think, I think that only she and Mo knew about him. Am I right, Marie? Yeees! I can see by your face that I am.'

'Gabrielle!? What's he talking about?' Nicholson's voice rose a pitch. He grabbed Marie's arm and pulled her to his side, giving her a shake. 'WHAT! Is he talking about?'

Nick watched carefully. He couldn't make a move yet, he was still too far away from them… and he wasn't sure that his broken arm would be good for more than one hit. But his shot in the dark had paid off.

Palfrey, and Marie by the look of things, had been known to Tantalus, and that animal was not interested in crusades and lost souls. He was in business. Surely, a business built on his own sick pleasures, but a business nonetheless. Nick knew they'd taken photographs, evidence the file Jas had found in the office, and it was only a short step from there to think that they'd sold them on to Tantalus. And more too, he was inclined to think. Let's see.

He took a step closer. Simon was too busy demanding to know what was going on to notice.

'He's trying to muddy the waters, you idiot! And doing pretty well, wouldn't you say?' She shook herself free from his grip and stood massaging her arm. Nick caught her eye, and they both knew that the other was going to make a move. The question was, when?

'Simon?' He looked round at Nick. 'They sold pictures, my man. To a weirdo. And I'd bet a pound to a pinch of pig shit, that if you went back to the boathouse, you'd find a video camera.' He made a point of looking at Marie. 'I'm right again, aren't I?' He looked back to Simon. 'They couldn't have cared less about your mission, crusade, whatever you call it, they wanted the kicks, the sex, the fucking MONEY!'

Nicholson's breathing started getting louder as his fury grew. In through the nose, out through the mouth, great, hissing lungfuls, powered by betrayal and madness.

'True? Or not true, Gabrielle? Well?'

He moved like lightening, the speed surprising even Nick. He backhanded Marie across the face and sent her sprawling, but not before she had clipped her head on the wing of the van. Down she went, out cold. Nick relaxed a fraction. Nicholson had done half his work for him. Nick slid another step closer.

'Please, don't think I don't see what you're doing, Rob. You may think I'm mad, and I may well be, but… I'm not stupid. Common mistake, don't feel cheated. This is not good, this whole thing, not good at all.'

He stared at the unconscious form on the ground, idly digging in his ear, thinking.

'This would have been so simple, should have been so simple, but you… you appear out of nowhere and spoil it all. I'm really disappointed with Gabrielle, oh, and Graham too. That was very naughty, what they did…it is true, isn't it?'

Nick shrugged. He certainly couldn't have cared less if it was true or not, it had got him to this point. Nicholson may have been over fifty now, but he was fit and fast. Nick had already had one severe lesson about underestimation, he didn't want another.

Nicholson heaved a heavy sigh and went to the open door of the van.

He kept looking at Nick as he reached into the cab.

'Oh well. What must be, must be.'

Again, the speed with which he moved caught Nick on the hop. Nicholson leapt away from the van, swinging the wooden bat high above his head. Nick launched himself in the direction of Marie. He could see where this was heading. His foot shot out from under him, slipping away on the loose dry earth. He assumed a painful splits position and had to roll over to get up again. By the time he had regained his feet, the bat had already fallen on the unconscious woman's head at least three times.

Nick rushed him, dodging the expected blow from the bat, but running straight into the bunched left fist that swung round to meet him. He went down onto his back, feeling the air rush from his lungs. Stupidstupidstupid, he thought, rolling to one side and feeling the breeze from the passing bat waft in his ear.

Still lying on his back, he swung his legs round, catching Nicholson just above the ankles. He heard rather than saw Nicholson crash to the ground. Up onto his knee, one leg bent beneath him, ready to spring, Nick saw the bat had landed several feet away, next to Marie.

Both men looked at it, then at each other. Nick saw his old friend smile. It was the smile of a predator, no mercy in it whatsoever. Nicholson reached behind him, feeling under his denim jacket, and pulled out a fisherman's baiting knife. That was familiar; Nick felt the scar under his ear throb and even from where he was kneeling, the damn thing looked sharp.

They both moved together. This was what Nick had feared all along, getting in too close. He knew his arm wasn't up to it. He had to get in first. Nicholson was unaware of Nick's disadvantage. As they clashed, Nick grabbed the wrist above the hand that held the knife and blocked the blow from Nicholson's other arm with his injured one. The pain was excruciating. He drove his knee into Nicholson's groin and almost immediately, felt him go limp. He did it again and saw the knife drop from his grip. Again. Holding him by the lapels now, ignoring his arm's complaints, driving his knee deeper and harder. Through it all, they had barely made a sound, just grunts and groans.

Nick let his opponent drop to the ground. He moved quickly now, heading to the back of the van. He closed his eyes before grabbing the doors and flinging them open.

David lay in the back on an old eiderdown, like the one that Nick had seen when he searched the house. The boy was strapped up with duct tape, wrists and ankles, and had an old rag stuffed in his mouth. There was a livid bruise on his cheek.

Nick leant forward, touching his neck, feeling for a pulse. There it was. He looked round the back of the van and found the roll of tape. He was calm now, cold and calm.

He went to where Marie lay and felt for her pulse. Weak, but there. That might work to his advantage, if she survived. He would need someone to say that he was an innocent in all of this. He snorted. He'd never used the word innocent to describe himself before.

He ripped lengths of tape from the roll and wrapped Nicholson's hands and feet. He went and got a five litre bottle of water that he'd seen in the back of the van, and poured it over the unconscious man's head.

Waiting until he was sufficiently awake, Nick carefully placed a strip of the tape over his mouth, watching him all the while. He smiled at him, making sure he could see what he was doing. Nick picked up the knife and held it up, running his thumb along the blade. Sharp enough.

Like a magician, he dug into his pocket and showed Nicholson the two glass bottles and the three keys. He saw recognition and… what?… horror? Panic? Pleading? Probably. He bent and put them on the ground. Nicholson twisted wildly to see what he was doing. Nick brought his heel down, smashing them and then grinding them into the dirt. That got a satisfying moan from the bound man.

Nick stood over him for a moment, wondering. Their eyes met, and Nick saw nothing remained of the man he thought he had known.

He hunkered down beside him and calmly slit his throat.

~~~

The storm had arrived over a week ago, a great crashing monster full of crackling lightning and raucous thunder. And water. Gallons of the stuff. And it seemed to Flute that it had been raining ever since. So much for summer, he thought, tossing his pen onto the desk and stretching.

He stood up and looked out across the car park, a stark and empty space since the pack of newshounds had departed. So was his office, for that matter, since all the boards had been removed to make way for another desk so that his new civilian typist could help him and
~~~

Cavannaugh correlate all the notes and evidence from the Cupid investigation.

Ballantyne/Slattersdyke was in a prison hospital, sore of head and chattering away quite pleasingly. The whole bloody mess, Cupid, everything, was the most bizarre, sickening and, ultimately, tragic tale in which he had ever been involved.

The report from the lab had shown that the bottle found in Mo Palfrey's hand had contained blood. They had found the remains of two others at the old mill, after the call had come in. Each with blood in them, or what was left of it. And the blood belonged to each of them. Their pact had been made years before and kept as a reminder of their history and how they had helped each other survive.

Blind love, he thought. Blind, stupid promises, borne of despair so deep he didn't think he would ever truly understand it.

His thoughts returned to the telephone call that had sent them out to the old mill. He had listened to the recording at the emergency telephone centre many, many times. That it was Sloane, he had no doubt, but the man had just vanished from the face of the earth. He would find him eventually, of that he was sure.

Bill Rockingham poked his head round the door and said,

'Bit of a kerfuffle over in Torquay, Sir. Some of our uniforms are heading over there to assist.'

'Sorry Bill, I don't understand. Why…?'

'Fire at a big house up the posh end. But reports are saying that the neighbours reported gunfire and that there's a group of children milling about in the street, wearing nothing but dressing gowns.'

'Children's home?'

'No Sir. Your opposite number got a call from a man saying that he might want you to go and have look round this place, once the fire boys have been in. Said the damage wouldn't be too bad and that…' he paused, not sure how Flute might react, '… and that Cupid would have been at home there and probably was.'

Flute kicked his chair across the room. Sloane!

One day, my friend, he thought, grabbing his coat, one day you and I will be having a quiet chat.

~~~
~~~

Excerpt from the Exeter Evening Herald, 14th September, 2007:

'... another brutal killing. Geoffrey Packard, a wealthy local entrepreneur and owner of the import/export company, Olympus, was found with his throat cut in a quiet park situated near Exeter city centre.

The circumstances of the death are unclear, but sources tell us that a note was pinned to the body. There is no indication of what was written on the note. Police have not confirmed that...'

Excerpt from the International Weather Report, Exeter Evening Herald, 14th September, 2007:

FLORENCE: SUNNY - 29 degrees.

Current estate agent speak called them studio flats, but the houses round the edge of the park would always be bedsits as far as Nick was concerned. Student country. He sat in the car, parked beneath the branches of a rapidly shedding tree, looking out at darkened windows and shadowy gaps. The open space to his right was an odd, triangular shape, surrounded by a low brick wall and high, ragged hedges. The wrought iron gate stood open, giving lie to the sign that said the area was for the use of local residents only.

Time to move, he thought, glancing in the rear view mirror. The figure bound and gagged there, sensed he was being watched and began to struggle.

'Not a nice feeling, is it, Mr Packard, having no control over your destiny?'

Nick pinned the note to the still-warm body, thinking that it had all been too quick. He had wanted him to suffer. He had to hope that there might be some truth to what the religious fraternity believed: that somewhere, Tantalus - or Packard or whatever the vicious, perverted little fuck had called himself - was paying for what he had done, and would do so forever. And if that's the case, thought Nick, then I don't have much to look forward to.

He took a last look at the note, and walked away.

'For Miranda' was all it said.

About The Author

Max Brandt started writing more years ago than he cares to remember. He still has the first book he ever wrote: 'Pirates', about Blackbeard, 8 pages with pictures, aged 7.

He fronted a rock band for 25 years and occasionally writes lyrics but now spends much of his free time writing, performing and directing with the Inn Theatre Company.

He has a penchant for the Bard and spent the last 13 summers heavily involved in Dartmouth Shakespeare Week.

Max lives in Devon with his wife, Janie, has 3 daughters, no pets, a plant called Columbina and thinks shepherd's pie is the food of the gods.

See MaxBrandt.co.uk for further details.

Children from the Kundeni School planting trees

Be Part of the Magic Oxygen Word Forest

As well as delivering great content to our readers, we are also the home of the Magic Oxygen Literary Prize.

It is a global writing competition like no other, as we plant a tree for every entry in our tropical Word Forest. We publish the shortlist and winners in an anthology and plant an additional tree for every copy sold.

The forest is situated beside the Kundeni School in Bore, Kenya, a remote community that has suffered greatly from deforestation. Trees planted near the equator are the most efficient at capturing carbon from the atmosphere - 250kg per tree - and keeping our planet cool. The forest will also reintroduce biodiversity and provide food and income for the community.

Visit MagicOxygen.co.uk to buy the anthology and find out about the next MOLP, then spread news of it far and wide on your blogs and social media and be part of a pioneering literary legacy.

Visit CarbonLink.org for updates on our project.